DREAMWATER

DREAMWATER

a novel

by

Patricia Goodwin

Plum Press

Marblehead, MA

DREAMWATER

For Tim and Christina,
who made the dream a reality
and reality a dream

DREAMWATER

Acknowledgements

Since the writing of *Dreamwater* consisted mainly of my being a recluse for a year - special thanks to my husband, Tim Goodwin for his constant support and humor, and for providing me with such a sweet hermit's hut from which to write and study. Thanks to my daughter, Christina for her editing wisdom, her eternal patience and her graphic design skills. Thanks again to my dearest friend, Joan Perry for listening with eager anticipation and asking important questions like, "So, where is this telescope now, Pat?"

Amazon, you are the lungs of the earth! Thank you!

Thank you, Marblehead, ever beautiful.

DREAMWATER

Preface

I had to follow Ned Low to some very dark places. On the surface, he is the powerful, evil character we love to hate. But, Ned is more than that.

When Ned was kidnapped at the end of *When Two Women Die*, I knew in my heart what would happen to him. Upon researching the time period, my suspicions were confirmed. Because I thought the most obvious position he could hold was cabin boy, a lowly servant on the ship, the first thing I did was look up the definition of cabin boy. I found this sarcastic reference on urbandictionary.com: "Often buggered by the professional sailors onboard until they get shore leave." Buggered is a slang term for sodomy, though both terms have been used to mean other forms of sexual contact, or even loose living in general. Further research reinforced what I thought would happen. But, the clincher came from the articles (ship's rules) of pirate Captain Bartholomew Roberts, which stated "No boy or woman to be allowed amongst them."

From that rule alone I knew I was right. The fact that a rule needed to be made said very clearly that the situation was real. Ned would probably have been sexually abused. I felt, in *Dreamwater*, Lowther would have taken Ned for himself exclusively.

17th Century attitudes toward sex were very different than our modern ones. We think in terms of child abuse, and rightly so. As late as the 19th Century, however, child prostitution was rampant. Decent people will always find adult sex with a child to be abhorrent. Nevertheless, for many children in the 17th Century adult sex may have meant survival - a very sad kind of survival. Every day, Ned wants to "slit Lowther's throat" but he needs him to survive.

Pirates were savages. Not followers of rules, though historians will tell you, "Oh, yes! The ship's articles were taken very seriously." I think historians are referring to privateers, those civilized beings that bathed, dressed in silk and played violin. A privateer was a different animal. A privateer had a license signed and sealed by royalty to commit theft and bring the spoils back to his King or Queen. If a privateer killed while committing this royal theft, the law might look the other way.

Pirates were criminals. They had no license to steal or kill. They may have had articles but, from my research, I doubt a real pirate followed stringent rules. Even now, shipboard rules are in place to keep order, as a ship cannot sail in chaos. However, pirates were wild. They were almost constantly drunk, and often fell overboard because of it and drowned. To illustrate the bedlam that was normal on a pirate ship: the articles of the real pirate Ned Low included rules about drunkenness during the taking of a vessel, as well as rules against shooting pistols below deck. Sex between men aboard ship, where quarters were cramped and privacy nil, seems to have been a matter of convenience and mutual consent; it happened regardless of rules. The rowdy celebratory sex that occurs after successfully taking a ship in *Dreamwater* was a well-chronicled part of pirate revelry. Pirates' lives were based on risk and murder, thievery and instant gratuitous pleasures that were to be grasped quickly and savored lest the chance be wasted. Death was quite literally at their door.

In my research, I also learned this harsh truth: pirates loved to torture. Pirates were vicious. They celebrated their victories by playing with their victims in ways that rivaled the Inquisition. Every form of torture I mention in *Dreamwater* was documented and performed at one time or another by actual pirates or slave traders. For instance, as an adult, the pirate Ned Low really cut off and roasted the lips of a captain whose ship he had taken, and forced the man to eat them. Slave traders could be just as brutal as pirates, using torture to control their captives.

However, Ned Low is more than a villian. He has redeeming virtues: his strength, his vulnerability and his love for women.

In *Dreamwater*, Ned is taken up by the whores of Isabella as a kind of toy or mascot. Ned is also in love with Molly Treadwell. Ned Low is more sociopath than charming rogue, but his appreciation for women and especially his affection for the good and beautiful Molly Treadwell redeem him. And, yes, a part of Ned's attraction to Molly is his desire to have power over goodness. Perhaps to defile goodness, but after doing so, he is in love. Goodness wins.

In history, the real pirate Ned Low was a romantic. In his youth, he had been something of a playful thief back in

England. He tried to go straight in Boston, where he wed his true love, Eliza Marble. The real Ned Low did not become a pirate until his beloved wife died in her second childbirth. He had already lost a son. After some trouble during which Low killed a man, he turned to piracy. Low left his daughter behind, an action about which he expressed deep regret. Sometimes, when he was lucid and not drunk, he would "weep plentifully" for his lost child.[1] Because of his own romantic experience with love, Low always asked a man if he were married before pressing him; he would only press single men on to his ship. He was known to free female prisoners.

Loving Molly might be Ned's redeeming virtue and Molly may essentially be a good person, but her affection for the wicked Ned proves her youthful attraction to the forbidden: Molly is not completely innocent. Like a typical pre-teen, Molly is off dabbling in things she shouldn't – magic and romance with a bad guy. I had no intention of joining Ned with Molly. She threw her scarlet ball of yarn according to the courtship game in *When Two Women Die*, but when Ned's foot came down on it, and all the girls giggled, I realized Molly loved Ned. I had intended to marry her to another character. It was clearly an instance of characters taking off in their own direction away from the author's intention. I felt something shift in Molly and I followed her lead. I always listen to my characters and consider where they want to go. I am in charge, but after all, they are the ones who love and fear and struggle.

---

1 Edward E. Leslie, *Desperate Journeys, Abandoned Souls,* Houghton Mifflin, 1988, account of the captive, Philip Ashton of Marblehead, p. 95.

I want to talk about age. In *Dreamwater*, Ned and Molly are very young. Because of their youth, I wanted to stress in 1995 how advanced young people can be; that is why I made Pete and Sarah very smart at only ten, and why the ghost hunters are fifteen years old.

In the 17th Century, there was no age of consent, as we know it, because fathers gave their consent, not girls or boys. Children were betrothed or even married at age two or three, sometimes because one parent, or both, had died. Marriage was an economic necessity of life. A partnership of survival. A classic example of early marriage is in Shakespeare's *Romeo & Juliet*, when Juliet's mother chides her for being unmarried and middle-aged at fourteen. Elizabeth Treadwell herself was married at fourteen. Molly Treadwell, at ten. Therefore, we do have a marriage consummation scene between eleven-year-old Ned, who has been tutored by the prostitutes of Isabella on Isla Hispaniola, and Molly, who is a ten-year-old virgin.

Ned is also strikingly handsome. We seem to have a deep psychological need to be attracted to our villains. Some of our most popular villains are handsome. From Robert Lovelace and Alec D'urberville to Patrick Bateman and Tom Ripley, we love to hate an appealing villain. Ned is certainly good-looking. In *When Two Women Die*, when we first see him, I describe him thusly: "His sharp features cut a darkly handsome profile into the bright day." Some have called Ned a hero, because of what he accomplishes in *Dreamwater*, but I think we have blurred the line between hero and villain. Sometimes, in our stories, our villains become our heroes.

I want to take a minute to discuss the liberties I have taken with history. The real Ned Low, according to records, was born in London in 1690. I wanted Ned to be a character in *When Two Women Die* and I needed him to be at least nine years old in 1690, so I adjusted his birthplace and his age.

There were other, more inconsequential, details I altered for my own use in *When Two Women Die*. I changed Edward Dimond's house to be much simpler than historians believe because I disagree with them about the house. I think it was built much earlier than the 18th Century, because Edward Dimond was in Marblehead before the 18th Century. For the sake of drama and character, I wanted Ol' Dimond to be a loner in a very small fisherman's shack. I also made Elizabeth's house more humble, with a ladder instead of a staircase in order to add tension and danger to events that happened on that fateful stormy night when she and the children hid from pirates in the upstairs bedroom. I changed Roger Williams' name to "Codger Williams" for effect. By 1690 he was already dead when I needed him to ride down the road so that Rosie could throw raspberries at him. However, the real Roger Williams really did try to force the women of Salem to wear a veil over their faces and John Cotton really spoke against him. Just at a slightly earlier time. I wanted to show how attitudes were beginning subtly to shift in Salem toward the dangerous and frightening situation of the witch trials. In *When Two Women Die*, Rosie goes to see Ol' Dimond to ask his psychic advice about her pregnancy. In *Dreamwater*, just two years later, she will be arrested for practicing witchcraft with the old seer.

Dreamwater, like *When Two Women Die*, is full of magic and paranormal occurrences. Marblehead, with its simple historic homes, old winding streets and dramatic rocky shores, lends itself to mystery. Pirates are still sighted climbing over the rocks and the mysterious Englishwoman's screams are still heard at midnight. I hid Rosie, Molly and the baby, Lena in the "Witch Cave" in Nahant, possibly a site of ancient worship, where an accused witch and her daughter actually did hide in 1692.[2] Magic and the paranormal (more normal than we realize) were ever-present in our ancestors' lives and are still present in our own. We'd recognize these constant, daily phenomena if we only looked with open eyes and open minds.

Of course, in *Dreamwater*, I have a whole set of other characters in 1995 who are also struggling to make their dreams come true: Peter Treadwell is trying to come to terms with his young wife's sudden death, while his daughter sees and speaks to her mother's ghost; his son Pete wants to study ghost hunting, but finds himself caught up in internet dangers; Jo Simmons just wants to enjoy her new business and her new husband, but she is being stalked; Cassandra is working very hard on understanding reality as well as she understands her psychic visions.

We've learned a great deal about how to live since the 17th Century, as you will see, when you read *Dreamwater*. Now we have someone to call when we are in trouble. But, we still struggle.

---

2 Robert Ellis Cahill, *New England's Ancient Mysteries*, Old Salt Box, 1993, p. 32.

As ever, Marblehead emerges as an extraordinary place. A place of almost paranormal loveliness, a place of history, of magic, a place where people still strive, but a place where many, rich and poor, have divined how to live, how to find their dream and how to make it real.

Patricia Goodwin

Marblehead, 2013

DREAMWATER

"In my dream I drank fully of water,
but when I woke, I was thirsty."

Ned Low, 11-year-old pirate, Isla Hispaniola, 1692

DREAMWATER

The *Deliverance*, Isla Hispaniola, 1692

He was eleven years old and already he drank too much. He could feel it. He was crimmy of the mornings. His arms and legs shook. When he first set foot upon the ship, he never imagined it would be like this. Never. Who would have?

Ned Low stood at the rail of the Spanish galleon, *Deliverance*, George Lowther, captain and master, anchored off Isabella; his gaze turned out to the endless sea. The weather was fine and hot, as ever it was in that part of the world. The searing red sun was setting, sliding slowly into the sea. The white gulls flashed gold and scarlet as they tilted their wings.

He drank to make it bearable. He drank all the day and all the night.

Lowther drank too. He reeked of it, always. Reeking was the way of the ship; there was no getting away from the smell, the rot of it.

The first time was that first night when Lowther and his crew murdered the beautiful Englishwoman on the beach. She was a noble woman, but that hadn't saved her. Her fine speech hadn't saved her as she had begged for her life; God hadn't saved her though she had prayed and screamed to Him as her savior; her beauty hadn't saved her, in fact, her beauty had brought trouble upon her. He, Ned Low hadn't saved her; in truth, her screams had excited him. None of it, not beauty, nor God, nor fine speech nor anyone had saved her. That very night, terror had turned upon him when he was alone with Lowther in the captain's cabin; Lowther, a large and filthy man, had set himself upon Ned. Ned became as the Englishwoman, and Ned had never known such pain and degradation. He had not known such an act existed, and even now, he did not know what to make of it. Times, he also wanted Lowther to do it to him, and that made him furious. Flashes in his mind and nostrils of the man's private parts were images and smells he tried to erase daily with rum. One day he would have to kill Lowther. He wanted to slice his throat every night. One day, he would do it, and the body would lie rotting in the captain's cabin for days while he, Ned Low, commanded the crew.

Ned tipped the bottle and took another long swig of sweet rum. The horizon swayed a little like a loose line in a gale.

Still, truth be told, he was not sorry to be there, in the Jamaicas. Not sorry, on the whole that he had been taken. He could not have stayed at home for much longer. Times, he was proud to be so hurt. He did not know what such pride did mean, only that it was.

There were compensations alongside the terror. Warm breezes like the one that stirred his long black hair now, and ruffled the long, scarlet scarf that tied around his head, though times, to be sure, the wind was too stifling hot for comfort. Also, he mused, he enjoyed the women, dark women, who caressed him and soothed his pain. He never thought he would have had women so soon. The women had taught him much. He liked these exotic women. He liked their laughter, their colors, their softness - the music of them. They sang and danced at the ready to music he sometimes could not hear. The women loved to be generous toward him. Often, they gave him presents, like the silk scarf he wore. His black eyes were rimmed with India kohl. The women had done that. He wore a gold buckle, and a twinkling diamond on his right ear. The women had decorated him and played with him like a doll. He finally had a good pair of leather boots to make him proud. These he had paid for himself with money he had earned as a fighter, not a sailor, no, as he had no duties on board but to fight whenever the *Deliverance* took a vessel. He was no sailor.

Ned spat into the ocean.

He took another swig.

He was eleven years old, and he knew, one day he would have to kill the captain and seize the ship as his own.

Marblehead, 1692

Rosie Low peered through the telescope. She stood high on Burial Hill, looking out to sea. Her long red hair flew about her in the harsh wind; at times the blazing red strands stood straight up over her head like a halo of fire. It was early spring, and cold with wet weather. Rosie looked southeast into the horizon; and saw there in the circle of clarity that shone before her – her son, Ned far and away in the Jamiacas as he stood on the deck of the Spanish ship that had taken him.

The sea around him churned green and white with cresting waves. He wore strange clothes and earrings and stranger still were the black smudges around his beautiful dark eyes, his father's eyes. That frightened her. He had a look she'd never seen on his handsome face. He seethed. The corners of his mouth twisted in an obvious sneer. She'd seen him frustrated, angry, but never so quietly furious. Something was very wrong. She knew this in her mother's heart.

Rosie stared at her son as long as she could, until the telescope went dark, then light again and she saw the scene before her of fishermen and their small work-a-day boats in the grey harbor of a bitter day in March. Even the seagulls mewing a long call of foul weather appeared grey.

Icy bits of snow blew in her face as she began the walk back to Ed Dimond's small house that nestled in the well of Burial Hill like some rough-hewn hull of a ship lost long ago on these shores. The old man had become her friend in the last two years, since Ned had been taken. He'd shown her how to use the telescope. First, Ol' Dimond came with her and stood next to her on the hill to get the 'scope going. How he accomplished that, she did not know, except by his mysterious powers, for it seemed to her that all he did was mutter to himself while turning and twisting the brass dials on the polished neck of the 'scope with his craggy old hands. As soon as the tropics were revealed, Ol' Dimond would return home, and she would stand as long as the 'scope allowed, peering through the lens at her son. She did not heed the fishermen and the townspeople watching her and Dimond as they stood together or staring at her alone using the 'scope. She knew somewhere vague and deep in her heart how perilous the old magical ways were becoming, but she hardly took notice of the danger.

She had to see Ned. She'd seen him several times now. The novelty never ceased to amaze her, but she hadn't time for amazement now. Now, she had to be serious.

Rosie knocked on Dimond's weather-beaten door and entered without waiting for his answer. Dimond, a lean, healthy old man, tough and salted, strong as a man half his age, sat at his simple table; he was busy repairing a leather belt. Rosie placed the telescope carefully back in its place by the door.

"Thank you, Ol' Dimond. I saw him plain as if he were beside me."

"And, you did not like what you saw?" Dimond asked her.

"Nay, I did not. He seems bravely enough, but broken hearted. Too thin and wan."

"Aye."

"Do ye know something about it, Ol' Dimond? If you see something I don't, ye have to tell me!"

"These are dangerous times, Rosie Low."

Rosie ignored him, still considering what she saw of Ned.

"His eyes are blackened with the dark ash of India."

Dimond sighed.

"Ye must leave him to his own devices, Rosie. Ned is strong as thou hast made 'im, and bravely, as you d'say. Think of yourself now. Your children."

"What of the children?"

"Rosie, ye cum 'ere to use the black arts, but there are those keeping watch over ye."

"Who is watchin'?" Rosie asked, still somewhat distracted by having seen her son.

"Selec'man Ambrose Gale be lookin' out fer witches."

"Should I not cum, then, Ol' Dimond? 'Tw'd be hard, now that I've been. A hard thing to give up."

Dimond rose from his stool.

"Nay, Rosie. 'Tis too late to make a difference. Tha' must come as often as ye like. For they cum for thee soon."

Rosie could barely comprehend the old man's warning she was so wrapped up in her son's condition. She'd heard of such happenings over Salem way. The knock on the door of the justices and the horror of one's friends and neighbors turned into a mob waving torches and fists. In her heart, the Jamaicas, though far off, seemed closer and more real. For all Rosie's seeming frivolity in happier times, she was a practical woman. She knew provision would be made for her children. Her dearest friend Elizabeth, as long as she drew breath, would not let her children starve. And her own Nan, at eight years, was old enough to cook and take care of the little ones and organize the household. Deep in her heart, she calculated this as a mother duck counts her ducklings without knowledge of mathematics.

But, what of Ol' Dimond who had helped her? Would this faithful old man get in trouble because of her?

"If they come for me, Ol' Dimond? What of ye?"

"Ah, a true wizard canna be caught."

The *Deliverance*, Isla Hispaniola, 1692

He had found a hiding place. It was his only refuge. Deep in the cargo hold, he had found a trunk. Some forgotten bounty from a raid: a woman's trunk full of silks, sweetly scented. This he had pushed to the far end of the hold behind all manner of hogsheads, boxes and sacks. He hid there sometimes, while Lowther drank himself blind. There, he could sleep unmolested, for there were parts of the ship like this dark corner, where the captain never came. The men left him alone, as he was Lowther's, and not a sailor. They had little, or nothing, to say to him. Still, each time, he made sure no one saw him go down. Deep within the folds of perfumed silk, while he listened to the rats streaming round him like a tide, he rested completely; he let go his limbs as he never could in Lowther's bed, to float, as in the womb.

Marblehead, 1995

The first day of June was brilliantly sunny; psychic and novice real estate agent Cassandra Diamond Hawkes was showing the Herreschoff Castle at Crocker Park. The postcard colors dazzled her eyes: sparkling blue sky and sea; bright green grass in the park and bleached white clouds billowing like snapping sails. White seagulls dipped and soared and cried out in the rapture of flight. As if in concert, her wild red curls flew about her face in all directions.

Outside, Cassandra introduced the property. "Of course, you probably already know from the brochure that the castle was built in the 1920s by an eccentric artist, who sold it to an equally eccentric yacht designer, Herreschoff." Cassandra explained to the potential buyers, a wealthy couple from Minnesota who wanted something different for a summer place.

The man turned to his wife and whispered, "She outta know eccentric!"

His wife shook her head in disapproval.

Cassandra had heard worse.

Once inside, they climbed a stone staircase, approaching a suit of armor that stood at the top of the stairs. Cassandra had to pick up the long Fortuny skirt she was wearing in order not to trip on the steep stone stairs. The silk fabric had begun its life as a silvery blue, but was now faded to a sun bleached purple. There was a hole in the knee from where she had fallen once. Now, she picked up the skirt in order to walk, like a woman from another century. She'd thought it was the perfect dress to wear to see a castle, but, really, she told herself, she had to stop thinking that way. People couldn't see straight when she dressed in a romantic manner; they only saw a mess, and also, they couldn't hear a word she said. She had to dress normally, she realized, so that people could react to her normally. She was learning. Dealing with reality was still very weird to her, weirder than her visions.

They were passing the suits of armor. She had to tell them, though she knew their reaction would not be good.

"Of course, the suits of armor must stay, due to a clause in the deed. It is highly recommended that you do not move or remove the armor."

"Why what would happen?" The man inquired. He was very tall and built like a truck.

Cassandra stopped the tour.

"We can't be responsible for what could happen."

"What could happen?" The man laughed.

Cassandra never understood this disrespectful kind of humor.

"Well, if the suits of armor are moved out of disrespect for the – well, the suits of armor (here, the man laughed again) forces might – forces might cause a disturbance. The armor could be keeping these forces at bay."

The man shrugged. "Well, if I buy this place, the armor is going. An auction or a yard sale maybe, or the pawn shop."

His wife, a neat and slender woman, reprimanded him.

"Don, maybe we can think of something else."

"What? The basement? Is there a basement?"

"Yes," said Cassandra.

"A dungeon, or what? Will we find chains and the rack?" He laughed. "We'll have to check that out before we leave."

Cassandra knew the man and his wife could not see the heads of the suits of armor turn in his direction.

Cassandra sighed and changed the subject.

"You'll see the magnificent sea views from this window. Beautifully framed by the stone."

As the group looked out the window, Cassandra saw, to her sudden horror, old Mrs. Herreschoff, now dead for more than twenty years, naked to the waist, mowing the castle's lawn.

Mrs. Herreschoff waved a cheery hello to her.

"Men don't have to wear a shirt in this blasting heat! Why should I?" Mrs. Herreschoff called out.

Mrs. Herreschoff appeared as an elderly woman whose naked breasts sagged and flopped with the motion of her mowing: she pushed the old rusted mower over the bumps and lumps of the old lawn; sweat poured down her wrinkled throat and soaked her linen shorts. A group of little boys huddled behind the stone wall, peeking and giggling, throwing stones and laughing as each stone was hurled through the air.

Cassandra wanted to stop them, but she wasn't sure they were really there. Just as Mrs. Herreschoff was nearly hit with a stone, police arrived, running up the green hill. One of the cops threw his police jacket over the old lady's shoulders.

11

"What are you doing? I live here! This is my house! I'm mowing the lawn! I have work to do! Get out of here!"

Cassandra watched as the police dragged Mrs. Herreschoff away from her own house. All of them, police, woman, and boys vanished like mist before her eyes.

"Yeah, nice view." The man from Minnesota replied. "Very nice. Is this the only window with a view of the ocean? That's too bad."

"Yes, the rocks block the view of the ocean." Cassandra answered, realizing he had seen nothing unusual. "Except, of course, for the lovely deck on the roof. We can go there now."

It was then that Cassandra saw the ghost of Beth Treadwell standing in the rose garden wearing a pink summer dress, glowing in the sun like a transparent flower, smiling at her.

Villa del Stella Negra, Isla Hispaniola, 1692

Ned was staring out the window of Jordana's room, his gaze, as always, fixed upon the open sea. The jungle ran right up to the edge of the town. Flowers spilled over the walls like dripping blood: grotesque flowers that resembled human organs, pulsating red and orange, glistening in the tropical rain, like looking into a man split open, a sight Ned had seen all too often. From the thick shadowy growth, weird creatures ran wild: huge bright birds, monkeys, snakes and insects so large they startled Ned for they were like tiny demons dashing across the floor or over the walls and ceilings of the rooms; rooms which seemed non-existent, like flat planes around chaos, having no effect whatsoever to comfort the human beings within. He did not trust the jungle. He did not like to be any where near it. Like most pirates, he favored the open sea.

There, on land, the tropical heat enveloped him. He, who had longed for warm breezes, often felt stifled by them. The heavy air moved through his hair and shirt as the hands of a lover, but it was not refreshing or bracing, as the cold winds of March would be in Marblehead. The tropical heat bore down upon him, pressed upon him from all sides. He was not sure it was not the breath of hell.

The villa was throbbing today. Built in Italianate style, the villa curled around itself in a square: three stories of lavish wrought iron balconies ran along the inside where the women gathered and strolled and called to each other, their elbows and bosoms resting on the railings; large, open windows faced the sea and the town of Isabella on the front; the jungle pressed against the villa at the back. A fountain gurgled and splashed in the center courtyard. Ned listened as the women's arguments flew about him in a peculiar island language, a language made up of parts from all over the world, mostly from the Française and the Hispaniola, some Englaise, some Portuguese, Italian, Dutch, Arabic; no on knew any more what the original language of the old island had been. Indeed, every king in Europe thought he owned Hispaniola, Jamaica and Cuba. In fact, none of them did. No matter how many officials they sent to ride in carriages, or flags they flew from the few government buildings, Lowther told him only thieves and whores ran things. Things ran themselves, it seemed to Ned. Ran over themselves like demon insects.

Each sound begat another: a rat terrier barked at some invisible devil, another dog barked at the first dog, and yet another, till several dogs joined in a chorus of complaints. Like the dogs, the women argued constantly about anything, about everything. They screamed vicious names at each other. Ned did not know how the women didn't kill each other; the curses they hurled at each other would have made him murderous. Adding to the cacophony, captured jungle birds screamed from their cages. Music played: strumming of strings, piping of flute, pounding of drum and singing - whether singly or in chorus, the women, right in the midst of vicious arguments, threw up their voices in dreamy, half-conscious song or lifted their feet and their arms in swaying dance. Ned moved silently each day through the chorus of women, dogs, birds, shops and carts in the street, men shouting, bells from the Spanish church. He especially loved the odor of the women, the perfume, the sweat; like the cooking of their food, constantly surrounding him, bubbling as though through him, spicy and deep.

Jordana watched him from the bed. Her little vervet monkey, Bobo balanced above her on the tip of the bedpost where he was engrossed in eating a plum.

Jordana sat cross-legged, half-naked in her silken skirt, with only gold and jeweled necklaces and her own long hair to cover her bare breasts. Her thick black hair fell in cascades of curls, strands of which clung to her neck, moist with sweat. Her honey colored legs peeked from the folds of silk. Jordana wore two emerald cuffs round her ankles, and the ever-present jeweled dagger at her waist. The bed was littered with the usual debris of her day: half-eaten sweetmeats; warm, rotting fruit; game cards; tarot; ribbons; beaded scarves and little rings of bells that were toys for her pets.

"What is out there, Peti' Low?" Jordana asked him, half-mockingly. "What do you dream of now that you are in Paradise?"

Ned chuckled, just a bit, under his dark demeanor.

"Do you dream of the golden haired girl? The one you left behind on another shore?"

Ned had never told Jordana of the beautiful Molly. The fair-haired Molly. The blue-eyed Molly. He could see right now the halo of golden hair around Molly's head. He could see her blue eyes sparkling like sun on the sea.

Ned mentally shook the image away, lest Jordana read his thoughts and send a devil to Marblehead.

Jordana smiled knowingly, knowing that he had cut her neatly off from his thoughts.

Jordana did not know her exact age, but she was close to Ned in years. Already, she had been sold as a virgin over a hundred times, until her eyes had hardened and no man could be fooled, not even in his cups. She had the devilish face of a minx: her brows tilted in such a way that Ned felt she always mocked him, her snub nose turned away like a disinterested cat that was still observing.

Ned left the window then and joined her on the bed. He was fully dressed, which frustrated Jordana just a little. She stroked his leather breeches with her hand. She aroused him, surely, but he resisted. He did not like to be so easily manipulated.

Instead, he admired the honey color of her skin, her bare shoulder round and glowing as the flesh of a new melon. Ned leaned toward her and licked her shoulder. She tasted sweetly of the almond oil she smoothed upon herself.

Jordana smiled and tilted her head flirtatiously. She puckered her full lips for him.

Her eyes were black pools.

Ned leaned to kiss her waiting mouth, but as he did, Bobo leaped between them, chattering wildly, kissing her himself, handing her the plum he clutched in his hairy palm.

Jordana giggled.

"Bobo, Bobo, you like to be between us, eh, Bobo?"

Ned sighed. The monkey shrieked triumphantly at him.

Jordana motioned to Ned with her dark finger, telling him to lean in closer.

"Mon Peti' Low," Jordana whispered in his ear. "I do not have to send the Devil to Marble Harbor. He is already there."

"What do you mean? What devil?"

"Himself." She shrugged.

Jordana lifted the plum to Ned's lips. He took a generous bite.

Jordana thrust the juicy plum into her own mouth.

"Return to me tonight, Peti'. I will tell you what you cannot guess."

"Tell me now."

"I will tell you when I will tell you."

Jordana lifted the plum to Bobo, but Bobo didn't eat. He turned and spat at Ned.

Ned grabbed Bobo by the tail and swung him off the bed. He hit the wall. The monkey picked himself up, spat and yelped; he toddled, yelping, out of the room.

Jordana began to undress Ned. He laughed, and so did she. He never laughed so freely as with Jordana. He kissed her mouth still open in a laugh, kissing her as she took off his shirt and licked his belly. A guttural moan escaped her as she watched him tear at the silk skirt till it fell from her, leaving her naked but for the gold necklaces, the jeweled anklets and the knife at her waist. She pushed him down on the bed and climbed on top of him. She groaned deeply as she rubbed her soft, downy mound against him once, then twice till she found

17

his ready cock; and gasped with pleasure as he slid into her, for though she was a prostitute, Jordana never took Ned's cock within her for granted. She leaned back, and cupped his balls in her hand and squeezed. That drove him mad, she knew it; she smiled knowingly as he cried out. Her dark nipples peeked out from the strands of gold, and he lunged at them. She giggled, leaning forward so he could suckle them. Then, she fell upon him, and he closed his eyes as her perfumed hair covered his chest, his breath quickened, "Peti' Low, mon cher," she whispered into his ear, a whisper he could feel inside her on his cock, she was putting a spell on him, he didn't care, "Mmm," he moaned, he laughed, if he said her name now, he would be lost. "Peti', mon peti'," "You canna 'ave me," he said, in rapture, "I already have you, you are mine." She whispered. What did he care? She was sweeter than any other and he was in her sweetly now.

Marblehead, 1995

Bob Simmons loved to take the *Handtub* out at night. Marblehead was always beautiful, and in fact, he liked to take her out any time of day, but there was something about the quiet on the dark water he craved: the Old Town hush you could almost hear, and the solitude. It was crazy, Bob thought, he loved people, loved being around them, but the seduction of being alone on the boat drew him out at night.

The air was humid and heavy with a slight stirring wind. The lights of Marblehead twinkled in the distance and the moonlight traveled on a bright silver path over the dark, rippling waves. When he was younger, Bob had made a game of following the silver path; he did so now, and just as it had when he was young, the path slipped ahead of him every time he tried to ride it. Bob chuckled a bit at his futile efforts. The *Handtub* hummed rhythmically, chugging and purring along. With immense satisfaction, Bob listened as the waves lapped delicately against the boat and the buoys; crickets trilled busily; on occasion, a bird chirped in its sleep.

His wife, Jo was busy tonight. She'd gone back to real estate. She had taken Cass on as a kind of protégé, but as it turned out, Jo and Cass were a great help to each other. Jo was a whip at business, and Cass, to hear Jo tell it, could pick a house for a buyer like picking apples in a supermarket. They made an "odd couple" crack team.

Bob was enjoying life. He'd retired from fishing; he just didn't have the heart any more since Beth's murder. He'd taken a town job with Marblehead Parks with plenty of benefits and good pay. His ex-wife had gotten remarried too, so that was a bonus. Jo had lost most of her settlement when they'd married, but she didn't seem to care. "I have everything I need," she liked to whisper in his ear after they made love and cuddled in bed. He liked to think that was a reference to his manhood and his lovemaking abilities. He knew money was the reason she'd gone back to work. Still, she seemed happy. She said she'd had enough of playing around. The housing market needed her, as she put it. Jo and Cassie, he thought, look out real estate! He chuckled. He was laughing a lot lately, he realized. He wore his full dark hair a little longer than he had when he was younger. And, he'd lost a lot of weight. He had abs again, something he hadn't had since high school. Jo played tennis and Bob had never even held a tennis racket before he started going out with her. Of course, his friends said it was all the sex with his hot wife. He laughed out loud again.

That was when he saw, or thought he saw, a mist forming over the water. A pink mist. That was strange. Bob shut down the motor and let the *Handtub* drift silently. The mist seemed to grow taller. Sea fog? Sea fog was beautiful at night; though it could be pretty dangerous. Usually silvery white and hugged the water. Usually all over the place, though, not just in one place.

Bob realized, suddenly, he was in the spot where Beth had been found. The old lobstering spot. No one fished here now. Too sad. For everyone.

The mist floated in a liquid, almost holographic shape, it grew taller, pinker, and a yellow spot seemed to glow from the top, almost like a head.

Pink and yellow? Bob's ears started to ring, at first pleasantly, then sharply, and alarmingly, almost like a shrill otherworldly scream. Bob shook his head. He blinked.

The mist was still there, shimmering, like the figure of a woman standing on the waves.

It couldn't be!

"Beth?" Bob spoke aloud, not expecting an answer.

His ears stopped ringing.

The lighted mist sprinkled into the ocean like spent fireworks on the Fourth of July.

For several minutes, Bob was alone with moonlight and the gentle lapping of water against the boat.

Just as he turned the *Handtub* around, the pink and yellow mist reappeared and seemed to float behind him, following the *Handtub* back to shore; it appeared several times as if to reinforce itself, as though knowing he would try to tell himself nothing had really happened.

The *Deliverance*, Isla Hispaniola, 1692

Lowther was sotted. Ned had to wait a long time for the old pirate's head to nod forward on his large and grotesque chest. He himself had pretended to drink all night. It wasn't hard to fool Lowther when he was drunk. Ned watched with satisfaction as the disgusting man breathed heavily, rhythmically and began to snore.

It was nearly midnight. He would have to hurry.

He opened the cabin door slowly; it creaked. Again, slowly, it creaked the more.

He'd oiled it once, but the pirate had noticed. "What's this?" He'd declared. "Tha' mite slips out like a greased eel? Thou ar' nothin' more an' a slipp'ry eel! I'll show ye how to slip out!" And, he had beaten Ned, and worse.

With each creak, the pirate stirred a little, then less, and Ned managed somehow to break out.

With luck, the deck was quiet. The night was almost unnaturally still. By the helm, two of the men argued without much interest about the weather for the coming days. One pirate said, by the stars, a rogue wave was overdue; the other disagreed saying they were ever in the doldrums.

He was over the side quickly, barefoot, agile as a crab clambering over the ropes. Ned had taught himself to climb sideways and down, slip into the water without a splash; whence forth, he swam the quarter mile to shore. None of the other crew knew how to swim, but he was from Marblehead and John Indian had taught him.

Marblehead, 1995

Joanna Pritchard Simmons was trying to explain the math of real estate for the millionth time to Cassandra.

"It's really simple, Cass. You just –"

"Why can't I just use the online form? It morphs so nicely after you put the numbers in. It's almost alive."

"Sure, the form is fine, but don't you think you should understand it too?"

Cassandra scratched her head; her long, slender fingers disappeared into the huge mane of bright red hair.

"I guess."

"I mean, don't people ask you about it?"

"Uh, I guess."

"What do they say?"

"They want to go over the numbers."

"And, what do you say?"

"I tell them *you'll* go over the numbers with them."

Jo sighed.

She and Cassandra had started Simmons Hawkes, a small, private real estate business together and it was working out pretty well: with Cass's psychic ability and her business savvy they made an unusual but powerful team. Every now and then, Jo tried to give Cass a better grasp of what was really going on business-wise, but Cass really wasn't interested, or, more likely, she didn't really trust the numbers. She trusted, well, for lack of a better word, Jo thought, the force. In fact, Jo knew that Cass probably had used the force to pass the real estate exam.

Cassandra's eyes were already moving away, out the window to the large garden she had created in front of the office. Jo sighed again. Cass was a better gardener than number cruncher, but, she had to admit, the garden brought a lot of people in. They were literally attracted to the small, quaint office painted white with its peaked roof and pink gingerbread cut-out trim under its cheerful, signature pink peppermint striped awning and Cass's amazing flowers out front. Real curb appeal. It drew them in.

"I think the fairy roses need trimming." Cassandra said, almost to herself.

"Go ahead." Jo told her. "Wait, what are you showing today?"

"Three houses. Cottage Street, a condo in the old Methody house and –"

"Cass, which is the Methody?"

"58 Pleasant."

Jo nodded.

"They didn't drink." Cass remarked, half-consciously.

"What year was that?"

"1835."

"Ok." Jo was learning too how to go with the flow of Cass's energy. "What else?"

"Those celebrities want to see the Spanish villa out on the Neck – Villa del Sol."

"Ah! That's today! I need to be there!"

"Okay. They want oranges. Only in a big bottle."

"Oranges?" Jo queried.

"Orange soda!" Cass called out like she just thought of it. "They like orange soda. We should fill the refrigerator with it and maybe, two orange trees in that sunny window overlooking the pool."

Jo was impressed. She grinned at Cassandra.

"I'll pick up everything and we can drive it out to the Neck. I really want to see this first hand. Sounds fantastic! You really got the knack, Cass!"

Cass had told her that the celebrities who frequently came to Marblehead were not any more important than anyone else looking for a house, and she was right, Jo supposed. But, it certainly was more exciting for her; Jo loved celebrity. But, for Cass, it either flowed or it didn't – the force, that is, Jo told herself. She realized more and more each day, Cass really had a way with that force.

And, roses. Jo watched as Cass went outside and clipped away at the long strands of pink roses. Easter lilies in abundance bobbed their heads. Jo could smell their heavy perfume through the open window, lifting on the sea breeze. Beds of blue lobelia made small pools on either side of the doorway. People remarked at those when they came into the office. Cass had placed hanging plants by the doorway, and window boxes trailing with flowers. Jo didn't know the names of half of them, but she did love them. Heavenly blue morning glories climbed now almost to the roof. Cass said she'd have to get them down in the fall - that was funny. Jo could just see it, Cass on a ladder –

Just then, Jo saw a strange dark man with a balding head and full, black mustache standing across the street by the mailbox. Her heart lurched wildly. He was staring right at her! He looked exactly like Frank Girelli, whom she was sure was still in prison for Beth Treadwell's murder. It couldn't be! Part of her wanted to rush out and scream at him. Another part wanted to hide and not let him know she'd seen him. The old terror of the rape she'd endured at his hands, crept over her in powerful waves that made her stumble against the desk.

She picked up her phone and started punching numbers, three numbers, 911.

It seemed to ring forever while she watched the man who watched her.

"911, emergency."

"This is Jo Simmons. There's a man outside my office at 10 Atlantic looking at me. He looks suspicious."

Just then, Jo noticed that Cassandra had stopped trimming the roses and was also staring across the street at the same man.

"He's right by the mailbox. He looks – I know this will sound crazy – he looks just like – Jo didn't want to say his name, but she felt she had to – Frank Girelli."

No need to explain who *that* was to a Marblehead cop. Beth's murder had caused a sensation from Boston to New Hampshire, where Girelli had been found weeks later.

Unwashed and unshaven, he had been dragged out of a cheap motel in his boxer shorts by New Hampshire police.

A moment's delay and the voice on the other end of the phone said. "A car is right by you now. Officer Parker is in the area, she's gonna stop."

"Okay."

Jo and Cassandra were now looking at each other.

Cassandra shook her head, "No."

No, thought Jo, no what? It's not Frank? She wanted to call someone right now at the prison, which one was it, she didn't know. Tell me, she wanted to say, tell me he's still in there.

Jo's eyes filled with tears. She could hardly see the black and white cruiser stop in a blur of tears and the petite blonde officer in her blues get out of the car. Jo wiped her eyes with the back of her hand. Make-up smeared on her skin. She sniffed back tears. She could see Elise Parker talking to the guy. He was getting out his ID. Jo watched as Officer Parker looked at the ID. The man kept talking and looking over at Jo. Officer Parker walked slowly over to the cruiser, leaned in to get the radio, called in the ID, listened, put the radio down and walked back to the man who never took his eyes off Jo.

The man took his ID, put it back in his wallet and just stood there. Jo saw the officer wave him on. He hesitated, began to argue with her; she said something quite sternly, and he walked on. He kept turning, looking towards Jo, as he walked away.

Officer Parker then crossed the street to the office and entered in a flurry of the cheerful chimes that Jo and Cass had hung to welcome clients as they entered.

"It wasn't Girelli."

"Who was it? Why was he staring at me?"

"His ID says his name is Hardy, Ben Hardy from Illinois."

"Illinois! What is he doing here?"

"He said he was mailing a letter."

"He was standing there staring at me and Cassie. He stood there by the mailbox for at least twenty minutes! That's some letter! I never saw him mail a letter! It's too much of a coincidence that he looks so much like Gi-relli. Too much."

"Settle down, Jo. If you see him again, call us, and we'll arrest him for loitering."

"Loitering?" Jo repeated, incredulous.

"Yes, and whatever other law he breaks." Officer Parker sighed. "Jo, it might mean nothing at all, but I need to tell you, he was in Walpole. He was released yesterday."

"Who? Girelli?" Now she was truly alarmed.

"No, Girelli is still inside. This Hardy fella."

"Wha – what was he in for?"

Officer Parker sighed deeply. "Rape."

Jo felt her face go pale.

"Should I get a restraining order?"

Cassandra came into the office. Jo looked at her for a second, and then back to Elise.

"Maybe. Let's see if he comes back, then we'll deal with it."

28

"If he comes back?" Jo repeated.

"There's nothing I can do, Jo, until he breaks the law. He's been released. He served his time. He's not on parole."

Jo sat down. She just stared ahead. She was just getting her life back after Beth's death.

"Jo, I can't do any more right now." Elise said. "I'll keep a car going by all day. If you see him again, call us."

"Okay."

Officer Parker left the two women alone in the sunny and charming real estate office.

Jo's phone went off, a cheerful ring of girls laughing and background notes of music. Jo loved it because it reminded her of girlfriends hanging out.

She didn't pick up the phone. She never missed a call.

Jo turned to Cass.

"Tell me." She said.

Villa del Stella Negra, Isla Hispaniola, 1692

If in the daylight the villa was noisy, at night it roared. The Villa del Stella Negra lived up to its name by sucking life into it and spitting it out the next day, depleted of strength, means and innocence. At night, the women laughed slyly. The women sang, but not for themselves, not with that dreamy unconsciousness of daytime, not with that purposeless sweetness of dreamy day. No, at night they sang like sirens, to tempt the men, to tempt gold from the men, to devour the men completely. At night, the women became pirates. They took out of revenge. Even if they were beaten and misused by the men, the women kept on. They kept on. Ned respected the women. He loved them. He felt at home in their midst at Villa del Stella Negra.

When he arrived, Jordana was occupied. In the main hall a raucous party was underway: dancers and musicians filled the room with drums and throbbing music; roasted pig and fruit, wine and rum covered the tables; lanterns and torches threw light and flickering shadows over the celebratory grimaces of whores and pirates. Jordana sat on the lap of a wealthy Italian. She was smoking the hookah; she touched the pipe to her most secret part before lifting it flirtatiously to the Italian's lips. He threw back his head and laughed before taking it into his mouth. He sucked deeply while gazing into her dark eyes.

Ned sat down nearby to wait for her. Jordana smiled at him. She liked to be watched and admired.

Ned watched quite happily as the women danced to the drums, their bodies nimble as snakes; the floor pulsated under his soles with their pounding feet.

Suddenly, Ned felt his hand grasped and pulled. He looked down to see one of the small children, a boy, pulling him away, wanting him to go down the long corridor to the boudoirs.

"Mi'nuit! M'nuit!" Chanted the boy.

Midnight. Yes, he supposed there was some magical reasoning about midnight.

He cast a glance at Jordana, who shrugged, while he allowed the boy to drag him down the corridor lighted by torches. The children of the prostitutes ran like insects along the corridor. They giggled and pushed each other. They called out, and pulled at Ned, hoping to get a coin or a trinket. A few old pilgrims who had come to see the Oracle leaned against the wall, waiting their turn. They watched him pass, jealously. That pile of rags, Listen, sat in a corner, his blind eyes glazed blue white, his protruding lip drooling as he did what he did best – he listened. From far inside the villa, Ned could hear the women's working voices issuing from their rooms. Gossip flew about like bats in the night.

As he thought, he was being taken to Marion, Jordana's mother, one of the youngest and most beautiful women there. She was ideal, special, reserved. None of the men dared to beat or misuse either Marion or Jordana. All of the pirates were afraid of Marion; therefore all of her children were protected by the very reason Ned was being taken to her now – her gift.

Marion, wearing a scarlet veil embroidered with tiny mirrors that caused the light to spark around her, sat upon a large couch draped with rich rugs of various hues and patterns. She had recently given birth. She held the suckling babe to her dark breast now. Lanterns hanging round her head threw delicate patterns of light round the room. In truth, Marion glowed. Her suckling babe did also glow.

For a moment, Ned was frightened by her majesty. He stumbled backwards.

"Nay, come to me, Peti' Low. I will see you." Marion spoke in her lovely voice. A soft and caressing voice all men would dream of hearing: that Marion would say their name with such affection and regard.

Ned stepped forward.

Marion motioned him closer with her free hand, and he went. Marion gestured for him to sit, and he did, facing this regal black Madonna.

Two young girls carried a copper bowl of water, which they placed ceremonially upon a tripod in front of Marion. Marion handed the baby to one of the girls. She settled cross-legged at Marion's side, nestling the now sleeping child.

Marion waved her hand over the bowl. A blue smoke seemed to rise from the water, trailing her fingertips.

Ned was not necessarily impressed. He knew this mysterious smoke could be nothing more than a potion dropped from one of Marion's rings. Still, he knew he was about to be impressed a great deal.

"My dreams are troubled, mon petit. In the night I have seen votre mere, the one who bears the name of the rose, the one with the hair and the temper of fire. She will be arrested, arrête, stopped. I would laugh if it were not for the terrible ignorance of men. Many will be hanged by their throats, unjustly so. They cry out to me, mon petit, through you. They are all named from you. From your heart."

Ned did not understand, except that his mother was in danger. His heart beat wildly, in spite of him. He did not want to care.

But he cared.

Maybe it was the soothing culture of women there in Isabella that had wooed him to appreciate his mother at last, maybe it was her absence and her distance from him, but appreciate her he did, suddenly.

"Why are they hanged?" He asked Marion.

"They are innocent. But, they are accused."

"Of what?" Then, in his alarm, he paused to show some respect for her. "Please – of what?"

"They are accused of dancing with Satan." Marion sneered. "They do not know Satan, mon cher. But they will meet him. He will judge them in the court. Satan has been invited to the harbor of peace, Shalom, by the justices, the very ones who fear him so much. They have opened their souls to him and to his treachery."

"What can I do against the justices?"

"You will go, Peti' Low, you will rescue her. You will know exactly what to do. You will be well out of this place, for a great upheaval is coming.

One word of caution – hide her, mon petit, until you are ready to embark. Hide her in the sacred temples, the ones that are built of heavy stones, stones that are aligned with the rising sun, along the path of the snakes."

Marblehead, 1995

Peter Treadwell looked past all the other parents going to pick up their kids at the Sunny Day School. He wasn't interested in any of the hungry, divorced moms. They practically salivated every time they saw an eligible male. They disgusted him. He didn't care how tight their butts were or how many times they threw themselves into guys' arms to say hello. Every time they flirted with him, he thought he was going to puke.

It made him miss Beth so much.

He'd developed a cold, hard-jawed demeanor. Otherwise, he'd be sobbing.

The teacher, Miss Meghan waved him in. She was a pretty girl, slightly over-weight, but not much; it gave her a comfortable, motherly look. She had dark red hair, a round face and clear blue eyes. A few freckles were sprinkled over her turned up nose. Very pleasant looking girl, he thought, miserably.

He really didn't want to talk. He just wanted to get Emily and go back to work.

She was holding Emily's hand.

"Hello, Mr. Treadwell. Can we talk for a minute?"

"Well, I've got to get back to the shop. I got a lot of orders to fill."

It wasn't a lie. In the four years since Beth died, he'd gotten a lot of business, mostly out of sympathy, he supposed. He didn't care why. The business kept his mind occupied. He didn't exactly have a company, no name or incorporation, just himself working through word-of-mouth recommendations. He made everything from bureaus to cabinets, birdhouses to mailboxes. Historic house plaques with the name and date of the original owner of the house were popular, as almost every house was historic and tourists loved to stop and read the little signs in the shape of a gable roof. He had his own simple furniture style, a cross between Shaker and Colonial, which he supposed was in demand. Customers waited a long time for their orders, and they paid more too, as the work was exclusive and top notch. Sometimes, just for fun, he made a piece the old fashioned way, with wooden pegs instead of nails. He worked all day in the workshop adjoining his house, and after the kids went to sleep, sometimes he went back to the shop and worked into the night till he fell on the bed exhausted. Often, he didn't wash. He barely ate. He knew he was not right. But, for the time being, he had to work or fall completely apart. That's why Em was in day care. They called it a school, but he knew it wasn't much more than play. It wasn't ideal. Soon, he'd be able to get things back – no, not back to normal. Back to something better than this. Maybe. He hoped.

"Mr. Treadwell – well, will you sit down?"

She gestured to the children's tiny chairs.

"No, I don't think so. What is it? Is something wrong?"

"Emily, would you draw a picture for your Daddy, please?" Meghan set Emily up with crayons and paper. "There you go! That's great! I can't wait to see what you make!

Mr. Treadwell –"

"Call me, Pete." The Mr. Treadwell thing was driving him a little crazy.

Meghan sighed.

"I'd rather not, thanks. Let's go over here."

Meghan led him to another part of the room.

Suddenly, both their heads turned in Emily's direction when they heard her say, "I'm gonna draw you, Momma!"

Peter whipped his head around and stared at Meghan.

"She's been talking to your late wife, to Beth, for about two weeks now. I thought it would stop on its own, but it hasn't. The other children don't understand what's happening. Sometimes they cry for their mommies thinking somehow Emily's mother is here but their mothers aren't. Obviously, they don't see Beth. But, apparently, Emily does."

Peter looked at Emily happily drawing her picture. He walked over to his daughter and stood behind her.

She was drawing a little girl sitting at a table drawing a picture. It was the effort of a very young child not yet five years old; the figures were colored sticks, but he could clearly make out Beth in a pink dress standing by her daughter's side. Her hand rested on the little girl's shoulder.

"Daddy" Emily turned round. "Your standing right in Momma's way." Emily spoke in her own special way, changing l and r to w, t to sh. "She can't see the picture. Oh – ok. She said it's okay. She likes you there."

Emily continued drawing happily.

Peter looked at Meghan, who smiled gently, as if to say, "See?"

He really didn't know what to think or say.

The *Deliverance*, Isla Hispaniola, 1692

Lowther grabbed him by the belt and pulled him toward him.

That was the signal Ned knew well and dreaded.

Lowther took him from the front this time, which he hated because it hurt more and he had to kiss the grotesque man with his foul breath and rotten teeth; he also hated that his own cock swelled despite his will and climaxed, making him murderous, an urge he had to subdue if he wanted to live.

When it was over, Ned buckled his belt, a sound he was ever grateful to hear, the sound of his temporary freedom.

Ned had considered many different ways to change his situation. Slitting Lowther's throat while he slept was his favorite. But, the crew would not be fooled for long, less than a day, if he tried to convey messages to them from a captain in absentia.

It occurred to Ned to ask Lowther. To trick him into sailing north. He eyed Lowther as the old pirate slurped wine with lusty post-coital satisfaction from his cup.

"I have heard Captain," Ned began, "of a rich merchant ship laden with Spanish gold recently from Terra Firma that has left port at St. Augustine, it is rumored, for Salem Harbor and on to England."

Lowther stopped drinking.

"I have heard of no such ship. What's 'er name?"

"She is called *Propriety*."

"Ha!" Lowther enjoyed the irony. Ned was that glad.

"How be she laden?"

"With raw gold, sir, from the mines. Doubloons, and Spanish jewels as a gift for Queen Mary of England."

"I'll be damned! Spanish jewels – how? From the plunder of the *Teresa*?"

Lowther had been fuming over the plunder of the Spanish ship, the *Teresa* for months. He had missed raiding the *Teresa* north of Antigua earlier that year. Ned knew it was loot he would not want to miss again.

"Is this a trick?" Lowther wiped his mouth with the back of his sleeve.

The word stopped Ned for less than a second only, so quick was his mendacity.

"How so?" Ned made his face as innocent as possible.

Lowther burst out laughing.

"Ha! You have no innocence left, li'l eel! Thy face is already jaded in the body of a child."

Lowther liked to use the intimate thee and thou of lovers with him. Ned was willing to squelch his distaste.

He went on. "Nevertheless, the *Propriety* sails further from ye as we speak of it, bearing Spanish bounty to a foul English bitch."

"Ah, who has told you of this ship? Was it your consort, that brat whore?"

"She spoke of it. Others know. There is something of a race to get to her."

This last piqued Lowther's interest.

"Ah! Who is after 'er?"

"I heard tell the *Molly* (Ned felt himself cringe to so speak her name) is in pursuit."

"*That* scurvy crew!"

"And the *Destiny*."

Ned knew all three ships were headed north. That they pursued the cargo of the Teresa was a fabrication.

"Another lot of scoundrels! I'll show them whose destiny she be!"

Lowther slammed down his cup.

"By God, I'll discern whether thou be lyin' to me, thou slimy eel. Ah, no matter," Lowther reconsidered his mistrust. "I'm tired of lyin' low in this dung heap of women. We're sure to find somethin' tasty along the way. To Salem, then!" He raised his cup.

"To Salem." Ned agreed.

Suddenly a thought occurred to Ned. If Lowther was tired of him, so much the better.

"Are you really tired of my cunning, then, sir?"

"Eh?"

"For there may be another prize in Salem. What would thou say to a fair-haired boy? An innocent? And," Here Ned paused for effect. " - a mute?"

"A mute!" Lowther laughed aloud.

"Aye, a mute."

"Haaaaa! If he be truly mute, he would indeed be a prize. Drink w' me, ye the devil's own spawn."

Lowther poured a glass for Ned, who lifted it in salute.

Ned thought to himself how lovely it was to know a seer, to have Marion and Jordana together in his pocket. It had been Jordana who had told him that Molly's brother, his old friend Tom Treadwell was now mute since the murder of the Englishwoman on the beach. And, both seers, in fact, all the women at Villa del Stella Negra, would bear up his falsehood to Lowther about the *Propriety* and the treasure load of the *Teresa*. The *Molly* and the *Destiny* truly did travel north, but Lowther would be chasing a fantasy treasure. But, as he said, it was no matter. Other treasure and more adventures would be along the way to make up for it.

And, his own mother and the fair Molly waiting for him in Marblehead.

Marblehead, 1995

Peter stared at his children, assembled as he had requested around the dinner table. Only dinner was not on the table. Ten-year-old Pete was his spitting image: blonde, blue-eyed, and freckled. It was like looking in a mirror twenty-eight years ago. Six-year-old Sarah folded and unfolded her hands, not used to the formality of being asked to sit at table for a meeting. Sarah was a strawberry blonde with her mother's delicate features. Peter didn't want to think about how beautiful she was, and would always be.

Emily smiled at her Dad expectantly. She was kneeling on a chair with her small arms on the table. Emily was also fair, round-faced and cherub-like.

Peter was holding the drawing Emily had done in day care. He placed it on the table now so that all could see.

He watched their reactions.

"Emily drew this in school today."

Pete's face twitched just a bit; he made a face his father couldn't read.

"What?" Peter asked his son.

"It's Mom." Pete said, pushing the drawing toward his father. "What's the problem, Dad?"

Emily looked proud.

Sarah said. "Em's always drawing Mom."

Peter looked at his children.

"Emily has been talking to Mom, too. Haven't you, Honey?"

Emily nodded eagerly.

"Yeah, Dad, I don't see the point." Pete grumbled. "Em's always talking to Mom. So, she drew her picture, so what?"

"Ok, ok, I hear you. But, I have to ask you guys. Just bear with me." Peter ran his hands through his hair. He knew how bad this was going to sound. "Have any of you seen Mom? Or talked to her?"

Sarah shook her head.

"No!" cried Pete.

Peter didn't believe him.

"Dad?" Emily whispered.

"Yeah, Hun?"

"Mom says she's here now."

"She is?"

Emily nodded. "Ah, ha."

"Where is she?"

"Right there." Emily pointed behind him.

Peter whirled round so fast his chair nearly fell over. Nothing was behind him but the refrigerator.

"Wait a minute!" Pete said and he left the room. They could hear him hopping up the stairs to his bedroom. He came down with his Polaroid camera.

"This should show us something." He took a picture of the refrigerator.

"Sometimes you can see a spirit Dad if you take a picture." Pete told him.

Peter just watched in amazement, as did the Emily and Sarah. They were still amazed by the miracle of an ordinary Polaroid developing before their eyes, but their attention would be riveted to this picture for a different reason.

The photo slid out of the camera. Pete ripped it off and they waited. Peter saw his son's face change from casual to shock.

He handed the photo to his father.

A bright circle of light shone in front of the stainless steel bulk of the refrigerator.

"Could be the flash." Peter considered.

"It's not, you'll see."

As the Polaroid photo came more and more into focus, the circle of light became more detailed. Goosebumps spread over his arms as the image became sharper and Peter saw that the circle looked like an earth with distinct forms that seemed to be land and sea, or clouds; or a cell, a plant cell or a human cell. Clearly, the circle was more than light.

"This is crazy." Peter said, rubbing his arms to clear the goosebumps.

"Dad, it's not. I've seen these before; they're called orbs. Only real orbs have these kinds of details inside."

"Where have you seen them?"

Pete looked embarrassed. "In books. Ghost hunters snap them all the time."

"Ghost hunters." Peter repeated.

"Yeah."

"I can't - I couldn't - think of Mom as a ghost."

A spirit, maybe, he admitted to himself, not knowing if there was a difference.

"You kids'd better get to bed, it's getting late."

"Dad, you know, none of us like it either."

"Have you seen her, Petie?"

"Dad, don't call me that."

"Sorry."

"I think I did, but I'm not sure. I was looking out the window one morning, and I thought I saw her out on the water. It was so fast! She like went by like a white bird. I thought it was a seagull, a flash of white. But, I couldn't help thinking how much it looked like Mom - his voice quivered - on her board."

It was too much. Both Peter and his son burst into tears. Peter threw his arms around his boy who sobbed deeply, grasping a picture of his mother's spirit in his hand. Peter stopped sobbing right away. After a minute, Pete also composed himself, sniffed and pulled away.

The girls looked very serious. Sarah's mouth turned down and she started to cry in alarm at seeing both father and older brother break down.

Emily alone was calm. "It's okay," she reassured them all. "Momma is okay. She wants you to see her. She said..."

"What, Em? What did Momma say?" Peter asked his daughter.

"Momma said not to cry. She said you should not cry."

"No, you shouldn't, Hun. Momma's in heaven."

"No, Daddy!" Emily cried impatiently. "I don't cry! And, Momma's not in heaven, she is here. She can't go to heaven because you are *crying!*"

Peter was stunned.

He and Pete and Sarah just stared at the little one.

***

Later that night, Peter tucked the Polaroid of Beth's spirit into the mirror frame above the bureau in their bedroom. Besides looking like an earth or a cell, the photo also reminded him of an ultrasound image of a fetus in the womb. A new life.

His eyes filled with tears. He let himself sob exactly twice before he sniffed the tears back. It was a trick he had learned over the last few years to satisfy the physical urge to cry. Several tears fell to his cheek, and he left them there.

Marblehead, 1995

It was a few days later that Bob Simmons called him and said he had something to tell him. He came over to the shop pretty agitated, fussing with his baseball cap, an old faded thing that used to be red and was now pink with the amusing Marblehead saying embroidered on it in frayed threads, "Marblehead, A Quaint Drinking Town with a Sailing Problem."

"Pete, look I don't how else to say this except to just say it."

"Okay."

Bob just looked at him.

"Bob, are you going to say it?"

Before he could get the words completely out, Bob blurted. "I saw Beth!"

Marblehead, 1692

It was a hot, prickly day in late June when Elizabeth Treadwell stepped out the kitchen door of her cottage to pick sage from her garden. She did not see the seagulls silenced by the heat of day or the chirping goldfinches that swooped down, then up over her head. She did not have time to enjoy her garden as she usually did with its blue flax blowing in the sea breeze or the pale red rose buds spiraling open to the morning sun; instead, she saw her neighbor, Jane Pritchard, rushing toward her. Rushing, for Jane, meant stepping deliberately, pursing her lips as though she couldn't wait to speak, and alternately looking down at her feet and up at her destination – in this case, Elizabeth.

Jane obviously had something she wished to tell her. Elizabeth instinctively knew it was something she would not wish to hear.

"Good morrow, Goodie Treadwell."

"Good morrow, Jane." Elizabeth greeted her.

Jane looked just a touch disapproving of such an intimate greeting.

The skin on Elizabeth's arms twitched in the tension and the heat, as though bitten by invisible gnats.

Marblehead was very different than it had been just two years before, when her beloved Rosie had gambled down the very same path toward her door, flushed and happy, bareheaded, her flaming red hair filled with sunlight, her baby strapped to her back like a papoose, and her breasts swaying with their natural movement. In fact, she, Elizabeth, had walked out her own door many times with her own breasts under her shift, full and swaying, only to be reprimanded by Jane Pritchard, if not with words, at least with these same pursed, disapproving lips she faced now.

This time, Elizabeth was wearing her long, blonde curls tucked under her bonnet, which was tied tightly under her chin. The bonnet covered her ears so she could not hear so plainly what she would like to hear: the voices of her children, the birds, the ocean and the wind, though this last whistled in her ears with a weird new voice caught as it was in the crisp linen. She wore a collar, stiff and cumbersome every time she bent to task. She was tightly bound in her corset. She couldn't help thinking this proper way of dressing was a sad loss of physical comfort and freedom. Being so tightly bound made her feel old, much older than her twenty-five years.

"Your friend, Goodie Low, was seen dancing in the woods." Jane lifted her chin to demonstrate her superiority. She was almost breathless with the excitement of this revelation.

"Rosie dances often, Jane, with the joy that comes naturally to her."

It was true; Rosie could suddenly skip or twirl with girlish energy. It was something Elizabeth admired, as she could not break her serious manner to step a jig or hop in any undignified way. It just wasn't in her nature as it was in Rosie's.

"You know as well as I do, Goodie Treadwell, that only the Devil dances and especially in secret, in the woods."

"Rosie dances in innocence. It is a gentle and graceful expression of Rosie's innocence."

"Nay, only the Evil One dances! Dancing is from the Devil himself!"

"How do you know?"

"Why, I have heard tell!" She added. "And, Goodie Gale said she heard Goodie Low conversing with a bird!"

Elizabeth wanted to scream. Her own children talked to birds and animals. If Rosie had been seen talking to a bird, it was in jest.

"Well, Goodie Pritchard, you will only have to worry about *that* if the bird talks back."

Jane was visibly shocked; her pursed lips tightened.

"Who knows what Goodie Low hears when a bird chirps! Perhaps she is conversing with Satan! She has been *seen*, Goodie Treadwell, up on the Burial Hill with the old wizard, who is himself a witch! You should be careful, Goodie Treadwell, to tread carefully and live up to thy name. Thy careless statements could be taken ill, could be taken against even someone as exemplary as you."

"I hope I am exemplary! Mayhap I can do my friend some good."

"Be careful whom you call friend, Elizabeth. Be very careful, for God will judge thee."

"I have no fear of being judged by my maker, Goodie Pritchard. I welcome God's judgment. I know He sees me every day and I am glad of it. Good day to thee."

Elizabeth couldn't wait to return to her house and her daily work. However, once inside, she couldn't help but think household chores were a luxury. She felt she was turning her back on some responsibility.

Something outside pulled at her.

Her husband Tom was standing in the kitchen. He looked her in the face as she entered. His blue eyes were serious, and his dark blonde curls hung tired and uncoiled about his face.

"Ye must not defend Rosie so, my dear." He spoke seriously; it seemed to Elizabeth's eyes dazzled by the outside sun, that he spoke from the shadows of the room.

"How can I not defend Rosie? At this time when she needs me most? She is my dearest friend."

Elizabeth picked up the task she was doing before she had gone outside to pick sage, which she had forgotten when she saw Goodie Pritchard. She'd been slicing an onion for soup.

The knife slammed hard against the board as she cut.

Tom regarded her anger.

"And now ye be attacking the onions?"

Elizabeth looked up. She smiled a bit, and shrugged.

"Aye, and they be as innocent as my sweet Rosie."

"They say she has been goin' to Ol' Dimond to dabble in the craft, Liz. The charges be serious. Rosie be not so innocent, an' ye do know it. Ye know –"

"I do not know! I do not!" Elizabeth raised her voice in frustration. "If I do not know, then how can they? How can they know? They do *not*!"

"Lizzie! They will arrest her anyways! They have arrested many for less!"

Elizabeth eyes burned with onion and tears that streamed down her cheeks.

"They have been callin' her devil because of her wild red hair, and they do say she sings while she walks."

"They have said these things her whole life! And the lives of her ancestors before her!"

"Aye, but it is now that they are coming for her and ye must stand clear, Liz or they will come after you too! I could not bear it."

Her husband, who had just returned from weeks at sea, looked at her as a man shipwrecked and desperate for fresh water and good rest. Elizabeth saw tears in his eyes as well, and she collapsed on to the bench.

"Who will raise the children if anything were to happen to you, Liz? And who will take Rosie's little ones into their heart, but you?"

Tom knelt and put his arms around her.

"We need you. Liz. We need you so. Ye must be careful. Please, please, be careful. For all our sakes."

Marblehead, 1995

Jo waited for Cassandra to tell her what she needed to know.

"They think it's funny." Cassandra said. "Everyone in prison thinks they're the same guy or twins. They think it's funny."

Jo's skin was crawling, but she listened.

"They talked all the time about what they did."

"Why did he come here?"

"To make you squirm, make you squirm."

Cassandra was going into a reality dream. She could see the two men wearing bright orange jumpsuits, huddled together and laughing in the prison yard.

"Grey, everything is grey except for orange, the hardscape is making her sick, sending back a hard vibration to her belly, and the men are merling like ants; they watch them watching, some have cell phones, pass them, knives, pass, pass, little broken guns, pass, and knives, hide, hide. Thoughts of death and pain and blood tremble up from the hearts of men. He says where you are, what to do, the one who got away and they laugh. They laugh, they laugh."

Jo didn't want to ask. She did not want to ask.

Jo began to cry, sitting there in her clean, pretty and efficient real estate office that she had worked so hard to create with her new partner, and a new husband, and she just began to cry. There was a sign over her desk and over her head that was supposed to be a joke. One side read Marblehead with an arrow pointing toward Old Town; the other side read Real

World, with an arrow pointing out of town. Jo wasn't thinking of the irony of the cheerful sign hanging over her head.

Cassandra was still lost in her dream of *men in orange coveralls milling about a grey yard and the hurting malice that filled each one, actually hurting her, her head ached, stabbing pains in her back and stomach, her bones broken, her teeth knocked out...*

Cassandra groaned and doubled over in pain that was not hers.

"Are you all right?" Jo lifted her head from her arms.

"Yes."

...the confusion, the many cries in the night, she could hear, how to get, how to get, how to get, always how to get, the deep sorrow like eternity, like terrified bats flying blindly in the light, looking for that tiny opening to squeeze through already blackened and slimed over by their kind, how to get, how to get, how to get.

Jo finally stopped crying, just for a moment, her face wet with tears, "Is he, is he – I mean, will he?"

Cassandra came out of her dream just at that moment and said, "Yes."

Isabella, Isla Hispaniola, 1692

Lowther thought he was being cunning when he stumbled into the tavern instead of the brothel at Villa del Stella Negra to learn about the *Propriety*.

He thought, "I'll stay clear of those bitches and find out from ol' Listen down at the punch house."

Listen was so old, he almost disappeared where he lingered in the murky corners of rooms, making himself small, nearly invisible, only to come away with gems that fell from the lips of others.

Everyone knew to be cautious 'round ol' Listen. Lowther was never cautious; he considered caution beneath him. Let others be wary of him!

Lowther found Listen just as he thought he would: slumped in the shadows listening to a nearby table of men playing cards.

"Spadille, dos."

"Basto."

"Renege."

The card players, deep in their game, were oblivious to Lowther and the old man.

Lowther slid to the floor next to the old man who stank of years of filth and bodily soil. A large cockroach crawled out of the neck of Listen's garment, and even Lowther sickened a bit at the sight of it. In truth, Lowther did not look so very different. The pirate's clothes rotted on his foul body; he stank as though pickled in years of tobacco, rum, and spices. His broad features spread across his face; his scarred skin had gone dark from not washing; his dusty hair was matted and snarled.

"What 'ave ye heard of the Spanish loot taken 'board the *Propriety* from the *Teresa* out of Antigua?" Lowther whispered to Listen.

Listen was a pile of rags. His teeth were gone except for one, very long front tooth that hung over his bloated bottom lip. Listen's blind eyes were closed. He opened them as if to see who was speaking to him. He knew it was Lowther; he'd been expecting him. Listen chuckled. His cloudy, bloodshot eyes swam in blue milk. A small tear ran out of one of them and down his pocky nose.

"I hear the *Teresa* was laden with gold 'dores!" Listen leaned toward Lowther and hissed.

"Ah, ha! I get ye meanin', ol' Listen! I must have news o' 'er! Who took her cargo and where be they bound? Give me what I seek, an' there'll be moidores a plenty."

Listen was quiet. He seemed to watch the men playing at ombre somewhere in his mind's seeing eye.

Their game went on peacefully enough until one slapped his cards down and shouted, *"Yo soy el hombre!"* At that point, all the others rose and seized his hand to see for themselves. Cards scattered across the floor, fists slammed into jaws, a struggle for the coins on the table, chairs fell over.

Lowther reached for his pistol. He shot at the ceiling. Women screamed.

"Git yer bloody arses out of 'ere! Can't ye see I'm 'avin' a civilized discussion?"

The men, who were Spanish sailors armed only with knives, backed away from Lowther and his pistol.

Lowther pulled up one of their chairs. He slid all the coins on the table into his pocket. Then he turned to Listen, who stayed slumped on the floor.

"What news 'ave ye of she?"

Listen held out his palm. Lowther sighed resignedly and reached for his pocket, but instead of taking out a coin, he slid a small blade out of his belt and this he squeezed into the old man's palm.

Listen squealed and leaped forward. Lowther caught him and pressed the knife deeper.

"Now, tell me what I want to 'ear or you'll be scratchin' yer arse with a stump!"

"She be gone, far gone!"

"What's 'er cargo, then?"

"Silk. Silver from l'Álamos. Gold, raw from the mines in Mexico. Precious jewels as a gift to Queen Mary." Listen spouted exactly what Lowther wished to hear.

"Ah! How'd ye know?"

"'Tis said all about! 'Tis so! The *Teresa* went down not far from Antigua, in the Sargossa. Cap'n Vane of the *Propriety* took 'er cargo and burned 'er with 200 slaves aboard 'cause he couldn't stand the stench."

Lowther also hated the stench and burned slave ships as well. There was profit to be made, but slaves were more trouble than they were worth. He loved to watch a ship burn, blackbird or otherwise, but it gave him no satisfaction to hear of another getting his bounty.

"Where's the *Propriety* now?" Lowther twisted the knife. A fountain of Listen's brownish blood spurted upwards and spilled over both men's hands.

"The *Propriety* is fast sailing north to Virginia, then onward to Salem harbor."

"Ah!" Lowther released Listen. "If she ain't, I'll come back for ye neck!"

As soon as Lowther left the tavern, Listen hobbled away as fast as he could to where the youngest prostitutes waited for him. They cooed over him, and took his bloody hand in their own, washing him in a bowl of water. They put ointment on his wound. They wrapped his palm in a clean cloth. They kissed his palm and put it to their young breasts.

Listen had long lost the urge through weakness and years. However, he grinned his toothless grin and caressed their plump breasts with both hands, which was his promised reward for so misleading Lowther and clearing the way for Ned Low to go home.

Isabella Harbor, Isla Hispaniola, 1692

The first and only time Ned Low wept was the first time he had sailed away from Jordana. Since that day, he had sailed away from her exactly four times. Each time, his heart had grown harder, but as the *Deliverance* cast off on this the fifth time, his eyes filled once again with tears. He sniffed the tears back. He wasn't in love with Jordana. It wasn't that. He would miss her cool arms, her sweet scent and her steady comfort. He would miss being able to laugh.

He desired Molly Treadwell. There was a certain danger in it, in taking her for himself, that he relished. She was better than he; made for something better than he. She was the finest thing he knew to exist in the world. He knew he was in love with her. And, now, he was sailing toward her.

But, there was so much business in between.

Much to try him, excite him and, possibly, kill him. He did not know what awaited him. He had come to fear what might happen more than he ever had. He hated this weakness. It was a weakness that made him lash out. He would have to fight now against weakness. He could no longer drink as he had. And he could no longer hide so much in that silken trunk. He had to be aware of Lowther's every mood. He had to be certain Lowther would stay the course for Salem. He knew if they took a ship on their journey, and he was sure they would take at least one, if not two or three or more, then he would be a savage fighter to compensate for the terrible horror that tormented him. He thought betimes of the other men in the crew, tales told to him by Lowther: of Tim Hide, who had held his mother in his arms as she had sucked her last breath and died of starvation, how he relished killing every fat and well-fed passenger; of Jack Goodman, whose father had beaten him and his brothers till they were raw, how he killed to kill his father over and over; of Piccoli, the Italian, who was forced to sell his sister to a priest in order to free himself, how he loved to kill priests and clergymen. Ned thought of these men without compassion. He thought only of confirmation.

***

From the window of her room - for Jordana never left this room except to ride in her carriage or walk in her gardens or swim naked in her pool - the very same window where Ned liked to stand and gaze out to sea, Jordana watched as the *Deliverance* sailed from the haven of Isabella.

She listened to Ned's heart and she heard him declare his love for the fair-haired girl and his hatred for the man who held him prisoner. It was no surprise to Jordana.

Still, her heart ached. Many had loved her, but no one as darkly beautiful as the Peti' Low. No one as sad and as terrible. She knew who he was and what he would do. He was already more of a man than any other man she had ever met. She would never love another as long as she lived.

Marblehead, 1995

"Dad, maybe we should get a ghost hunter crew in." His son, Pete said.

Peter hesitated; he felt pretty glum. That would mean he'd have to admit Beth was – a spirit – was as close as he could get to the word ghost, even in his mind, without choking on it.

"Do we really need someone to tell us what we already know?" Peter asked, feeling like the kid. He supposed it was a good thing that Pete getting older and wiser but did he have to sound so wise at ten? Ghost hunters. Jeez, Peter had to admit, there were things he didn't know anything about that his son seemed pretty familiar with.

"Well, it's not so much that we don't know, it's that we might find out more."

He and Pete, the two dogs and Emily were driving to pick up Sarah at her ballet class at Marblehead Ballet and then they were going to get pizza for dinner.

Marblehead was especially lovely at twilight with the sun getting lower in the sky. At the moment, the sun was glaring gold on a slate blue field; in an hour or so the sky would be churning up brilliant violet and fiery streaks that forced you to pause for a moment to take it all in, to take a picture with your memory.

Peter was practically oblivious to the sunset when he was out with the kids; he took in the beauty half-unconsciously, through osmosis. Since the murder of that little girl out in California, Polly Klaas, and since losing Beth, Peter was quietly obsessive about driving his children and keeping them with him. He hadn't mentioned any of his worries to Emily or Sarah, but Pete had picked up on his uber-caution and silently cooperated. For how long, Peter wondered. Already, he went off occasionally on his own or with friends. He hoped he'd given his son enough ammunition by way of training to help him through any situation. Jeez, kids needed training nowadays; he realized, maybe they always had. He'd bitten the bullet and watched the J.J. Fassbinder safety videos with Pete about dropping his backpack, and running back in the opposite direction of the pedophile's car, about staying clear of vans, about making a lot of noise, and about telling someone. He hated talking about any of it to a kid. But, he had to be sure that Pete knew exactly what the danger was, exactly what "a stranger" meant, exactly what a pedophile wanted to do. Peter dreaded having the same conversation with Sarah and Emily when they were old enough to go out on their own. He secretly hoped Pete would enlighten the girls at some point. Pete took the lessons seriously. Peter was grateful, but he hated the whole idea. He remembered childhood as a time of complete and unconscious freedom being on his bike all day away from home: in summer, swimming, jumping back on the bike dripping wet, bareheaded and barefoot, catching a meal at someone's house or back at his own, jumping back on the bike again, roaming and exploring the town till dark when it was finally time to go home and crash on his bed. Winter was no different; he'd stayed out all day in winter too, sledding, skating on Redd's Pond, exploring, eagerly taking part in huge, town-wide snowball fights that went on for days. Now, he was grown-up and afraid. Afraid of what might happen next. Afraid of everyday surprises. And, yes, afraid of ghosts.

Emily was in her car seat in the back, listening to all the ghost talk. Peter thought, how much could she understand?

He stopped his old Volvo in front of the Marblehead Ballet and the two dogs started to go into their "dance" as Peter called it: twisting their bodies, whimpering eagerly, turning awkwardly in the confines of the back seat in anticipation of seeing Sarah. Tiger resembled a dirty lapso, and Pizza, well, Beth always claimed he was part Irish setter. For a second, Tiger's butt was in Em's face, then his face was in her face and he licked her absentmindedly and Em giggled. Then, both dogs looked anxiously out the window for Sarah. Then, they started dancing round again. While he watched the dogs' routine, Peter realized that Emily suddenly looked too big for her car seat. Was she too big for her car seat? Peter asked himself. What was happening? And why was it happening so fast?

The door opened and all the little ballerinas came running out. Parents grabbed little bodies in black leotards and pink tights. Peter got out of the car and Sarah ran into his arms. She looked so sweet in her pale pink tights and black leotard. She was still wearing her pink ballet slippers, so they had to go back in to look for her sneakers. He made sure he locked the car and started to tell Pete to be careful. Pete answered, "I know, Dad." without looking up from his book. Pete took a book with him now. He usually took one to the table too, and Peter had to tell him to put it away, but he was proud of him for reading so much. He supposed his son was a nerd. Oh, well, he always knew Pete wasn't exactly an athlete. He looked like a surfer with his long, tangled blonde curls and sandaled feet. Pete was tanned and sun-bleached, like most Marblehead kids in summer, but he spent most of his time outdoors lying flat on his belly on the grass with a book. Peter glimpsed the book's title: "Tales at Midnight: True Stories from Parapsychology Casebooks and -" Peter sighed. Pete was ten years old, but his reading material was over his Dad's head at the moment.

Looking for Sarah's sneakers took a while. When Peter walked in to the building, there seemed to be nothing but piles of sneakers in the entryway. He and Sarah finally found her pair; Peter sat her down on a nearby bench and put them on her.

"Hi, Petie!" One of the mothers called out to him, waving her hand and grinning with such brilliantly white teeth against her salon tan, Peter actually cringed a little. "Kill me now!" he thought.

"Yeah, hi, how are ya?" He replied.

"I love your scruffy look!" She cooed, waving.

Peter admitted to himself, he didn't shave very often, and might not have combed his hair since his morning shower. Did he shower that day? What day was it? Oh, yeah, Weds, Ballet Day.

"Who's that?" He asked Sarah.

'That's Martha's mom." By her deadpan tone, he knew Martha's mom was a pistol.

"Oh. She called me 'Petie'." Now he knew why his son hated being called Petie.

Back in the car, the dogs slurped their welcome over Sarah's face as she buckled her seat belt. Sarah leaned over and kissed Emily on the cheek. Pete was still reading his book.

Suddenly Sarah piped as she clicked her seat belt, "Pete has a girl friend named Sarah!"

"What?" Peter gasped.

Pete barely looked up from his book.

"She's not my girl friend."

"Is too! Her sister, Jade told me so in class tonight!"

Emily giggled. The dogs barked like they knew too.

"What's going on, wanna tell me?" Peter looked in the rear view at Sarah and over to Pete.

Pete sighed. "We're friends, Dad. Sarah Weaver. She has an Apple Blackbird PowerBook 540c with a track pad and a matrix color screen and I want one too."

"Paul Weaver's daughter?"

"Uh, huh."

Paul was Peter's lawyer. In fact, he was just about everyone's lawyer in town. His daughters, there were four, were charming and lovely girls. But, Peter didn't want to even *think* about his ten-year-old son and girls.

"What's a PowerBook? Dare I ask?"

"It's a laptop, Dad. An Apple. I could really use one."

"An Apple." He repeated foolishly, not really sure what that was.

"Yeah, Apple makes the best computers."

"How much?"

"I dunno, 3?"

"3 what?"

"Thousand."

"Who wants pizza?" Peter called out.

Pete didn't answer. Emily said, "I do! I do!"

Then, Sarah said, "Jessica Knight says that pizza isn't good for you and we should eat healthy foods."

"Who said that?"

"Jessica Knight."

Peter and his son exchanged glances.

"She's right, Dad. Pizza's not that great."

Emily piped in, "I like pizza!"

"So do I, Em." Peter said.

"Me too, but not every night, Dad." Pete told him, turning the page.

"So, you can actually read while talking about something else?" Peter watched his son's hand turning the page.

"Ah, yeah!"

"And, we don't have pizza every night."

"Every time we go out."

"So, what do you suggest?"

"Broccoli!" Sarah told him.

"Broccoli?" Peter winced. "I don't want broccoli on my pizza!"

"You don't have to have it on your pizza, Dad." Pete informed him.

"They do put broccoli on pizza, though. Don't they? They do at the King's Rook. Mom and I used to love their shrimp scampi pizza."

"Dad, that's so '80s!" Pete laughed.

"Yeah, I guess." Peter went off into a daydream memory of he and Beth in the romantic candlelight of the Rook's back room, snug and dark as a ship's hold, where the time worn wood of the tables had come from an old vessel, and the stained glass windows shone like jewels, where it was private, where everyone was quiet and content for a while.

Peter sighed.

His son looked over. He knew he was thinking of his mom.

"I'm tellin' you, Dad, we should hire a ghost crew. You might feel better."

"Yeah, maybe. How about Bertolini's? They have pizza *and* broccoli."

"Yeah, sure."

"Okay, Dad! But, I'll have pizza too!" Sarah chimed.

Kids and father burst into laughter at that.

The Atlantic, North of the Caribbean, 1692

Blood, monstrous masses of blood pouring at him, pouring through cracks in the deck, massing on the deck, ankle deep in blood; the smell of blood, rank, sour, fresh, fresh again, fresh again, turning sour on his lips, splattering his forehead, drying there, caking, more blood upon blood, more blood; the taste of blood, like rancid meat, tasting of fish blood, of sugar blood, of spiced blood; blood blinding him, spitting out blood, pouring down his face and neck, pouring down his legs, none of it his, all of it his.

Not a dream! His sword and his knife flashed over and over, slay or be slain, Ned fought alongside the crew, slaughtering all on board the *Destiny* till none but those Lowther would torture stood on deck. Ned was a good fighter, so Lowther had told him, and for that he was rewarded with more fighting. Something about his being strong and tall for a boy, yet smaller than a man, made Ned lethal in ways the others were not. He could climb and swing and surprise the enemy like a deadly gadfly.

Nothing was left. Lowther beamed with satisfaction as each trunk, crate and hogshead was lifted aboard out of the belly of the *Destiny*. As captain, he would take the lion's share. Later, each man would get his part.

"Cum thee, lad! Let us begin our real business!" Lowther called to him.

He knew what it meant. The torture of the captives. He, Ned was to bare the chest of the ship's captain, one Daniel Tate. He did so with his knife, slicing through his official coat, tearing the man's shirt from his back. Then, he slit the trousers down the front till the Captain stood naked in strips of his clothing. Two other men wrestled the man's boots from him and tossed them to the crew.

"Ah, you'll not be needed those no more!" Lowther growled.

He leaned in with his knife. Several passengers whose turn had not yet come gasped as Lowther's blade came close and drew blood just nicking the Captain's throat.

"Nay, 'tis not yer neck I want today, 'tis yer bowels!"

With that Lowther sliced Captain Tate's abdomen wide open. The Captain howled. Blood leapt from his belly and sprayed Lowther. Two ladies fainted anew; they fell face first into blood. Lowther had hardly begun. He yanked the Captain's intestine out and handed it to Ned, whose job it was to nail one end to the mast. This he did. The horror of seeing a child do this job was not lost on the onlookers.

Then Lowther began to whip the Captain with the cat-o-nine-tails and all the crew laughed and sang the pirate's song about freedom and revenge to which Captain Tate, or what remained of him, was made to run round and round the mast, slipping in his own blood, whipped and whipped, slipping and sliding, running against life, against odds, against hope, derided and smacked by the *Deliverance* crew, too shocked to die, whipped and whipped, running, stumbling, running, falling, finally dead. The captain's body jerked upwards in the death dance; the crew laughed anew, grabbing the rest of the passengers from the *Destiny* to do with as they wished.

Screaming and laughing, screaming from the captives, laughing and singing from the crew, about blood. "The life flows out of my enemy," They sang, some with fine voices, creating a terrifyingly weird mock opera. "I rejoice at the flow of blood from my sword/the blood flows for my vengeance of many lost years/I fight for my joy! I kill not for gold, but for joy!"

Lowther tapped his toe to the rhythm of the music provided by the crew's players of fife, fiddle and drum. His boot hit something odd. He looked down to see Captain Tate's gold watch on the bloody deck. He stooped to pick it up; it opened to a miniature of the man's lovely wife. Blood dripped from Lowther's hands down the woman's face.

"She's a pretty young widow now!" Lowther laughed as he slipped the watch into his own pocket.

He was closer now to the treasure he coveted. Only two ships away from the treasure of the *Teresa*.

In the light of the burning *Destiny*, in the euphoria of having fought and taken and being still alive, the remaining crew of the *Deliverance* – for they had lost three of their brothers and later they would bury them at sea, but for now – they stripped, greased themselves with hog fat, started up a good jig, drank till they were stupefied, and began a ritual writhing and churning of men that made Ned sick with apprehension. Men danced for hours along the decks to the pounding music with crazed joy. Blindly, they humped each other and the captives like mad dogs.

Ned could not help watching; he was so fascinated by this debauchery. Yes, it was happening, he had to tell himself. Lowther was busy abusing one of the two women who had fainted. Weirdly, Lowther was now naked under pieces of a woman's torn dress over his back and a feathered bonnet on his head as he thrust himself between the woman's bare legs. Several men stood by and laughed at the sight. It was dangerous to linger. Though none but Lowther could touch him, he never trusted the men in their blind celebratory madness. Twice he felt a hand on his shoulder, pulling him, and twice he fought the man off with his blade. Two men would show fresh cuts on their faces in the light of day.

Quietly, Ned slipped below to find his silken trunk.

He had to move several new trunks and crates before he found it. He crawled inside. The womanly smell of the silk made him near mad, and he hated to admit, he too needed to release himself. With blood that was not his own dripping from his hands, he did so in a sick frenzy, still hearing the clashing of knives ringing in his ears, thinking all the while not of Molly and of peace and loveliness, but of cold death, of blood-soaked slaughter and of Jordana's musky tunnel to oblivion.

Marblehead, 1692

When they came for Rosie, it could not have been worse.

The summer day was brilliantly sunny and blue of sky. The honorable men and women of town approached the Low lintel from the street side, just skirting the marsh. They were two Selectmen, Samuel Peach and Ambrose Gale; several of Rosie's neighbors, Goody Gatchell, Goody Pritchard, Goody Minot; two of their husbands, as the other was busy afield; and a small group of rowdy children throwing stones.

The assembly reached the front door; they knocked and received no answer. They knocked again.

"Goody Low! Goody Low! Ye cannot hide from the law! Show yourself to this company!"

No answer.

Selectman Gale pushed the old wooden door. It was unlatched.

The group entered the dark, silent home.

"Goody Low, by the name of His Majesties King William and Queen Mary, I am authorized to command ye to show yourself to us!"

No one spoke.

The group stepped forward cautiously.

"Careful! She may jump out at us in any form!" Selectman Peach whispered.

Suddenly, a fat, orange tabby cat snarled at them and darted out from under a table. It sprang across their path causing the group to shout in alarm.

"She is already sending her kindred spirits!" Goody Gatchell cried.

"I daren't go any further!" cried Goody Pritchard, and she backed away, but did not leave the shadows of the room.

"Hush, we must proceed."

The solemn and righteous group stepped cautiously forward until they reached the sunlight of out of doors again, at the back door of the kitchen. There, in the shade of a maple, they witnessed Rosie's newest and ninth babe, Edwina, called Lena, named after Edward Dimond, whom Rosie was sure had saved her husband at sea, peacefully asleep in her crib, her tiny mouth pulsating with dreams of her mother's breast.

"There!" Goody Pritchard pointed out the back door, being the first to spy Rosie, and she would praise herself continually afterwards as being the first to set eyes on her.

Three of the smaller children played about her. The oldest girl Nan worked at carding wool. Two of Rosie's sons argued and pulled at a rope that was for some reason incredibly desirable to both of them. It was a scene of domestic industry. But that was not how it was perceived.

Rosie was washing clothes. Her appearance and her task could not have made her look more like a witch. Rosie's bright red hair was half fastened, half tumbling down her bare shoulders and back. Since she hated to wear a corset while she worked, she was not wearing one. Her shift slipped down her naked shoulders and her full breasts shook with each movement of the stick she used to stir the pot – a pot that stood upon a tripod over an open fire. Sweat poured down Rosie's temples, under her ears, down her naked throat, and like a river between her breasts. And, she was cross. Very, very short tempered from the hot, tedious labor.

"Oh, put that rope down a minute will you, what're ye about with that thing? Come and stir a bit, there's a good lad."

When the Selectmen and townspeople broke out of the back door of Rosie's house, Rosie looked up cross and squinting into the light, stirring the steaming pot of clothes.

"Rosie Low!" Shouted Selectman Ambrose Gale, "You have been accused!"

"Look!" cried Goodie Minot. "She stirs the Devil's Brew!"

"'Tes me foul britches, ye damn cow, an' ye welcome to 'em!" Rosie growled defiantly, still stirring the pot. But, her heart was starting to pound a bit harder.

Rosie also stood quite near the wood, where it was cooler in the shade.

"Look! She be near the wood where the Devil himself do bide!"

"'Tes the very same wood that 'rounds ye house an' most of Marbley Harbor, ye dumb ox!" Rosie defended herself.

Of a sudden, two sparrows shrieked. With wings flapping, and feet joined together in a squabble, the birds fell from above and landed in the pot of laundry.

Rosie looked stunned. She knew instantly how this unfortunate event would be divined.

The ensemble of Selectmen and righteous citizens gasped all together with one voice and cried out, "Witch!" "Evil!" "See how the Devil do send his minions to her!" "Quick, Mr. Peach! Get 'er before she flies off! Quickly! Quickly!"

Rosie's face went white. The men grabbed her arms and pulled her from her chore, which she regretted having hated, that which she wished she could continue, and then make the dinner she knew she might never make again.

The children were also stunned. The boys grabbed on to the Selectmen's official coats in a vain attempt to pull the men from their mother, but their small bodies were thrust aside. The younger ones began to weep. The baby wailed from the kitchen crib.

Rosie nodded to Nan. Nan knew what to do.

Nan, also quite pale and near faint, solemnly returned her mother's nod. How she had dreaded this day! And now it had come.

Marblehead, 1995

Jo was out jogging at Fort Sewall. She loved the path that wound itself around the cliff overlooking the open ocean to the north – where the British had been sent on their way by the *U.S.S. Constitution* in 1812 - and the cove below to the south – where pirates had murdered that Englishwoman in 1690. It was impossible to ignore the past in Marblehead; layers of stories were always present in her mind. Fort Sewall was briskly cold in winter and sizzling hot in summer, and she loved it. It was bright and clean and it practically belonged to her alone at five a.m. There were a few regulars: the architect who flirted with her; the interior designer who constantly yacked on the phone while she power walked; the young mother with a curious infant on her back. Jo never flirted back with the architect, but she loved to flirt with the infant, making faces, saying hello, making the little girl laugh. None of the other joggers were there on this day.

Someone passed her. She thought she smelled alcohol.

A man jogged ahead of her now on the path.

He turned around and jogged backwards.

It was that guy, Ben Hardy! He was grinning at her, and he was weirdly jogging backwards!

Jo ran faster, as fast as she could, though she felt she could hardly breathe. In order to get past him, she had to run off the path, dangerously down the hill, over rocks and weeds that fell down the side of the cliff. She dashed around him while he laughed at her.

"I'm gonna get you!" He called after her. "You can run but you can't hide!"

Jo ran till she reached Front Street where a couple of older women were out walking their dogs. There, she stopped to catch her breath. She was pretty uncomfortable and probably looked it, because the women asked if she were okay.

"Yes, yes! Fine!" Jo managed, her breath scraping her raw throat. "I just need water." She unhooked the bottle from her belt and drank. The cool water barely made a difference to the heat in her throat.

The women nodded, unconvinced, and walked on.

Far up on the hill, she could see Ben Hardy waving to her.

She could tell he was laughing.

Marblehead, 1692

"The children are all at home alone!" cried Matt Low to Elizabeth and Tom, who stood in their kitchen and listened to him. "They came and they took my Rosie! My dear Rosie who never harmed another in her life! The little ones will not be comforted. The baby wails for the breast. Nan canna' do it all the way my Rosie could! Oh, what shall become of us all? How could they think my lovely girl was a witch? How could they?"

Elizabeth was silent. Rosie had been going to Ol' Dimond's house to look through his enchanted telescope and she had been discovered. Rosie had flaunted the rules for so long. Now, she was caught. Elizabeth was sympathetic, yet she felt powerless to help as she stood now wearing collar and corset feeling herself caught as a cloistered nun.

"Matt," Tom began, "Ye must know Rosie was going to see Ol' Dimond, and that he was teaching her his ways and mysteries. It was sure that she would be found out one day."

"I tried to stop her, Matty, but she would not hear me." Elizabeth told him. "She said she saw yer Ned, that Ol' Dimond showed 'er through his conjurin' 'scope and she could n'er give it up."

Matt sat down, exhausted.

"I know." He said. "I know, she did tell me. I cunna stop 'er neither."

"Matty, I'm not sayin' she deserved to be taken, I'm not." Elizabeth reassured him. "No one deserves it. How can anyone worship Satan? 'Tis madness to think so!"

"They do hate 'er for her passion and for 'er happiness." Matt said. "They do hate 'er fer 'er red hair and 'er cheerful beauty. The dried up sour old crabapples they be!"

He threw his head down on the very table where his wife had once wept for his safety at sea, and there he also wept. Elizabeth regarded his sorrow and knew the outcome would not be as happy as his homecoming. She did not think Rosie could possibly make such a cheerful return from the authority of the Salem judges as Matty had from the terror of the raging sea. Few had survived the self-righteousness of men – arrest – worse than a storm at sea. Rosie would never confess. Only a confession and repentance could save her.

As though hearing her very thoughts, Matt whispered aloud, "My Rosie will hang before she confesses to being a witch. She will not satisfy them thusly. She will not ever!"

Elizabeth touched his shoulder. His flesh shuddered under her palm.

"Rosie has asked me to help, Matt. Nan will bring some of the children to me from time to time to ease her burden. Dunna fret so. I will be helping as soon as tomorrow. Why, ye could bring the baby tonight and I will find a nurse maid."

"Who will suckle the babe of an accused witch?" Matt cried.

"I would, if I were nursing. I would straight off! Ye would not need to ask me!" Elizabeth told him.

Matt reached up and patted her hand.

"I will bring Edwina, then. Who will ye find?"

"Matt, I do know of a slave at Goody Tucker's who has just delivered safely of a babe. She will help us, I'm sure."

Matt looked at her.

"A slave? A slave will help us?"

"Yes! I'm sure of it!"

"That is where we are then. We are rightly named Low that now we are lower than a slave."

"Matt! We must be grateful to the Lord who provides!" Tom scolded his friend.

Matt's tears made tracks on his face.

"Suckled by a slave." He repeated miserably. "Will that turn my baby black?"

"Matt! Ye must not fret so! First, let us feed the child, then we will worry about the rest."

"I will bring Edwina, then." He said with no confidence. He feared greatly. Matt Low did not know what to make of what was happening in his town and to the neighbors he had known so well. He was used to seeing hard things away from home, used to the treachery of the sea, for instance, and how she could change from life-giver to life-taker in an instant. He was used to seeing men kill each other for little more than a turn of a card. But, home had always been quiet and true. He was not the sort of man who examined his thoughts, but if he were pressed to say exactly what he feared, he would say that he feared what new madness was to come for Rosie, for the babe, for himself, and for all.

Marblehead, 1692

That evening while Rosie was imprisoned, Elizabeth carried Rosie's hungry and lustily crying newborn to the house of her neighbors, the Tuckers. Many people walking by stared in her direction, but she did not care. She was glad of the mild evening and the cool salt breeze, reassuring on her face. Her neighbors could be damned. Except the Tuckers, of course, she added hastily to her thoughts. She needed them now.

The Tuckers were more affluent than most, as Mr. Tucker was a ship's captain, and quite successful. He was often away from home. His wife, Grace, was a cheerful, goodly woman with no children of her own.

The Tuckers had several slaves working in the house, the large garden and the stables. There was an outbuilding on the grounds for garden and livestock slaves. The groom slept in a tiny room in the back of the stable. In fact, the Tucker house occupied a large lot, very large for Marblehead, that nestled into a flat at the base of a cow path. Mr. Tucker was a very generous man who allowed the town to use his property as common land for grazing. Several cows, sheep and goats littered the grass as Elizabeth approached. They did not mind her at all, nor she them. In fact, on this night, Elizabeth preferred the livestock to most of the folks she knew.

The Tucker home was fine eggshell white saltbox with a brightly painted scarlet front door; there was a shining copper foot guard, brick stairs, an iron boot scraper, and a black wrought iron rail. The slave, Cuba, called Sarah by her masters, opened the door when Elizabeth knocked. Sarah was a slight woman whose dark skin set off the colorful red calico cloth wrapped around her head. Only the Tuckers would allow a slave to wear the exotic turquoise beaded earrings that dangled from her pierced ears. Sarah's breasts were full of milk: Elizabeth noticed right away that they swelled above her bodice and even wet her frock at the nipples. Sarah's baby was a boy, also called Cuba, after their homeland, as was the custom amongst slaves.

Sarah regarded Elizabeth. She knew what she wanted, of course, the crying babe made that obvious, but she stood for a moment enjoying her sudden power. She smiled, knowingly, and a bit arrogantly. She waited.

"Sarah," Elizabeth began, "is your mistress at home?"

"Aye, miss, she be in the parlor." Sarah stepped aside to allow Elizabeth to enter.

Elizabeth found Goody Tucker bent over a basket in front of the fire in the parlor. In the basket was her beloved King Charles spaniel bitch, Matilda and her newly born litter of squirming pups.

"Oh, Goody Treadwell! Come, look at Matilda's new little ones! I have yet to name them. Perhaps you could help me choose! I am all a flutter, you see, from comforting my dear Matilda in her distress!"

Elizabeth leaned over the basket with her friend's screaming child.

"I'm afraid I've come on an emergency of my own." Elizabeth informed her, gently.

"Oh! Oh, my yes!" said Goody Tucker, rising. "Yes, of course, you have. I have heard all about Goody Low's misfortune. Sarah! Sarah! Do come to Goody Treadwell's aid, there's a dear."

It was only then that Sarah, with a satisfied smirk, reached for the child and took her from Elizabeth's arms.

Elizabeth was both relieved and forewarned. Something in Sarah's demeanor gave her pause, but she handed over the agitated child nevertheless. Sarah took Lena out of the room, to the kitchen, probably, to nurse her. Elizabeth wanted to follow, but Goody Tucker insisted that tea be brought.

"It seems litters abound just now!" Goody Tucker giggled.

Elizabeth was shocked, but said nothing. She sat down on a small chair embroidered lavishly with flowers and butterflies.

A maid came with the tea. Goody Tucker asked her to take the dog basket to the kitchen.

"I am sentimental, I know. Dogs should be in the stable or the kitchen, but I could not bear it. I could not. Just for a moment, I had to have her by me." She sipped her tea. "You have so many little ones, I'm sure you understand."

"Oh, yes." Elizabeth agreed.

Goody Tucker prattled on about many things. Including the fact that her husband was away at sea, that he captained the ship, *Clothilde,* a ship owned by the illustrious merchant Philip English.

"Of course, we are that worried about Mr. English's current misfortune and we hope it will not distress us too terribly. Of course, I know nothing of such matters. Mr. Tucker is away at sea, you see." Goody Tucker added this last as though she were quite confused by the latest events.

Philip English and his wife, though of the wealthy merchant class, had also been recently incarcerated for witchcraft.

Elizabeth sat as patiently as she could. She was worried about Rosie's baby, not about Mr. English's arrest at this moment. Though somewhere in her shocked and muddled mind, she realized Mr. English's misfortune could also touch her own and the awful dark cloud that did seem to fall from news of this sort, that the moneyed class could be as vulnerable as her dear Rosie. What was happening? How was such topsy-turvy madness happening in her small and modest world?

"Where is Sarah's baby, Goody Tucker? Will she keep her child?" Elizabeth ventured, thinking practically of the supply of breast milk.

Goody Tucker stopped talking and thought for a moment, as though she were trying to recall who Sarah was. "Oh, yes! Oh, yes, of course, she will. We can afford it, and Mr. Tucker would not consider selling the little boy who will be useful enough in a few years. Besides, you know, Goody Treadwell, slaves are less likely to run off if they have family about them."

Goody Tucker changed the subject to one that interested her.

"Will you help me choose the names for my new little ones? Do you think Christian names are blasphemous for pups? I'm sure they could not be!"

"I'm sure not."

Elizabeth regarded the details of the room. The walls were hung with thick gold and green wallpaper on which the pattern of a mansion, river, trees, horses, and elegant people in formal dress repeated over and over. The lavish wallpaper was in turn covered with elaborately framed paintings of men and women in silks, a rather obese lady holding an apple, landscapes of rivers and trees and a few paintings of dead game and dogs, lacquered and glistening in the candlelight. A cupboard of rich, dark wood shone against the shimmering walls. Within the cupboard, through highly polished leaded glass, Elizabeth could see fine blue and white dishes twinkling with light. Ladies and gentlemen in strange exotic dress embarked on journeys in carriages upon these dishes.

"I see you are looking at my Dutch collection, recently purchased by my husband in Amsterdam and Paris. Lovely, aren't they? I assure you, they are au currant. The most recent designs from the forbidden Orient."

The floor beneath Elizabeth's poor shoes was a golden wood, dazzling with shine, covered here and there with deep carpets and rugs of patterns so varied and colorful, Elizabeth's eyes became confused and she had to look away. She longed for her simple dirt floor at home from which green plants sometimes took root.

The tea was brought in paper-thin teacups, so small and delicate, Elizabeth hesitated to lift hers to her mouth. The cup was searing hot to her lips, and she jumped back a bit, but soon managed. The tea was bitter, and not a flavor she was used to, not raspberry or blueberry, or mint, but something harsh and black.

Goody Tucker never stopped talking, mostly about the town, her neighbors, and her little dog that had just given birth.

"Yes, I did see her, Goody Tucker, when I came in, yes, of course, yes, you are very fortunate in your pet."

"I wonder how she is now. Mary! Please bring Matilda to me! I must see her immediately!"

Mary appeared to say, "Yes, Mum." Then, she left and reappeared slightly disheveled, confused, and to Elizabeth's mind, embarrassed. "The dog is asleep, Mum."

"Oh." Goody Tucker hesitated to be so maneuvered by a servant. "Yes, of course she is. She must be that fatigued!"

"But, I fear I must be going, as it will be dark soon, and I must bring the baby home."

"Oh, yes! Yes, of course!"

Elizabeth was startled as Goody Tucker rang a little copper bell that had rested on the little mahogany table by her side.

The maid appeared and curtsied.

"Mary, will you tell Sarah to bring Goody Treadwell's child. Thank you."

Elizabeth didn't correct her. In a few minutes, too long for Elizabeth's comfort, Sarah brought Lena back. The child slept peacefully, her cheeks puffed and flushed with blood, her little chin tucked in with comfort and satisfaction.

Elizabeth took the baby from Sarah, thanked her, and Goody Tucker, and said her goodbyes. She could not wait to get away from the Tucker house.

"We'll see you tomorrow, of course." Goody Tucker called out, waving farewell.

Elizabeth looked back to see Sarah standing at the door, smiling smugly.

Something was wrong. Instinctively, Elizabeth checked Lena's clothing and blanket. These were covered with long silky brown and white dog hairs. A few silky strands still clung to the child's damp chin.

Elizabeth blanched; she could feel the warm blood rush from her face.

The slave had given the baby to nurse on the dog! Her back stiffened. Though she wanted to turn and run back and accuse Sarah, to pummel her mercilessly, Elizabeth stiffened her back the more, and walked on instead. So *that* was a slave's comment on a white witch's infant child. Elizabeth supposed such an act would seem like justice to a slave. But, her heart broke at the insult to her dear friend and to the innocent child. She supposed there had been little harm done the one time, but she knew she could not take the child back.

There was only one thing she could do.

Marblehead, 1995

Peter Treadwell had agreed to meet, just meet, with the ghost hunters. One of them, the lead ghost hunter, Justin was the older cousin of one of his son, Pete's friends. Justin came from a very wealthy family and he had all the latest equipment, which Pete was practically salivating to see in action.

They were meeting at Peach Ice Cream. Neutral ground. Peter had told his son, "You know, this is your mother we're talking about." But, he told himself, Beth had believed in spirits. Beth had mentioned once or twice when they were renovating that she hoped the old ghosts liked what she was doing with the house. They had purchased Edward Dimond's historic home, an old saltbox that was supposed to have a ship at its core. They had found some ancient timber beams, but not a hull as expected. Beth had been devoted to its authentic restoration. But she had worried that the spirits might not appreciate the initial demolition. Taking her lead, Peter had been a little concerned about the old ghosts doing something eerie in the presence of the ghost hunters if he met the crew at the house - something he wasn't ready to witness. Old Marblehead. The house was at least three hundred years old and God only knows who or what was still lurking there. His back shivered at the idea of spirits and strange occurrences. Made him miss Beth. She understood these things better than he did. He missed her every second. He did hope Beth was still around him. At the same time, he also hoped she'd moved on, maybe to heaven, maybe to another life. But, according to his baby girl, Emily, her mother was right there with her. Emily held his hand at that moment, so Peter guessed Beth was also standing with them.

The outdoor ice cream parlor was crowded with what Peter liked to call "skinny people eating ice cream." Gorgeous people, really, fashionably scruffy and tanned, like shipwrecked gods and goddesses. Marblehead was hard-core about working out. A steady stream of joggers ran by the house and workshop all day long. Peter never had to worry about working out because he *worked*. He was pretty fit from lifting heavy boards and equipment all day. He got plenty of sun, too, out in his workshop yard. Nevertheless, Marblehead jogged by all day long, from before sunrise to late at night. Just then, as if to illustrate his thoughts, a petite blonde woman, very pregnant and very athletic, ran by wearing a Triathlon T-shirt stretched over her belly, pushing a jogging stroller in front of her. Hard-core.

Then Peter saw someone who wasn't exactly skinny. Emily's day school teacher, Meghan. She was wearing a blue dress and sitting by herself on the stone wall that ran around the flower-filled terrace adjoining Peach Ice Cream with the rest of the businesses in the tiny shopping enclave: a small market, an antique store, a photographer's studio and a bank. From the look of her, Meghan was thoroughly enjoying her ice cream cone. He liked that. Peter watched her for a second while Meghan licked with enthusiasm at the thick globes of vanilla and some other flavor on her cone, a slight smile of satisfaction on her face. She swung her round legs, which were crossed at the ankles, like a little girl. She was surrounded by daisies, roses, and what-not, flowers that to him were no more than small dots of color he could not name that blurred before his inexperienced eyes. Beth would have known the names of every little colorful dot like each were her own child. The flowers framed Meghan's plump form with an out-of-focus soft haze like one of those Impressionist paintings. Peter lost his breath a little at the rush of emotions then brushed the feelings off. He got a hold of himself and walked forward to say hello.

"Miss Meghan." Just as he said her name, Emily thrust herself past him, and grabbed Meghan by the legs. In a moment, she had crawled up on to Meghan's lap, with a little help from Meghan's free hand.

Emily kissed Meghan's soft cheek and hugged her deeply.

Meghan kissed the top of her head. "Hello, dear!" She laughed.

Peter started to hold out his hand to be shaken; he and Meghan both laughed because her hands were quite full of Emily.

"How are you?" Peter asked.

"Oh, fine! How are you guys?" Meghan replied with a sweet smile, kind of dimpled, with a bit of ice cream still on her lips.

"Chocolate?" Peter inquired, pointing to her lips.

Meghan shook her head and wiped her mouth with a napkin.

"Maple walnut!" She giggled.

Peter looked around for his son and didn't see him.

"Mind if I sit down?"

"Of course not. Pull up a chair!"

Peter laughed and sat down next to Meghan on the wall, being careful to keep a respectful "teacherly" distance.

Peter sighed in an attempt to relax. Here he was at an ice cream shop on a beautiful summer day, surrounded by flowers and beautiful, happy people and he was nervous.

"How are you?" He asked Meghan.

"I'm well, and you?" She smiled.

"Good, good."

"Are you getting ice cream?"

"Yes!" Cried Emily.

"In a minute." Peter said.

He really didn't want to move from Meghan's side for some reason. And, he noticed, neither did Emily. That is, until she saw a cute little white dog. Em jumped down from Meghan's lap and ran over to stroke the dog's fluffy fur. The dog's head flipped from one kid's ice cream to another in hopes of getting a bite.

"Mr. Treadwell…" Meghan began.

"Peter, please. Mr. Treadwell sounds so old."

"Okay. Well, I guess, it's okay since I won't be Emily's teacher any more."

Peter just kind of nodded for half a second until he realized what he had just heard.

"What?" He asked foolishly. "Why not?"

He wondered if she'd been fired. No, that couldn't be. She was too good at her job to be fired. Thoughts flooded his brain in a weird panic. He hardly knew Meghan but he had come to count on her being there every day for Emily. Emily needed Meghan. That much he was sure of.

"What's going on?" He asked with a sinking feeling in his stomach.

Marblehead, 1692

Elizabeth could not waste any time on anger or regrets. Nay, nor on horror or distaste. The babe had not been properly fed, and would need to suckle again soon. Elizabeth's anger gave her new energy. She hurried to Rosie's house, which was closer than her own.

There she found Nan a bit overwhelmed, but doing a fair job of keeping order at the Low household. Nan was a plainer version of Rosie. She had not been blessed with her mother's brightness. Her hair was a lank, browner shade of red; her cheeks were pallid and her spirit quite ordinary and plodding. Elizabeth could see that she was serving the evening meal of corn grits and dandelion greens on a soiled table in sticky trenchers. But, perhaps she was used to such a mess. Rosie had never been a tidy housekeeper, being more likely to sit and sing to the baby than sweep the floor or clear the table.

Elizabeth told Nan what she was going to do; she packed a few diaper cloths and pilches for the baby. Most were still damp from Rosie's washing that day. On the way, she could not help picking a few flowers for her friend, as Rosie herself would have done. Wild roses, though the petals fell in a frothy white shower as she walked.

Rosie was being held in the root cellar behind the larder of Selectman Peach's kitchen. She could just picture the servants going into the larder for onions or apples or flour and banging on the locked door to torment her dear Rosie with taunts of "Witch!" and "Demon!" Such thoughts made her shudder for her friend's wellbeing. Though Rosie, she was sure, would make things worse for herself by swearing an oath or two back at them. How she loved her!

Once at the Peach house, a cornflower blue saltbox with dark green shutters, Elizabeth thought for a moment of going round to the back and bribing a servant, but she walked straight up to the front door instead.

Just for a second, she felt her own husband's disapproval of what she was doing pull her backward but she shook off such doubt and knocked on the dark green painted door.

Elizabeth stood as tall and proudly as she could, holding the still sleeping babe.

The kitchen maid, Ruth Gatchell's middle girl, Addie opened the door. Addie was an overweight girl with pocky cheeks and oily hair falling out of her maid's cap.

She laughed when she saw Elizabeth holding the baby.

"What do *you* want?" She asked.

"You will tell your master I am here and I have brought the child." Elizabeth told her, pushing her way into the fine house.

Another fine house of shining wood floors, thick rugs and rich, heavy curtains.

Once inside, Elizabeth decided not to wait for the master of the house. She strode right through the hall to the rear of the house where the kitchen was, and on, past the cook and the kitchen maid both of whom stared at her: the cook dropping an egg on to the table, missing the bowl; the kitchen maid, letting fall from her wet hands a porcelain dinner plate on to the floor where it smashed to pieces. The cook did not know whom to reprimand first, but she wisely chose the kitchen maid as Elizabeth strode right into the larder.

At the rear of the larder, Elizabeth stood at the locked root cellar door.

"Open it!" She commanded.

"Ye do not give orders in this house, Goody Treadwell!"

"Call your master then and he will open it! Call him now!"

The shouts and commotion brought the footman, who in turn brought the master, and the mistress, who was cutting roses in the garden and could hear for herself that a commotion was happening just a few feet away.

Master and mistress of such a fine house were unaccustomed to standing in the kitchen areas. Servants and slaves were likewise uncomfortable to loiter next to their masters.

Selectman Peach's sensibilities were quite overcome by the presence of the baby, who woke and began to fuss. In the violence of all the shouting, Lena's whimpers grew to full-throated wails that intimidated the Selectman into fumbling for his keys and opening the lock.

Peach was confident opening the door would not risk security. The only escape of a witch they'd ever had had been from a public house on the docks. Mr. Peach felt sure no such violation was possible from the security of his watch.

The door opened to reveal Rosie sitting on a box. A small pallet lay in one corner of the room and a pile of straw in the other.

Rosie looked exhausted, disheveled and dirty from sitting in such a bare room, but she beamed with affection upon seeing her friend and her child.

"Dear one!" Elizabeth exclaimed. "I have brought the babe."

Rosie took the baby gratefully, and just in time, as Lena's fussing had become the unbearably painful howl of a newborn.

"There, there," Rosie cooed, as a crowd gathered at the root cellar door. House maid, cook, kitchen maid, footman, and master and mistress stood powerless as the baby suckled noisily on her mother's breast. Baby and breast melded as one, so robust and rosy and justly linked to each other they did seem.

Elizabeth stood as a sentry by Rosie's side, her chin just a bit too proud, she knew. Selectman Peach cleared his throat with authority.

"Return to your tasks immediately!" He ordered.

Mrs. Peach clapped her hands, and the staff flew away like pigeons.

"The child is nursing every two hours, Mr. Peach. I beg you, she is an innocent, and must stay with her mother."

Elizabeth did not wish to plead, but she also did not wish to offend. She would have liked to smack the cheeks of both master and mistress as badly behaving children, but she did not.

She waited.

"Please sir, please madam, please show some compassion for an innocent child." Elizabeth ventured.

Again, Selectman Peach cleared his throat with authority.

"Addie!" He called to the maidservant.

"Yes, sir?" Addie appeared from behind the doorway where she obviously had been lurking.

"See that a crib is brought for the child." Peach ordered. "And, bring a blanket."

Goody Peach hurried off to see that her husband's orders were carried out properly, and, of course, that an old blanket was brought and not a new one.

"Thank you, sir, madam." Elizabeth curtsied as best she could, for she had never had the occasion to do so before.

Rosie knew better than to giggle. She solemnly bent her head over her little one.

Elizabeth put the flowers down next to her on the box, where they would surely die from lack of water. More petals fell. She sat at her friend's feet amongst the petals. She placed her hand into Rosie's. Rosie gripped her flesh so hard, Elizabeth thought she would cry out, but she did not. Both women kept their gaze on the suckling babe as though babe and breast were life itself.

Selectman Peach stood for a moment and regarded this scene, which appeared to him to be a religious mockery. An innocent suckling from the teat of a devil monger! Indeed! He disapproved strongly, but for some reason, he dared not speak. Some power overtook him, he would say later, some witchcraft, and under his own roof!

Marblehead, 1995

"Mr. – Peter, there's something going on at the school that I don't approve of and I can't stay there any more." Meghan explained, her voice starting to shake. "I think you should know the teachers and some of the students, in fact, many of the teachers' own kids are taking steroids."

"What? Why? Steroids. Little kids?"

"Yes."

"Why?"

Meghan sighed. "Well, with little kids, there's a lot of germs and kids and teachers get sick if they don't have some sort of edge. It makes sense, but I can't – I just can't work in that environment."

Peter was silent. He wasn't really sure what he was hearing, it sounded so odd.

"There's more. The little ones cry, Peter. They cry all day, non-stop." Tears were beginning to gather in Meghan's blue eyes.

"They cry?"

"Yes."

"Why, is someone hurting them?"

"No. Not exactly. They cry because they can't understand that their mothers are coming back for them. They're too little. I'm talking about the toddlers especially, but the infants too." He saw that Meghan's eyes were filling with tears. "I don't want to sound unprofessional. I'm a trained teacher, but, after all, there are limits. It's too much, all day long, hours and hours of crying when their mothers are having their hair done or going to spin class –" She stopped herself.

"I'm sorry. I didn't mean to get so emotional. I don't want to ruin your day."

"Hmp." Peter made a sound that was half sigh and half garump.

"Look, it's my thing. The feeling now is that women have the right to do whatever they want and I believe that, I do. The kids are well cared for, in a way, as well as they can be, but – she paused - I just think they're too young to be away from their mothers. Just too young." This last she seemed to add deep in her own thoughts.

"They don't understand that their mothers are coming back." She told him. "I've seen them sobbing for hours, pushing and pushing their bodies into the little fence we keep at the doorway, the last place they saw their mothers.

Oh, God, I'm sorry. What a conversation for ice cream!"

Meghan wrapped the remains of her cone in a napkin.

All Peter could think of was that Emily's mother, Beth, was not coming back. Then, he quickly realized, Emily saw and spoke to her. Now, he wanted, for the first time to meet that ghost crew.

"Listen, Meghan," Peter began, not sure how he was going to say what he was feeling, "I don't want, I mean, Emily – Emily needs you. I don't want you to feel guilty about your decision, I mean, what are your plans? Would you consider a nanny position? With us?"

Meghan sniffed and looked up at him with big, wet blue eyes, freckles over her nose, flushed cheeks. Dark red hair framing all of this homespun beauty.

"I don't know what I'll be doing."

"Well, please consider the idea, because frankly, I don't want to send Em back there without you and we're gonna be needing someone. Even just for a little while, please think about it. Em loves you." He added.

"In that case, if you don't mind hiring someone who cries so easily, then, yes, I accept. I'd love to take care of your children."

"Great! You can start right now!" Peter saw his son walk into the ice cream shop in the company of four older boys dressed in black who could only be the ghost hunters. "Em needs an ice cream and I have a meeting."

The ghost hunters were strange.

Justin had a ring through his eyebrow. The others had more piercings in weird places (*Was there any place that wasn't weird?*) and skulls and bones, pirate style on their shirts. Their piercings and clothes alone would have been enough to make Peter get up and leave at one time. Not today.

He looked over at Meghan and Emily eagerly buying Em's ice cream. He was supposed to pick up Sarah in a while at a friend's house. He guessed he could stay till then.

Salem, 1692

Jonathan Corwin's house in Salem village was of the medieval style, painted black and faded to a blackish brown. Dark roof peaks jutted into a night sky streaked with shimmering blue clouds out of which a glowing moon slid. On the outside, the house was as solemn and silent as death.

Inside, Judge Jonathan Corwin; Selectman John Peach, Selectman Ambrose Gale, both of Marblehead; Reverend Samuel Parris, recently arrived from his Barbados sugar plantation to take up his Salem ministry, whose daughter, Betty and her cousin, Abigail had been stricken ill by Salem's witches; Judge Samuel Sewall of Marblehead; Chief Justice William Stoughton, up from Dorchester, and several other men of distinction in Salem, including Bartholomew Gedney and Judge John Hathorne, were in attendance around the long mahogany dining table. No food or drink was served. The only light in the quiet room came from the glittering brass chandelier above their heads. The faces of these serious men were illuminated as saints leaning toward one another in earnest or devout purpose, perhaps to ask their Lord the truth. Instead, these fine men were carrying out a distasteful duty. One that had befallen them from the hands of Justice. The distribution of property. The property of the damned.

"How came the lands and property of Rebecca Nurse?" Hathorne read from a long list. He was a tall handsome young man with high noble brow, full moustache over delicate lips, a sympathetic appearance that was incongruous to his severity.

"To the Village of Salem, pending verdict." Stated Bartholomew Gedney, a small, stout man with a frustrated look.

"How go the properties of Philip English, 14 buildings, 21 sail vessels, wharf, and warehouse?"

"I shall be taking custodianship thereof, we need not trouble ourselves with those matters here." Jonathan Corwin stated. "These are complicated transactions that require much negotiation with his bank."

"Aye, aye." All heads nodded in agreement; the others were not surprised that Corwin would overseer the English property.

"How go the lands thereof Wilmott Redd, including ponds, fisherman's shack and farm?" Hathorne queried.

"To the Village of Salem; she is accused of sundried, detestable acts of witchcraft. A most unsavory old hag." Ambrose Gale added with a grimace. Gale looked to be a serious and careful man. He had begun as a fisherman, but was quickly accumulating lands. He wanted to be a merchant, and would be soon if his plans went well. He was already popular among the fishermen for supplying them rum.

"Her lands are not unsavory. The pond itself is large and valuable to the town. It will be much appreciated as common land." Gedney replied.

"Aye." Several grunted in agreement.

A few scratched at their wigs, which were becoming itchy in the close, humid air of midsummer. William Stoughton watched this display of discomposure with an air of censure.

He was a man of dignity who never scratched or belched or fidgeted in his seat.

"How goes the orchard of Bridget Bishop, the tavern and accompanying lands?" Stoughton demanded; his dark brows converged like a hawk's, his mouth, lipless and weak, disappeared into his chin.

"To the Village of Salem, forthwith!" Hathorne read triumphantly from the papers in front of him.

Harumps of approval went up from the group, as this parcel of lands was particularly attractive, as attractive as its owner, and as tasty a morsel as a bite of Bridget Bishop's sweet flesh would have been. A taste many of them had enjoyed, and now were relieved to bury in unhallowed ground where none could see.

"Apples!" Came a cool steady voice into the shadowy room.

"What say you?" Hathorne asked the men.

Barely a whisper did he hear, a breathy female voice.

"Apples!" She repeated.

"I say! I demand to know, gentlemen, is this a jest?"

The men looked up from their papers.

"I heard nothing." Replied Reverend Parris.

"Nor I." The other men agreed.

"Perhaps the wind is whistling through the flue, John." Corwin remarked, "It murmurs on occasion."

"There is no wind, I would there were! Let us continue. There is more business to attend to – the lands of – Giles Corey -"

"He still refuses to plea. And, he has deeded his Ipswich meadows and goods to his sons-in-law." Gedney offered.

"He is a stubborn man of violent temper. He has accused his own wife of witchcraft, saying she did strangely hinder his prayers, but not before he did murder a man, 'tis said, by stomping him!" Reverend Parris ventured with real fear of Corey. He had never met the man, but had heard many tales upon arriving in Salem.

"I have heard he has inhuman strength at the advanced age of eighty!" Gedney told them.

"Aye, I have heard he lifted an oxen and threw it in the river! After which he mowed all the day with no rest, outlasting men half his age!" Parris added with more confidence.

"An unpleasant, obstinate man and a bully." Judge Sewall agreed. He had been silent up till then, but he had met Giles Corey a few disagreeable times.

"That will change when he faces pressing, sir! Pressing is the penalty for refusing to answer the charge! Then, he will be mild, I guarantee it!" Judge Corwin pronounced.

"Apples! Apples! Apples!"

This time all heard the voice. Altogether, their faces turned upward as the flames of all six candles in the chandelier burst high and flickered out. The room fell into darkness, as there was no fire in the hearth due to the heat of summer. The leaded windows, open to catch any slight movement of the stifling air, all together suddenly and with great violence, slammed closed.

"Who is there? I demand you show yourself!" Cried Hathorne.

Then, slowly as though in reply to Hathorne's command, came the odor of rotting apples into the room. They all smelled it, through the closed windows, though it was July, and not October, the month of harvest.

"Light the lamps again, and let us continue." Hathorne said stubbornly.

A servant was called, the candles lighted, the windows opened, and the men went on with their important work.

Silence and the heady wine of rotten apples attended them.

Marblehead, 1995

Peter turned his attention back to Justin, an alarmingly skinny boy of about fifteen with dark hair and startling big blue eyes. One of Justin's blue eyes was used as their ghost hunter logo, under the script, "Eye of Night." One blue eye sat atop his black baseball cap, only Justin wore his cap backwards so that the eye was at the back of his head. Funny. He and Beth once had a comical argument about which was stupider, a baseball cap turned backwards or a baseball cap turned to the front. They laughed a lot at that. Of course, Beth had worn a pink Marblehead baseball cap turned to the front, with her blonde ponytail bouncing in the back. But, he had to admit there was something kind of silly about baseball caps on guys who weren't on a baseball team. Unless, they were on a ghost hunter team. Maybe.

"Mr. Treadwell, do you know any psychics?" Justin was asking Peter. "Mr. Treadwell?"

"Oh, um, sorry. Me? No! I don't think so."

What an idea! Wait, hadn't Beth actually known someone?

"Dad? Didn't Mom know someone?" Pete asked him, as though reading his mind.

Justin piped in. "We usually work with a psychic. We don't like to go through a house without one. We have a psychic we use, but if you know someone, I'd prefer it, so that you can feel more secure with the findings."

Was this kid fifteen? Peter asked himself.

"Ok." Peter replied. He turned to his son, "What was her name?"

"I don't know but I can find out." Pete told him. Pete made a mental note to himself to look through his mom's old personal phone and address book later. He knew where it was, but he didn't want to get his dad upset so he didn't mention it.

"Mr. Treadwell, I understand your daughter is able to communicate with her mother's spirit?" Justin asked him.

Peter just couldn't believe what he was hearing. How could this kid be talking to him like that about his wife?

He must have looked as offended as he felt, because immediately, Pete and Justin started to talk together.

"Dad! It's okay!"

"Mr. Treadwell, please I don't mean any disrespect!"

"Dad, Justin's gonna have to talk to you about things." Pete told him.

"Yeah. Yeah." Peter answered, nodding his head.

Peter held his head down, thinking about Beth. Suddenly, the lovely upscale ice cream shop with its flowerbeds and cute tables and chairs seemed to be swirling in water.

"Dad?"

Peter's eyes were filled with tears.

"Yes. My wi-fe talks to my little girl, Emily. She's over there eating ice cream."

Justin nodded.

"I always ask that all children and animals be absent from the house during the investigation."

Peter looked up. "So, she won't be there."

"No."

"She won't be able to help you."

"No, Mr. Treadwell. The psychic will do that. And, the equipment."

"Equipment?"

Justin went on to explain the equipment. Pete's eyes were ablaze with interest. Peter's glazed over. He really couldn't comprehend the details. He heard "Polaroid." He heard "micro cassette recorder" and "night vision." Wonder where he got *that*, Peter thought. Also, he said something about a thermal something or other, "very sensitive, for measuring temperature variations." And, a flashlight.

"I have a flashlight." Peter said, foolishly.

Justin asked a few more questions about the history of the house: how it had been built in the 17th Century by the psychic Edward Dimond; how it was said to be part ship; how the psychic he would use was Dimond's ancestor; that she had once lived in the house; how it was next to Old Burial Hill where many of the original settlers of the town were buried. Peter answered yes to all. Justin nodded and made checks down the list of questions. He asked if Peter had ever experienced any psychic phenomenon there. No, Peter answered. Pete also shook his head, no.

They made an appointment. How about Saturday night at midnight? Ugh, he was going to have to stay up late.

"Why so late?" Peter wanted to know.

"It's the witching hour, Mr. Treadwell. The hour when day truly turns to deep night. Spirits find it easier to communicate with the living during the darkest hours. We'll arrive around nine, but we'll begin at midnight. We'll be there all night."

So they made a tentative date for Saturday. Waiting on whether Pete could arrange it with Beth's friend, the psychic.

A ten year old and a bunch of pierced teenagers dressed in black with skulls and bones on their shirts and a psychic!

What was happening to him? And now, he also had a nanny. Should he ask her to live in, he wondered? How else would she get there early enough to help?

Marblehead, 1692

The eyes of Molly Treadwell were bluer than the very sky, bluer still than the sea.

This thought filled the heart and mind of Daniel Pritchard as he gazed into them. Daniel did not dare to look at her mouth, with its disturbing Cupid's Bow on top and its upward curl at the corners. He hardly dared to consider kissing her; the idea was so powerful to him.

The two were walking side by side as Molly was on her way to the well curb and Daniel had intercepted her as she had passed his house. He had waited at the upstairs window till he saw her fair head appear along the beach path. Then, he had run breathless downstairs and out to meet her as if by chance.

Molly carried a pail but she was not only on her way to get water. Molly had another errand in her mind and heart.

"Hullo, Molly! May I help carry your pail?"

"Yes! Hello, Daniel."

Molly handed Daniel the empty pail. Now, she would have to get water and return home, she sighed in her heart.

Daniel was silent for a moment only. Then, he began to chatter nervously about fishing, his chores, the news from the docks, most of which Molly already knew, or did not really care to know. It would be like her telling him of weaving or carding or wiping the baby's bottom. She smiled and nodded nevertheless.

Daniel was gratified. He liked nothing better than to be beside her. He was more than happy. He swung the empty pail energetically, almost in celebration as he walked.

Molly dearly loved Daniel. She knew he would make a fine husband one day. A practical and loving man. His blonde curls bounced gaily as he walked; his warm brown eyes smiled at her.

But, it was no use. Her sights were set on another.

Marblehead, 1692

"This order of business I feel we must come to now." William Stoughton spoke, finally wiping his brow of the sweat that was accumulating there. "The old man known hereabouts as the Wizard of Burial Hill, one Edward Dimond."

Parris, who had been leaning backward in exhaustion, for they had been at this meeting for hours, suddenly sat upright in his chair.

The men from Marblehead regarded each other warily.

"You don't mean," Judge Sewall began.

"I don't mean, what, sir?"

"You don't mean to accuse Edward Dimond?"

"Is that a question?"

Sewall and all were silent.

"I not only mean to accuse him, sir! I mean to arrest him!"

"Edward Dimond is of advanced age, sir. He is more or less a recluse, who bothers no one." Ambrose Gale suggested.

"He bothers, sir! He bothers! I hear tell the man is bothering with witchcraft, spells, demons, potions and incantations in the dark of night upon the hill!" Stoughton insisted.

"Edward Dimond has aided many. It is thought that he has saved many vessels." Judge Sewall ventured, as he knew several men who had been saved aboard the *Rosamund* not two years ago.

"Be careful, Judge." Stoughton interrupted. "Careful, sir. Else you will implicate yourself as accomplice to witchcraft."

The men fidgeted in their seats to hear a judge so harshly reprimanded.

"Mr. Stoughton, you come from miles away. You cannot know the gravity of what you are suggesting to us." Judge Sewall answered.

"I am Chief Justice of the Court of Oyer and Terminer and by the Supreme Authority of Their Royal Majesties King William and Queen Mary, I am suggesting, sir that we do our duty by those who have entrusted us with this sacred task and to whom we owe allegiance!"

"Aye!" Reverend Hathorne replied. "The man has been a blight upon the good name of Marblehead for decades. Who knows what atrocities are being committed against God upon that hill!"

"I propose we write a warrant to arrest Edward Dimond for witchcraft forthwith!" Stoughton insisted. "That will be our final act of business tonight. Tomorrow we will arrest him!"

"Tomorrow!" Hathorne agreed.

The men around the table who did not know Edward Dimond looked purposeful. Those who knew Edward Dimond looked horrified.

Marblehead, 1692

Molly patiently allowed Daniel to carry the pail of water home to her mother. She patiently waited while her mother thanked Daniel, while her mother praised him, while her mother offered him refreshment.

Elizabeth was grateful and happy to see Daniel in her home and with her daughter. His mother, Jane had changed toward Elizabeth since Rosie's arrest, becoming even more severe, if that were possible. Daniel was important to her, and her daughter, Elizabeth thought, though Molly seemed to have cooled toward him.

Daniel didn't notice the change in Molly's attitude toward him, so smitten was he by the nearness of her delicate beauty. Daniel was staring now at Molly's profile. The way her nose turned upward just slightly, her narrow childish brow, her curls the color of sunshine that spilled from her bonnet and framed her rosy cheeks. Nothing so lovely existed in Marblehead, except perhaps the rosy red of dawn over the blue ocean – no matter, such natural beauty only reminded Daniel of his beloved Molly.

Molly sighed inwardly as Elizabeth invited Daniel to dinner. Molly had planned to sneak up to Burial Hill on her way to the wellcurb that afternoon, and now she found herself inconveniently back home earlier than she wished. She had heard tell from her mother's own lips that Goody Low had seen her handsome son, Ned in his ship flying over the oceans of the Jamaicas through Ol' Dimond's magic telescope and this was a sight Molly wanted desperately to see! The fact that Goody Low was at that moment incarcerated behind the kitchen of Selectman Peach's house did not stop Molly's heart from wishing to see Ned for herself, even for a flashing moment. The urge to get herself up to Burial Hill was powerful.

She could not go out again that night. She would be needed to help with the children. Daniel would walk home alone.

She would have to go in the morning.

Marblehead, 1995

Jo and Cass rode out to Villa del Sol in Jo's Iris Blue 1962 Karmann Ghia with the top down. Jo had won the car from a German yachtsman after several bottles of champagne and a drunken game of bocci. Those were her last crazy days after Beth's murder before she got tired of craziness and married Bob, who was always there for her, always so steady, caring and - calm. She needed calm.

The back of the car was filled with two cases of orange soda and two small orange trees. The colors of the day were enough to knock you out, Jo thought – bright blue sky, green trees bouncing with oranges, sparkling bottles, Iris blue car, Cass's red hair blowing in the wind, her own jet black cap of hair blown back. The sea air smelled great, crisp and clean!

How was it that rats came to Paradise? Jo pondered. She could not shake the torment of having seen that man who looked like Girelli stalking her.

She didn't want to let him steal into her new life. The missed call had been from Bob. She needed to call him back, to tell him. Not now. Not yet. Now she wanted fresh air blowing through her hair, sun and sea, and Hollywood stars.

At the villa, she filled the hidden, cabinet-paneled stainless steel refrigerator with sparkling orange bottles and had just placed the last orange tree when she and Cass stopped what they were doing to admire the long, white stretch Hummer pulling up.

Jo quickly brushed a bit of soil from her hands and ran out to meet the potential buyers, a rap star, Fly By and his girl friend, Miami, a professional celebrity who had become world famous from a blurry sex tape that had been released without her permission.

They were beautiful. They were so often seen together that the media called them "Biami." The tall, black chauffeur got out and held the door. Jo saw a long leg clad in white linen pants with a startlingly white shoe peek out. Fly By, dark brown skin against white linen suit with '80s exaggerated broad shoulders, stepped out. He turned and held his hand for his lady. Again, a long leg, foot wrapped in gold gladiator sandals, white toenails; next, the white linen dress was revealed, deep cleavage of tanned breasts, Miami stepped out of the limo, looked up with her expensive sunglasses, broad hat, jet black hair.

Jo didn't look too shabby herself in a short summer dress of red cotton that fit snugly and showed off her slim figure. Cass wore a loose floral summer dress and flat shoes. She looked dainty and country to Jo's sophisticated casualness.

The rap star held out his hand to be shaken.

"Hello! Welcome to Marblehead! I'm Jo Simmons." Jo felt a little thrill go through her each time she said her new name. She shone with enthusiasm.

"Fly By. Nice to meet you." Fly By thought her smile was for him.

The beautiful Miami stepped beside him, her head down as she looked at her silver mobile phone. She raised her head and looked fully into Jo's face with her mind somewhere else. She was impossibly lovely with heavy make-up, but she was a woman who was obviously so naturally beautiful, Jo realized, she would have looked perfect without make-up.

"Well! Would you like to see Villa del Sol?" Jo asked them both.

"Yeah! Lead the way!" Fly By answered her.

Jo opened the oak paneled front door to the dramatic entry.

"Nice!" Fly By approved of the foyer that vaulted over their heads to a skylight of clear blue sky. A twinkling crystal chandelier nestled the curve of the stairway.

Fly By's white suit was dotted with rainbows.

Miami's lovely face turned from Jo and looked at the staircase curving to the skylight. She said nothing, which seemed fitting for the serenity of her face, now covered with rainbows from the chandelier.

"This way." Jo told them.

Jo walked in front of Fly By, but somehow Miami walked in front of Jo. Miami's famous behind was overly large, but heart-shaped, and moved with an almost liquid, languid motion. There it was, right before Jo's eyes, the famous ass.

"Hey! You got orange trees!" Fly By called out in delight.

Miami turned her head, "Oh, yeah. Nice."

"Oranges grow here, man?" Fly By asked Jo.

"Well, no, only in summer, and only in pots. You can bring them indoors in the fall."

Both stars nodded their sunglassed faces in unison.

The orange trees flanked the view, the blue horizon of Marblehead, the seaward side of the Neck that swelled on and on to a vanishing horizon of sky and sea. One seagull broke the constant blue with its bright wings.

Both stars stared out at this immense blue; they were quiet.

Then, Fly By broke the silence with, "If the rest is like this man, you got yourself a deal."

Miami nodded coolly.

Jo smiled. "I think you'll enjoy the privacy of this side of the Neck. The kitchen is right through here."

Cass was waiting for them in the kitchen.

"My colleague, Cassandra Diamond Hawkes."

Everyone shook hands. Jo described the kitchen, "You can see the kitchen is a lovely white marble countertops, cream cabinets, stainless steel chef's stove, pot filler, marble backsplash…"

They were still looking out at the view.

"Let's go out!" Jo said, enthusiastically. She opened the accordion doors.

"The pool is salt water, easy to maintain, a simple, clean design, blue tiles."

"The pool is small." Fly By remarked.

"It's rather large for New England." Jo hated admitting any disadvantage to a house. "And, there's a cabana with a full bath." She gestured toward the small cottage behind her.

Cass could tell they were getting thirsty.

"Yeah, let's see the bedrooms." Fly By spoke a bit impatiently.

Jo sensed the strain, but didn't know why.

"Would you like something to drink, first?" Cass suggested.

"Oh, yeah!" Fly By answered.

They all followed Cass back into the kitchen where she opened the hidden refrigerator door to the brilliant sight of several tall bottles of glistening orange soda.

"Oh, man! You knew I was comin'!"

Fly By tipped a bottle to his lips and handed it to Miami who did the same.

"I just love it when she does that!" Fly By admired Miami's casual tilting of the large bottle to her red lips.

Cass poured four champagne glasses full of orange soda, and they went on to the dining room, study, up to the bedrooms, where Jo had installed long sheer white curtains in the master suite that billowed nicely as she opened the French doors to the beckoning terrace.

Jo said, "His and her walk-in closets, floor to ceiling shoe racks." No one seemed to hear her.

Miami looked out at the vast blue, empty except for a two serene sail boats.

Just then, a tall ship, a three-masted, 17th Century Spanish galleon with dark green sails and black hull, gracefully dipped its bow into a view unmarred by any modern obstruction, looking for all the world as though it had sailed there from history.

Jo shrugged, "That's just Tuesday here in Marblehead."

All seemed lost in the sudden beauty of the antique ship, all except Cassandra who saw *a pirate ship, nodding its head like a snake curled upon the waters, like a black swan curling her neck, her back arched, her wings nestling an evil crew of men ready to slaughter, ready and waiting to pounce like venomous snakes, they had been there before…*

Miami turned her serene face to Fly By, who, as though in a trance gazing at her beauty, said, "We'll take it."

Jo was ecstatic, even when Cass explained to her later that Fly By might rent it when he wasn't visiting. Jo was in the throes of delight in having made a good sale; she truly loved finding a great house for a great client. The money made it even more fun. She loved the idea of helping Bob and herself make a good life. The whole process just felt – efficient!

They sat down at the Villa's white marble breakfast table and wrote up an offer for $5.2 million, $500,000 below the asking price.

But, Jo's hands were shaking after the famous couple said good-bye and she and Cass were getting back into the Karmann Ghia. She wondered why; she'd made impressive sales before. Immediately, she realized, she was trembling because she was going back to the office and that man could be outside again watching her. She glanced at the glove box, where she had stashed a loaded pearl-handled Chanel pistol she'd bought in Paris once as a joke.

It wasn't a joke now.

Marblehead, 1692

Molly did not sleep that night, so excited was she about the possibility of seeing Ned through Ol' Dimond's magic glass. She rose early, before light, even earlier than usual, and left the house quietly. She knew she would not be there for her mother that morning and she would be missed. But, her heart thrilled with the idea that by the time her mother opened her eyes to begin her day, she, Molly, would have looked through the magic telescope all the way to the Jamaicas!

Molly wondered, as she made her way, past the Pritchard's house, if Ned ever thought of her the way she thought of him, even a tiny bit as much, since he had taken her charm of red woolen yarn on the very day pirates had kidnapped him. Pirates! What adventures was he having? Somewhere in her sensible heart, as she hastened along the path, Molly knew she was being foolish about Ned, when Daniel was the more suitable husband (after all, who would want to marry a pirate!) but she could not help it. Ned was exciting! Daniel was not.

In fact, the boring Daniel was rising earlier than usual also. He wanted to get an early start on fishing. He had an idea of bringing a fresh catch to his mother for the evening meal, and, of course, to Goody Treadwell. He was just looking out the window at some seagulls that mewed and circled high, which he thought threatened a morning storm, when he saw Molly come hurrying – was she on her way to him? His heart sank as she passed right by, her lovely head down, not even looking at his house. Where was she going? He peered out the window and watched her pretty shape as she began to climb Burial Hill.

Burial Hill? There was naught up there but a few graves, and Ol' Dimond in his hermit's hut. Surely Molly had no reason to go there! What had a pretty girl to do with such a decrepit old man and so early of the morn? Then, he remembered that Goody Low had been arrested for going to Ol' Dimond to learn the craft. His heart beat even faster, if that were possible, even faster than it had upon sighting his love.

Daniel dressed quickly and went out, following Molly up Burial Hill at a distance so that she could not see him. He was already far behind, and he did not call to her. Something stopped him from calling out. He was embarrassed about following her, yes, but also embarrassed for her to be making such a strange journey at a strange time and in a strange manner.

What was she doing? He did not want her to know he saw her.

Daniel did not think much beyond these confused inquiries of a mind not yet fully awake, or he would have noticed the party of men dressed in black who were convening by the meetinghouse as the red sun just peered over the ocean turning the horizon scarlet.

Molly reached Ed Dimond's door and hesitated a moment only before rapping soundly upon its ancient wood.

"Ol' Dimond, Ol' Dimond! Are you within? 'Tis Molly Treadwell come to ask a favor of ye."

With the impatience and self-importance of youth, Molly rapped over and over till the door swung slowly open and Ed Dimond stood before her. In truth, he was bent more than standing, wearing old clothes that smelled of salt and fish as old as he. Molly held her breath.

"Child, they are coming for me this very morning. I will give ye the 'scope, but ye must be quick about it. Ye must be gone afore they get 'ere, dunna forget!"

Dimond reached for the telescope that stood in its usual place behind the door. He handed it to Molly, who was a bit taken aback by the device's sudden weight in her small hands.

How did he know what she wanted? She didn't care! She did not know how to use the telescope, but she hastened nevertheless to the eastern most point of Burial Hill to look through its magic lens.

Daniel followed right behind her. He glanced at Dimond as he passed.

Dimond stood quietly by the door and watched the two young people run to the edge of the hill.

"How they run!" Dimond thought, "Closer and closer to their demise."

Molly reached the edge of Burial Hill and raised the telescope to her eye.

She wished, she wished so hard to see him! At first, there was only a blur, a red blur, which she thought must be the rising sun.

"Oh, get out of the way, sun!" She cried out.

Then the blur seemed to move. The image changed, clarified, and there was Ned! He had a sword lifted in one hand and in the other a knife and he was covered in blood! Blood flew into his face and over his bosom! A hateful expression distorted his handsome face, his brows converged and his mouth twisted in anguish and rage. His teeth clenched like a wild dog and he did seem to growl.

Molly dropped the telescope, and fell to her knees just as Daniel reached her.

"Molly! Molly!" Daniel cried.

Molly looked up at Daniel for a second only with the blue eyes that he loved. Then she turned and vomited on to the grass.

"He was covered in blood." She whispered, and vomited again.

"Who was covered in blood, Moll? What did you see?"

Molly did not want to tell Daniel what she had done. Sickened by what she had seen, she still wanted to keep it and think on it a while; it was her own, after all.

Daniel lifted the telescope and looked out to sea as he had seen Molly do.

He saw nothing unusual, just the rosy sunrise on the harbor and the boats getting ready to go out.

"I don't know what you saw, Mol', but 'tis dangerous I'm sure to look through this magic scope. 'Tis the very kind of thing that got Goody Low arrested for witchcraft and I'm not sure she wasn't guilty of it."

Molly did not listen; so busy was she with vomiting last night's dinner.

"Well, we should return this to Ol' Dimond. Come." Daniel told her, offering his hand to lift her from the grass.

"I will carry the 'scope!" Molly offered, wanting to keep it close to her.

"Nay, I will, it's trouble I tell you. Come, let's go."

The two made their way back to Dimond's hut just as the officials, Selectmen Peach and Gale, Magistrate John Hathorne, Reverend Samuel Parris, some women from the village, two of the afflicted children, Abigail Williams and Betty Parris (who had tagged along out of a dire curiosity to see the old wizard for themselves), and Judge Samuel Sewall, who had made sure he was there to offer any condolences to the old seer: all came to the old man's door.

Molly appeared disheveled, with vomit on the front of her pale blue dress, and Daniel carried the telescope. Before either of them saw the group, a woman yelled.

"He bears the magic 'scope!"

"She has been cavorting with the Devil in the dark of night! They are both witches!"

Abigail Williams fell on the ground and wailed. Betty Parris followed her, writhing on the ground. Both children jumped in pain, and cried out that they were being pinched by Molly and by Daniel.

"See how they are afflicted!" Cried their uncle, Reverend Parris.

Molly did not know what to do. She felt it must be obvious to everyone that she was not touching the girls, but her heart hit hard against her chest nonetheless as she watched helplessly and in horror of what was being said about her!

Daniel began slowly to realize what a nightmare they had walked into. A nightmare that was not their own and was about to overtake them. He was powerless before it.

Reverend Parris grabbed their arms and held Molly and Daniel to the side as Judge Hathorne called out to Edward Dimond.

"Edward Dimond, Seer of Burial Hill, you are under arrest for witchcraft and other deeds against our Sovereign Lord and against Our Sovereign King, His and Her Majesties, King William and Queen Mary. I herewith demand that you show yourself and submit to arrest!"

The door creaked slowly open, but Ol' Dimond did not stand there, as he had to greet Molly. The room was empty.

The officials searched the small house, turning over tables, opening cupboards and even drawers to see if Ol' Dimond might have made himself small enough to hide there. A cat snarled and hissed at them; she leapt upon Selectman Peach and scratched his shoulder through the cloth of his coat. He cried out, "The Devil has marked me!"

But, no Edward Dimond was in the house.

For a moment, exhausted and breathing hard from their efforts, the men dressed in black official coats, stopped to catch their breath. Parris still clung to Molly and Daniel.

"Well, he cannot have gone far. He will be found eventually." Hathorne declared.

Just then, as the party was about to turn and leave, Judge Sewall saw, but dared not say to anyone, two blue eyes only, open as though from inside the wall. The Judge shivered though the day was warm. He would swear to himself later, he had seen the watery blue eyes of Edward Dimond blink at him with eyelids of wood, as though part of the wall!

Marblehead, 1995

By eight p.m. the same day they'd met with the ghost hunters, Peter and his son were sitting at the kitchen table staring at the phone. It was a white phone that Beth had commissioned a Marblehead artist to hand-paint with green leaves and flowers that trailed off the phone and out to the walls and woodwork. The design and the work were very intricate and pretty, though the paint on the phone handle was slightly worn away.

But, that's not why they were staring at it.

Peter and his son had been discussing the idea of calling Beth's psychic friend, Casaandra Dimond Hawkes.

"Dad, I'll call if you don't want to, I don't mind." His son had said, a small piece of paper with Cass's phone number on it in his hand.

Such a small piece of paper, Peter thought, for such a big decision.

Peter sighed deeply. He played with a fork, tapping the old wooden table with the prongs; it made a soft sound. Peter listened to the sound; he liked wood, it made a welcoming sound to everything that touched it.

"Dad?" Pete asked as quietly and patiently as he could.

"She was kinda kooky." Peter mumbled, like a mopey child.

"Of course, she was kooky, Dad, she's a psychic."

Peter sighed again. What a freak show. Ghost hunters in black, rings through their faces, skulls and psychics. He felt old and out of it. Tired. The dogs at his feet looked up at him and yawned in unison. Yeah, me too, Peter thought.

"I really want to give it a try, Dad. Let's just do it. I don't want to be always wondering."

"I'm not sure it'll prove anything."

"I know, maybe not, but it's something. You know? These guys have had some good results."

"What kind of results?"

"Dad, look, this is Mom. I don't wanna start talking about other people's ghosts, okay? I think we should do this. I want to."

"What did Emily say?" Peter asked.

Pete smiled, "Em says we're nuts 'cause Mom is here."

Peter smiled too. That little girl always brought them together.

"Okay." Peter nodded his head. "Okay, let's set it up."

That's when the phone rang. It was Cassandra, wanting to know what time she should arrive for the ghost hunt.

Marblehead, 1692

The officials threw Daniel Pritchard and Molly Treadwell into the root cellar along with Rosie Low and her baby, Edwina. The magic telescope was taken as evidence and kept in a locked cupboard at Reverend Parris' home. In fact, Abigail Williams and her friends stole it one night and took it into the woods where they saw nothing through its lens but giant vampire bats, teeth bared and claws open, flying at them.

The jails were overfull of witches now, from Ipswich to Quincy. A few had escaped, as they could not be guarded properly because of the sheer numbers. Officials shook their heads in despair that Salem and all its surrounding areas were indeed bedeviled.

Elizabeth had come downstairs to a cold kitchen that morning. She wondered, of course, what was wrong. Where was Molly? But she had to hurry and feed the children. After which, still concerned, but sure that faithful Molly would turn up, she had stopped by Rosie's to make sure Nan was not in need of anything. Not till she was near the Peach's house, did she hear a commotion of several townspeople who ran to her to torment her about her daughter being arrested as a witch.

For a moment only, Elizabeth thought they must be mistaken by some rumor, but she quickly realized the truth when she remembered that cold and empty kitchen, and the sudden rush of panic overtook her.

Panic stopped her breath, panic worse than that for her own death! Molly! Sweet and clear! Beautiful! Innocent! What had transpired to make such a mistake happen?

Elizabeth ran up to the door of the Peach's house. She wanted desperately to bang her fist upon it, but she did not. She composed herself outwardly and rapped gently.

Addie Gatchell opened the door.

"Ah, back agin' are we?" She said, smugly.

Elizabeth wanted to smack her ugly face. She did not.

"I must see – Mr. Peach, please." She almost said "her daughter," but that would never get her inside.

"I'll see if he is a'wailable."

Addie tried to shut the door in Elizabeth's face, but Elizabeth quickly stepped in and the force of Addie's hand still moving, slammed the door behind her.

She and Addie faced each other. The girl's filthy breath was sickening. Elizabeth knew instantly that she had some stomach ailment, rigid bowels, no doubt that were backing up into her mouth. That was the cause of the greasy hair and pocky skin too as much as her failure to wash and keep herself clean. A dog or a cat could do better to clean themselves, Elizabeth thought.

Addie left Elizabeth in the hall and went to find her master, but Elizabeth did not wait as she was told. She walked briskly toward the kitchen as she had done once before and stopped by the locked door of the root cellar.

"Molly!" Elizabeth whispered at the keyhole. "Molly! My dear, are you within?"

A shuffling of skirts from within, and Molly's sweet, breathy voice on the other side of the door.

"Mother!"

Elizabeth's legs nearly gave way to hear her dear girl locked up. She fell against the door.

The servants watched this drama in silence, for they knew the master was on his way. His footsteps approached, heavy and hard upon the wooden floor upstairs.

"Molly! What has happened?"

Silence, then. "I daren't say."

"Oh, Molly, what have ye –" Elizabeth stopped herself. Any mention of a guilty act on Molly's part would go against her later, especially with all these ears and eyes upon them now. Besides, Elizabeth could not have cared less for what Molly might have done. She cared only for how to get her daughter out of this terrible trouble.

Mr. Peach's footfalls were now on the floor above their heads, down the hall, down the kitchen steps, beside her.

Elizabeth looked up at him with the most piteous mother's face she could muster.

"Mr. Peach," she began.

"I'll have none of this, Goody Treadwell! None! I have succumbed to your begging countenance once before when I allowed the babe to suckle her mother, demon to demon, as far as I am concerned! I'll not listen the more to your entreaties. I know what you wish for, Madam, and you shall not have it. I was witness to your daughter's debauchery on Burial Hill where she cavorted with the old wizard and his magic tools of devilment. I saw her torture the children with pinching and pricking. She shall stay incarcerated, Madam until her trial at which time she may confess and do penance."

The kitchen maid, cook, footman, and Addie, all in a smug row smiled at Elizabeth's confusion and terror.

Elizabeth could hear Molly weeping, and Rosie's voice trying to comfort her.

Elizabeth, stunned and horrified, allowed herself to be shoved out the kitchen door where she fell into the street. She remained there in front of the Peach's house, on her knees, for several hours. She held her hands in prayer and entreaty to both God and Selectman. In her shock, she did not recognize the difference.

Her husband, Tom came for her at nightfall, having heard while he was out fishing that day. Another boat had pulled up alongside and the crew had told him his daughter had been arrested that morning and his wife was outside her cell praying.

Tom knelt beside his wife and prayed.

After half an hour, he told her it was time to go home. She allowed herself to be lifted and she walked back, leaning on his strong arm, to take care of her other children, as he reminded her.

In time, they heard that Daniel had been moved. They did not know where.

Marblehead, 1995

In accordance with the rule "no children or pets," on the night of the ghost hunt, Sarah was staying with a friend; Emily, Tiger and Pizza were with Meghan at her house. Pete, who was technically a child, was present. Peter never thought for a moment that he shouldn't be, Pete was pretty excited, and yet, somewhat solemn. He really took this ghost hunting seriously. Peter would never have asked him to leave; it seemed to be his show too, as well as the ghost hunters'.

The night was warm; pale clouds hung in the dark sky and the air smelled heavy with rain. Peter watched anxiously at the front window of his white saltbox house with gold shutters that nestled Old Burial Hill on one side and faced the ocean on another. He could hear the contented rhythm of crickets and ocean waves through the open window, and the trills of an owl waking up. The old burial ground was quiet. Peter wondered what kind of activity the hunt would stir up this night.

When the ghost hunters arrived, around nine o'clock, they pulled up in an old Woodie station wagon, the kind that surfers had used in the 1960s. A tall man with striking, long white hair and a black moustache, got out of the driver's side, walked over to Peter and held out his hand to shake.

"Hi, I'm Justin's dad, Frank Finley, also known as his driver."

Peter shook his hand, and laughed, "Yeah, I almost asked if I should pick him up."

Frank laughed, "Well, he's got a lot of equipment, so I usually drive him and his crew."

"Care to help with any of this stuff?" Frank asked.

"Sure!"

Peter helped carry boxes of cameras, recorders, wires and microphones. The crew kept their heads down, spreading wires around Peter's house until the place looked like a spider web. Around eleven o'clock they were almost finished; Pete ordered pizza, so they all sat down to eat. Cassandra was expected around midnight.

"Mr. Treadwell?" Justin began, as the eating wound down. "I need to ask you a few questions, if you don't mind."

"Sure."

"It would help a lot if you could tell us where your wife has been seen…recently."

"Well, my friend, Bob Simmons thought he saw something over the water out by where Beth was - killed."

"What did he see...exactly?"

"He saw a mist, a pink mist in the shape of a woman on the waves…" Peter hesitated. "She had a pink dress."

"Okay. Did anyone else see her? Besides Emily?"

"I did," came a voice. Cassandra was standing in the kitchen doorway. She was early. Peter was glad to see her even though she was wearing an old dress that looked like rags.

"I saw Beth up at the castle."

"Which castle?"

"Oh, the one at Crocker Park, the Herreschoff Castle. Mrs. Herreschoff was mowing the lawn with no shirt on, and Beth was there wearing a pink dress and she was laughing."

"With no shirt on?" Peter asked.

"Yes, she was a ghost, although, she really did that and got arrested. Well, just detained and sent home."

Everyone stared at Cass, but no one laughed. In fact, Justin was writing in his notebook.

"Thank you. Anyone else? Anyone see or hear anything here in the house?"

"I saw her over the water too. From the house." Pete replied. "I think she was windsurfing."

"What did you see exactly?"

"A flash of white. Could have been anything really." Pete admitted.

Justin wrote it down anyway.

"Cassandra, are you getting anything right now?" Justin asked.

Peter guessed dinner must be over.

"Yes, I'm always getting something." Cassandra replied.

"What?"

"My ancestor, Ed Dimond is always here. I saw him often when Beth and I would meet to make the video."

"The video?"

"Yes, Beth was making an historic video of the town. I was narrator."

Peter hardly remembered that. It struck him as sad that he could have forgotten.

"Is he here now?"

"Yes, but he's not in the room."

"Okay."

Justin looked at his watch, some sort of bulky device with lots of circles on the face.

"It's midnight. We should begin, officially." Justin said. "Lights out. Equipment on."

Now Peter was in the dark in his own house, a very weird feeling, that is, unless he was stumbling his way to the bathroom in the middle of the night. Here he was in his own kitchen, in the dark, with a very strange group of strangers, and the table covered with the remains of dinner, something Beth would never have left. No, nor him either. He always tidied up...Justin was calling him from the living room.

Peter got up from the table and, his natural night vision kicking in, he walked comfortably in the dark.

"It's 12:02 a.m.; we are in the living room," Justin spoke into a small, hand-held recorder. "I want to ask all the living people to be silent and let those who have passed speak. Please keep all other noises to a minimum to not interfere with any possible communications. If there's anyone here, we are open to hearing anything you wish to tell us. Please just speak and either we will hear you or the recorder will pick up what you have to say."

The room became so quiet that Peter heard nothing except the occasional shuffling of someone's feet and a self-conscious cough.

"Cassandra?" Justin asked.

"There are several spirits here right now, but they are not speaking."

Suddenly, the recorder sputtered static.

Cassandra seemed to be listening.

"Apples!" Cassandra reported. "She is saying 'apples.'"

"Apples?" Justin repeated. "What does that mean?"

Cassandra was listening again. She did not tell them what she saw: *the tall, buxom girl with flowing dark hair, defiant chin and blue eyes that once had sparkled with mischief. The revelations she was seeing of justices lifting their black robes to show their erections, justices dancing and twirling ridiculously, kicking up their heels.*

"She doesn't live here, but she wanted to be heard. She is a very strong spirit. She is able to travel from place to place. She lives – lived and died in Salem. They stole her orchard before they hanged her for witchcraft. She says she lay wi' most of 'em, and they were tha' afraid of 'er speakin.' (Cassandra lapsed into dialect for a second.) She likes to speak whenever anyone will listen." Cassandra felt the room was stifling now with the smell of apples, both fresh and rotten. "Do you smell it? Apples?"

Yes, Peter could smell apples. He was astonished. Maybe there was a half-eaten apple still on the table? He never had *that* good a sense of smell, all the way from the kitchen.

"I can." Peter said.

Justin and the rest of the crew could not. Pete did not.

"She's grateful to us for listening."

"Ask her, Cassandra, if she knows anyone here, please." Justin asked. He and Pete also took several Polaroids of the living room.

Cass listened; she nodded.

"Her name is Bridget Bishop. She was a tavern owner in Salem, and they took tavern and orchard from her and murdered her as a witch. She has come to know Ed Dimond, who is here. She has come to know –"

Peter hung on her words. This strangely dressed woman with wild red hair.

"She has come to know Beth Treadwell."

"Is Beth here?"

"Yes."

Peter was stunned breathless.

"Will she speak?"

"Yes."

Suddenly, from out of nowhere, one of the kids' toys, a tugboat, let out a strong whistle, "Woo, woo!" Peter didn't remember it being that loud.

The group looked at each other.

"Was that her?" Justin asked Cass.

Cass smiled, "Yes."

"She sounds happy." Peter said, without thinking.

"She's happy to be here tonight." Cass said. "To see you and to speak to you."

Peter couldn't believe it; he struggled not to weep.

"She wants you to be happy." Cass told Peter.

He couldn't take it. Peter threw his hands up over his face; he sat on whatever was under him and burst into tears. He forgot his trick of only sobbing twice.

The whole crew was silent, waiting for his tears to pass. When he stopped a few minutes later, Cassandra said, "She almost didn't speak. She didn't want to upset you."

Peter nodded.

"But, she wants you to know something. She would like to whisper to you in private, but she cannot. She can only speak through me. The whistle was a joke. She can still laugh.

There's something important. She wants you to live, Mr. Treadwell, to pick up your head and look around you and see all that is beautiful and alive and live.

And love."

Peter could not speak.

"But – there's more –" Here Cassandra felt *the orange and grey shapes begin to move in front of her eyes, to shift and gather, to separate and grow large and small, close and far off, then too close, the shapes wanted to infiltrate paradise –* "Jo Simmons is in danger. Right now! You must tell her husband. *She tried to help me, she tried, but it was too late…*"

"STOP!" Peter cried out.

142

Cassandra was frustrated. There was so much more she wanted to say.

Marblehead, 1692

"Molly," Rosie asked after the girl stopped crying. "How did ye cum 'ere?"

Molly looked at Rosie. She knew she was looking at, with the exception of Edward Dimond, the only other person in the world who would truly understand what she had done. Molly's mother knew what Rosie had told her, but her mother had not looked through the telescope. Here, the only two women who had looked through the telescope sat facing each other.

"I have seen him."

Rosie regarded her. She hesitated.

"I have seen Ned." Molly explained. "Through Ol' Dimond's telescope."

"Gah!" was all Rosie could get out.

Molly's eyes began to fill with tears again and Rosie was startled to have somehow made her cry.

"He – he – was covered with –" Molly began to realize that she was speaking to his mother, but now she'd started, she had to go on. "Blood!"

Rosie was silent; her complexion went grey.

"He was fighting, Goody Low, and I do believe the blood was not his own, but the blood of his enemies."

"Ah!" Rosie exclaimed. "How did he fight?"

"With a sword, Goody Low, and a knife. He did slice men in half, and in a flash, I did see a man's arm fall off." Molly felt as though she might swoon.

Rosie was impressed. She was that glad that her Ned was not hurt, and was hurting men who might harm him. She cared not for the men who were dying, but only for Ned who was killing them.

Molly did not know how she felt. She had never seen such a slaughter and so quickly seen, in a flash before her eyes. How long did this battle continue? How was Ned now? Was he also slaughtered? Molly shuddered to think of him hurt. But, Molly was frightened. Not just for Ned. She was frightened by the violence of Ned's world. She wanted no part of it. She wanted to go home and do her chores. But, here she was, in a prison for a crime she did not understand was wrong. The idea that she had seen Ned from so far away did not seem to her so unnatural. Always, she had known that Ol' Dimond's 'scope was magical, why was that so horrible or devilish to folks? And, what had she done to those children? She did not understand that. She would never pinch or prick another person. She had not touched them, yet they had cried out. Was she imprisoned now for hurting the children, or for looking through the telescope, or for going up Burial Hill in the first place? Folks had gone up the Hill to see Ol' Dimond forever! Ol' Dimond had been helping townspeople for as long as she knew, how was it somehow wrong – *now?*

Rosie, lost in her own thoughts, her pride in Ned, now looked at the troubled child. She embraced Molly, and pulled her close.

The girl sobbed in her arms.

Rosie kissed her forehead. "Thou must call me Rosie, now, m' dear. We are together now in this jail and we will help each other."

Isabella, Isla Hispaniola, 1692

Jordana started from her afternoon sleep. She had been dreaming that the Devil had imprisoned the sun and the blue sky in darkness where none could ever see the light and the heavens again.

She opened her eyes to see the deep blue of her own sky, the dark green sea and the black skeletal masts of the ships resting in the harbor. Bobo was beside her. His liquid brown eyes looked into hers. He blinked, as if to say, what will you do now about this sun and this sky forever hidden away? They are not your sun and not your sky. Will you be careless? Or, will you help the one whose sun and sky they are?

Jordana considered a moment. Perhaps if the light-haired one were hung for witchcraft, Peti' Low would return to her, Jordana.

She knew he would always return to her – if he continued to sail the seas.

Bobo jumped up and ran to a table of fruit, where he snapped up a mango and bit into its sweet skin, causing juices to fly over him like an ocean spray.

Jordana held out her hand and Bobo tossed her a mango, and she did the same, biting its skin and causing her naked breasts to be sprayed with sticky juices.

Bobo laughed and chattered. He sprang out the window to look for adventure in the busy street.

From her bed Jordana took one more bite then threw the rest of the fruit out the window.

She nestled into the bed, enjoying the smooth silk traveling over her legs. She sulked. She sighed.

Then, she dutifully closed her eyes and sent her lover a dream, a dream she knew would spark passion in him for another: one who was fair not dark; sweet, not pungent; virtuous, not treacherous, and in every other way, not like him, not like the pirate and the dark one Jordana *was* like, and coveted so much.

The *Deliverance*, North of the Carolinas, 1692

Ned also woke with a start, for he had dreamed the Devil had thrown the black bag over Molly's head and hung her, so suddenly, the image flashed before his eyes like the blink of an eye and was gone.

He sat up in the bed next to Lowther who was snoring horribly, his foul mouth open and drooling on to his fat, hairy chest.

Ned rushed naked out of the bed to the windows at the rear of the captain's quarters where he hung his head out to breathe the fresh air. The wake of the ship threw spray over his face, and he was glad of it, but he vomited nevertheless, heaving from his belly with the panic of not knowing what to do, not being able to do or go anywhere, and not being able to help himself or anyone. What did it mean? He daren't dismiss the dream. Molly was in darkness he kept repeating to himself. That bright girl was now in darkness.

It was one thing for him, Ned, to be so imprisoned, but not for Molly. He wished he could fly. He turned to see Lowther again on the bed. The desire to cut the man's throat was stronger than ever. He wished like a child that he could do so, and then slice the throat of every man on board and sail the *Deliverance* right up the beach of Lovis Cove to save his dear one.

And, his mother, he reminded himself.

The ship that moved beneath him moved too slowly! Surely, he could not last the journey! Weeks of slow torture spread before him like fields of hell fire. What was happening in Salem? What could he do?

Ned threw on his leather trousers and walked barefoot and quickly to the deck where the crew smirked and whistled to themselves. Ned brushed past them all and climbed the rigging till he stood as alone as he could be, in the crow's nest peering out to sea, willing the ocean to speed backward, to speed the *Deliverance* on to Marblehead.

Marblehead, 1995

Peter didn't kick them out. He knew Pete would be brutally disappointed if he halted the ghost hunt, and, well, he didn't want to be an asshole about his grief.

He and Frank sat in the kitchen alone while the crew went over the rest of the house. The lights were still out, but a small candle flickered on a dish between them, and they each had a cold beer.

"Justin will go over the evidence later, then he'll report back with his findings."

"You take this pretty seriously." Peter said.

"Yes, I do. I am a medium as well, like Cassandra."

"So, are you getting anything?"

Frank didn't want to say that Peter's wife was standing behind him and she was looking sad and concerned.

"Yes, I am. There's a lot going on."

Peter shook his head, "Man, I don't know if I can ever shut my eyes again."

Frank smiled, "It's all good, you know. They've been here the whole time."

"Who?"

"Well, Cassandra's ancestor, the old seer, Ed Dimond is here. He's very powerful and independent. He can travel through space *and* time."

Peter was shocked at Frank's casual attitude about such outrageous claims. His face must have looked like it.

"I wouldn't say it, Mr. Treadwell, if I didn't believe it."

"It's just so hard for me to believe." Peter admitted. "But, I know, I know Beth had a lot of respect for Cassandra's ability and – her – lineage."

Frank nodded.

"Anyone else?"

"So far, Bridget Bishop has come, as you know, to be heard. She was silenced so long ago. Ironically, she lives now in a town full of practicing psychics and witches. They all know and accept her like a living person, just like we accept our neighbors. But, it's not enough. She takes every opportunity to tell her story to someone new."

"She was hanged as a witch?" Peter asked.

"Yes. Apparently, she was very pretty and flirtatious, and she owned some very valuable property, an apple orchard and a tavern."

"So, they took it all."

Frank nodded. "They took a lot of property."

"Makes you wonder."

"Yes, it does. Bridget's apple trees still dot Salem, but the full orchard itself is past. Bridget's spirit is one who is tortured. Her property has been built over. Perhaps that gives her no peace. It's very interesting to me that she likes to be around modern-day witches, and that she has come here tonight where Ed Dimond lives. You see, Mr. Treadwell –"

"Call me Peter."

"Peter, it's amazing to me that in 1692, during the witch hysteria, only the innocent were hanged. The real witches and seers, like Edward Dimond, managed to escape being caught by the authorities. Tituba, for instance, was accused, but never hanged. She was a slave who came with Reverend Parris from Barbados. Some think she may have started the whole hysteria when she and Parris' niece were caught practicing old island magic in the Salem woods.

This is a mysterious place. You know, Marblehead is built on granite, and granite has been known – well, in a sense – to have a heartbeat. There have been some good findings using ultrasound."

Peter nodded. He wasn't sure what he was hearing. There seemed to be a lot of that going on lately. One thing that haunted him – he supposed the word *haunted* was appropriate – the sound of that toy, that "Woo, woo!" It had been so happy and cheerful, just like Beth. It rang in his ears. Haunted him.

"Why doesn't she talk to *me*?" Peter asked. "She talks to Cassandra and Emily, but not to me."

"We can't always explain how the dead communicate to the living. If it's any comfort, Peter, I've heard this complaint before from other grieving men and women whose loved ones chose someone unusual to communicate with, while not communicating to the ones closest to them in life. We can only say that different channels are open at different times. What might seem odd to us could be the most sensible to those in the spirit world."

"I just wish she would talk to me." Peter repeated, hanging his head like a sulky child.

"Maybe she has, maybe she is."

Peter looked up.

"How do you mean?"

"Keep your eyes and ears open – and more importantly, your mind."

The Atlantic, off the coast of Virginia, 1692

They smelled the suffering before they saw the ship. It was the *Molly*, bearing cargo of rum and sugar, and slaves out of Africa. Ned was already sickened with his dream of Molly and to smell what he knew would be more horror and dread coming his way, sickened him the more, but not with fear. No, he had long since lost the first thrill of battle. The screams, that had once delighted him, now seemed ridiculous. He was no longer a child when it came to being impressed by a severed limb flying at him, nor by the fountain of blood that did spring from a man's neck when he lost his head, or the way the body tottered headless and tried to walk. He had long since lost the fun of it. Though the other men laughed and danced at their slaughter, Ned no longer even smiled.

Ned was bored with slaughter. What sickened him was the necessity of it all. Only keeping alive interested him; he anticipated the fight only as a means to keep himself and his blood intact.

He had come to terms also with the ship's name, *Molly*, for he knew that they would take her and she would be destroyed. He braced himself to destroy her.

Lowther knew exactly how to take a ship. The Molly had thirty guns, but she would not fire them. Lowther knew she would be facing at the sight of another English ship.

"Fly the St. George!" Lowther called out, long before they saw the *Molly*, the English flag was raised, the red cross of St. George on a field of white. When she came into sight, she would come close, trusting herself to another English ship, eager for news and the company of fellow Englishmen.

They waited on deck, all hands at the ready. The stench grew and grew in strength. The sun beat down and the smell of horror came closer. In time, even before she was sighted, they could hear the far-off screams and the ghostly wailing of women.

"Agh! Blackbird!" Lowther complained. "A nasty business." He spat, anxious, Ned knew, to have it over. Lowther hated slave ships.

The orders were to take the cargo, the guns, any passengers, and burn the rest.

But, the crew wanted more. They wanted to play.

A half hour more of waiting. The crew smacked their lips in anticipation. Men lined the deck. Men lined the mizzen, the rigging, the rails. Each man wore a clean white shirt and a black sailor's cap as a camouflage of respectability, except for Lowther, who sported a bright blue coat with shiny gold epaulets and buttons that he'd taken from an English captain.

The *Molly* came into sight, her captain and crew also lined up and waiting. The *Molly's* Captain named, Merriweather, and crew, though of a merchant, wore navy blue and white uniforms. It was late in the afternoon, off the coast of Virginia, the twilight sun shone directly on the sparkling white uniforms that shuddered in the wind like flags. Ned knew the first class passengers nervously waited below, in their lounge, around their tea table.

Lowther hailed the *Molly's* captain. "Ahoy!"

Captain Merriweather answered "Ahoy!"

Lowther added, "God save the King and Queen!"

Captain Merriweather replied the same. You could see the Captain's chest sigh with relief. Planks were set between the two ships. The silence as before a storm became a vacuum while the pirates waited and the *Molly's* crew and passengers breathed collectively easier.

Ned smiled, knowing what was coming.

Of a sudden, the St. George came down and the Black Jack took its place. Lowther's own flag, a dancing jack brandishing a sword, on the black background of death. The switch of flags was an old trick that should not still work, but it did. The horror on the faces of captain and crew at being so fooled delighted everyone on board the *Deliverance*. The *Deliverance* crew shouted with joy and near flew on to the deck of the *Molly*.

Ned saw little more than his knife and sword as he fought aggressively to keep his own blood and limbs. When the carnage was over, the *Deliverance* owned the *Molly*. Both ships decks were seeped in blood. Sails splattered and torn. The stench and the cries would have been unbearable if Ned had had any remorse. But, he had none. Except that it existed at all. And he was in it. That's the way it was for all pirates. Revenge. It was so simple, Ned thought as he breathed heavily after the exertion of battle, pirates were savages. Pirates fought with a knife between their teeth, with claws open, with wings they flew from mizzen to deck; they had naught to lose, not family, not home, not country, they believed in nothing –

except revenge. When the fighting was done, the pirates' chests pounded with heavy breath in their anticipation of the torture. They taunted the prisoners. The pirate song never failed to terrify the captives; the song they sang of a lust for revenge and the justice of revenge at those who were masters on land and in polite society, which the prisoners had foolishly abandoned, to be where pirates ruled. "I kill for revenge! I love to see blood at the stroke of my sword! I shed blood, you only shed tears!" The prisoners were paralyzed with terror. The pirates eagerly lapped up their terror. They fed on it. "I come, as God from above!" They sang, "To strike down those I loathe!"

Ned knew their singing was but the prelude to horror.

He and Lowther watched from of the *Molly's* quarterdeck, a place of honor where only the captain and first mate should stand, of which they had taken possession. The passengers especially stood wide-eyed to witness this nightmare reversal of order.

The *Deliverance* crew brought up some of the African slaves. The chains came with them, all in a line, chained by ankles and wrists, men and women. With axes, the pirates chopped off feet and hands to remove the chains. The amputated slave men and women fainted or rolled their eyes back and passed into a daze.

"Didn't think 'twould get much worse, did they?" Lowther joked, to which Ned gave a slight smile in acknowledgement.

The screams of the rest, the *Molly's* crew and prisoners alike, rose to a pitch that almost erased sound, and the pirates laughed as they stripped themselves and lay on top of both slave women and men alike, but especially enjoying the flesh of women, Ned thought, as their hands crushed the women's breasts and cupped their buttocks to increase their pleasure. Crewmen and slaves alike were fondled, and it was a game of torture for the *Deliverance* crew to see if they could further shame their victims by arousing them to climax while raping them.

The gentile passengers were horrified; they screamed and moaned. Little did they realize they were waiting their turn. The Captain was held, hands behind back. He protested loudly. Lowther reached into the man's belt and pulled out his pistol, which he then put into his own belt.

"An English doglock an' bran' new! Thank ye!"

Captain Merriweather hollered something very official sounding. Lowther drew his knife and sliced off Merriweather's lips. Lowther then called for a fire, and a small pit was made. The pirate roasted the man's lips as all watched. Lowther bit into the meat and chewed, causing a great roar of appreciation from the *Deliverance* crew. Then he spat out the chewed lump as though it tasted foul, and all laughed anew.

"Enough!" cried Lowther, who then organized the transfer of the *Molly's* cargo to the *Deliverance*. "Take only ten cannon, lest we sink with our greed. Take all the rum and sugar. Then we will see to the passengers."

The transfer took several hours, while the first class passengers, three men and two women, one of them pregnant, and two little girls waited in terror.

Ned could see how exhausted the prisoners were. Torches were lit. By their light, he saw Merriweather slumped into his chains; his shiny uniform caked with blood. Ned watched the children's innocent heads flip back and forth in confusion; they wept with fear and clung to their mother's skirts. He knew it would be over quickly for the children.

The children were thrown overboard immediately. Then, the pregnant woman was also thrown to the dark sea.

Blood in the water had attracted the demon fish. The *Deliverance* crew leaned over the rails with torches to watch; they cheered as each piece of flesh disappeared into the jaws of the demons. As he looked on, Ned wondered without emotion, what kind of world was it that Nature herself rose up to conspire with pirates?

The single woman, who was not beautiful, but overweight and plain, was stripped naked and used by several of Lowther's men.

"More than she would ever have in 'er whole life, eh?" Lowther joked, nudging Ned.

Ned barely moved his lips in a sneer.

The male passengers and the captain averted their eyes, which made Lowther laugh the more.

"Ah, it's time to go home, men." Lowther pronounced.

The crew followed Lowther home to the *Deliverance*. Once aboard the home ship, Lowther gave the order to torch the *Molly*.

"Let us send these slaves back to their native land!"

Ned knew the slaves of Africa thought they would return to their homeland in death, unless, of course, their limbs had been sliced off. He felt no remorse for those who had lost feet and hands; he was amused by it, as his fellow pirates were amused, and thus, satisfied in their torture.

As the *Molly* drifted away in the dark night, Ned watched as the flames rose from the sails and the ribs of the ship glowed with fire. The odor came to them of wood and blood and flesh cooking. The screams and wails of slaves and free men alike filled the night with a music sweet to pirates: the satisfaction of pain, the justice of suffering, the triumph of revenge.

Isla Hispaniola, 1692

Sometime near the end of May, Marion ordered her household to leave the shore and climb the hills behind Isabella for safety. Amidst trembling and rumbling of distant aftershocks, they camped for three weeks drinking fresh water from a spring, eating fruit from the trees and sleeping soundly within a circle of fire, while to the south Jamaica heaved and tore itself wide open with earthquake, spitting forth rogue tsunami waves that drowned the islands. Thousands died in Port Royal, Jamaica just south of the belly of Hispaniola, whilst Marion, Jordana, the new babe, Mari, the whores, their children and their slaves, even old Listen, waited in safety for God to rest from his savage rage.

Marblehead, 1995

The ghost hunters left at 5 a.m. Peter fell asleep on the bed he had shared with Beth. He'd torn off every bit of clothing he wore and left them in a heap on the floor. He fell asleep in darkness, naked and exhausted.

It happened so fast he didn't have time to question it. The sun's first rays broke through the sheer curtains and stung his closed eyes. He opened them. Squinting into the light that appeared pink and orange, he saw her. The curtains billowed around her. Her blonde hair curled over her shoulders. Her skin shone with light. Unmistakably, Beth stood in front of him. She was so beautiful, radiant and naked. He responded by becoming aroused.

She held out her hand, and he reached for her. Before he knew what was happening, Beth was with him, beside him in the bed. He pulled her to him and enveloped her eagerly.

"Beth!" He wanted to ask, "Am I dreaming?" but he didn't care if he were dreaming.

He touched her everywhere and she was warm. Her breasts met his touch with softness and warmth. He remembered each and every curve of her. He entered her; she was warm and moist; her arms tightened around his back, her mouth opened for his mouth. How he loved her!

"Beth!" He climaxed too quickly, he was almost disappointed, but he looked straight into her sparkling blue eyes and he was happy.

She smiled sadly, then kissed him fully and disappeared like air from his embrace.

Marblehead, 1692

Elizabeth woke to the roasty aroma of bread baking and, she thought, "Molly!" She threw her clothes on her body, and picked up her shoes in her hand, and fairly flew down the ladder to the kitchen where she saw, incredibly, Tom and Peter, Sarah and Emilie, four blonde heads together, busily doing for themselves.

Tom was lifting a finished loaf of bread from the oven. Sarah was slicing the thick wedge of newly ripened cheese that her father had bought from the Simmons' dairy when last he'd sailed to Gloucester. Peter tended the boiling kettle. Emilie placed each a cup.

They had no milk. Goody Pritchard and her husband, John were not speaking to the Treadwells since their son, Daniel's arrest. Elizabeth had not dared send any of the children there to milk the cow they had shared in happier times. They would do without.

The kettle whistled on the hearth. Tom carried it to the table, where he poured the steaming water into the teapot full of blueberry leaves.

"Mother!" cried Emilie. "We have made your favorite, special breakfast – warm bread and cheese with blueberry tea!"

Elizabeth was weak with emotion at seeing her dear children working for her, and at not seeing Molly: the emotion was so powerful her knees nearly gave way.

Tom came to her, and steadied her. He was a tall boy of eleven years, very pale and thin, but stronger than Elizabeth at this moment. He guided her silently to a place at the table. He placed a trencher in front of her filled with hot crusty bread and melting cheese.

"Mother, you must eat well!" Emilie said in her childish way of speaking, mushing her words just slightly, changing l to w, t to sh. It brought tears to Elizabeth's eyes. But, Elizabeth knew she wept for Molly, and Rosie, not for soft words.

Elizabeth did not want to eat. She wanted to sob, but in spite of herself, her belly cried out for the delicious aroma of the hot food. She bit into the crusty bread, and chewed the sweetness of the soft grain. She swallowed half expecting what she ate to come back up into her mouth, but it did not. She drank gratefully from her cup. She took another bite, chewing deeply, savoring the warm cheese. She felt guilty for so enjoying herself. She began to weep anew; she sniffed away the tears, which fell anyways into her meal. The children did not speak. They allowed her to eat and sob.

When she was done, Elizabeth thanked them each with a kiss. She wrapped two pieces of warm bread stuffed with cheese separately in cloths for her daughter and her friend. She also took a small basket of clean diapers for the baby.

She gave the children some instructions for their day. She kissed Tom especially; she knew he had led the others.

"Take care of them," she told him.

He nodded, for, still, he did not speak.

***

Elizabeth walked to Selectman Peach's house, which had become her daily vigil.

She took her position as she did every day, opposite the house. On the hot, sandy street she knelt and faced the grand house in supplication and prayer.

Elizabeth remained there all day. The sand bore into the soft flesh of her knees, right through the fabric of her skirt. The hot sun baked her, but she did not mind any of it. She thought only on Molly and Rosie and the baby who were inside a dark, close windowless room, where the heat from the adjacent kitchen was bound to be horrendous. At noon, Addie came out and took the bread and cheese and the basket of diapers from Elizabeth's hands. Elizabeth hoped to God she would give the food to Molly and Rosie, and not eat it herself. Addie gave her the same smirk she always did, so Elizabeth could not tell.

Their trial was less than two weeks away.

Elizabeth begged for mercy.

The townspeople walked past her on their way to their tasks and errands. Some spat on her, others pushed her, or deliberately walked into her. Boys liked to jeer at her, "Witch Mother!" They called her, and threw rocks. Occasionally, a rock hit her. Today, she was struck on the side of her face and she fell to the ground, whereupon the boys burst into laughter and more derision.

She could just discern the forms of Addie Gatchell and two other servants crowding together at the window to stare and laugh at her predicament.

One person Elizabeth did not see looking down at her was Selectman Peach himself, from an upstairs window.

Elizabeth righted herself from the stoning and knelt.

Judge Sewall, who happened to be passing, also witnessed the violent scene.

"Get away, ye hooligans!" Judge Sewall slapped one of the boys, whom he grabbed by the collar and thrust aside. "Get ye home!"

"Goody Treadwell, ye must not remain here in the street."

Elizabeth looked up to see the man reaching for her, gently helping her to her feet.

"Oh, Judge!" She cried. "You can help me!"

"Yes, of course, Madam."

"Please, sir, please help me! My child, my dear, sweet Molly! She is accused, sir! She is innocent, innocent! Never did she know the Devil, never sir! She helps me daily, she serves God, sir!"

Judge Sewall was quite taken aback by the sincerity of the woman. For a moment, he hesitated. His kind nature immediately wished to help her. But, he had seen the child in question with his own eyes holding the awful telescope, cavorting with the old seer, and then, he had seen – God only knows – or the Devil only knows - what he, a solemn judge, had seen, there in the wall of Edward Dimond's house – eyes! Eyes had stared back at him! Whom could he tell about *that?*

Not even this child's mother would comprehend what he had seen, no, nor would she condone it!

Nay, the judge knew, she would condone anything that would save her child. Therefore, he could not help her.

"Ye must go home, Madam. Ye cannot be in the street or I will arrest ye myself."

The idea that she was breaking the law horrified Elizabeth! Is that where she was now? Such a simple act of kneeling was now something to be arrested for?

Judge Sewall lifted her to her feet.

"Come now, get thee home!

Elizabeth looked into his eyes. He had a generous face, round and soft, seemingly gentle. She knew he had most recently seen five of his infant children go from their mother's womb into the ground. He knew the sorrow of losing a child.

"You know something." She said. "You know Molly and Rosie are innocent of witchcraft. You know, sir! And, yet you continue to accuse the faithful."

Yes, he knew something. In his old heart, he admitted to himself that he was getting tired of all the accusations and the nightmare of deaths of those who once had been deemed faithful. Old Rebecca Nurse's accusation and her hanging had most horribly confounded him. Not the least, he had buried five newly born children in recent years and the sadness bore on him. Death now clouded his exhausted eyes. How many of his children would continue to be born only to die while their flesh was tender and new? How much was such premature death a judgment from God? He was confused and frightened about where his responsibility lay and where it had gone awry. Still, for now, it was safer to go along with the tide. Until he could clear his mind, that is. And, his heart.

"I know nothing, Madam. Except that you are disturbing the peace and disobeying a judge."

For a moment, Elizabeth considered getting arrested and joining Molly and Rosie in the room. But, she knew she could not bring them food nor help them in any way nor take care of her other children or Rosie's, if she were in the room too.

Suddenly, Elizabeth felt tired. So very tired.

She allowed herself to be lifted. She stood a moment and looked at the lovely house, all shiny and clean; the painted door shone, the garden nodded with flowers glowing in the sun. You would never know terror was within.

Elizabeth cast one sad look on to Judge Sewall, a kind and honorable man who, despite his goodness, did not have the courage to stop the epidemic of death that had caught her sweet child in its grip. Her stomach sickened with panic. Every day, Elizabeth heard, more had been hanged for imaginary crimes. Hanged, hanged, hanged, every day, folks she knew or had heard of. So close by! In Salem! Or Danvers way! Bridget Bishop, a comely, cheerful lass who had worn a scarlet bodice, hanged! Sarah Good, hanged. Susannah Martin! Giles Corey of Ipswich accused! Wilmott Redd accused, her pond and lands ceased! John and Elizabeth Proctor accused! Rebecca Nurse, an elder, godly woman, accused and hanged. Philip and Mary English! All their property ceased. A shadow flew over

Elizabeth's heart, could that be the reason, and just as suddenly, the shadow fled. She could not grasp a thought.

She was so very tired. Hardly could she put one foot in front of the other to make her way home. Home! How terribly guilty she felt for going there.

Marblehead, 1995

The next morning Peter woke to the smell of coffee. He threw his clothes on from the pile next to the bed where he'd dropped them the night before and hurried downstairs, almost hoping to see Beth in the kitchen making breakfast.

He rounded the corner at the base of the staircase and slid into the kitchen like a hockey player on ice.

Meghan smiled back at him. She thought for a second that he was disappointed, that he had expected to see Beth.

Oddly, he was relieved.

"Meghan! Boy! Am I glad to see you!"

She laughed, blushing. She was glad.

Peter saw that she was wearing a blue tank top and cut-offs. He could see her shape clearly, and she was full-figured, but trim.

Emily, who was sitting at the table eating a large stack of pancakes, jumped up and ran to him.

"Daddy! Meghan says I can have all the pancakes I want!"

"Oh, really? How many is that?"

"I dunno." Emily shrugged, skipping back to the table.

"That stack looks bigger than you!" Peter kissed the top of her head.

"No, sir! It's not bigger than me, Daddy!"

"Hope you don't mind my barging in, Peter." Meghan said.

"Nope! That's why I gave you the key."

Peter poured himself a cup of coffee. He sat down at the table, next to Emily, and allowed himself to drift off, staring out the kitchen window at the ocean. For a blissful moment, he was content. Then, the odd occurrences of the night before filtered back to his mind. What had actually happened? Had he made love to Beth? He knew he had. He hadn't been dreaming. He'd touched her for God's sake and she'd felt warm! He took a sip of hot coffee and felt it surge through his throat to his stomach. Just like that, he thought, just like hot coffee. He had felt her: she'd been warm, even hot when he was inside her, she'd been hot and wet and wrapped around his penis and her insides had sucked on his penis like they had when –

"So, how'd it go last night? If it's okay to ask." Meghan interrupted his thoughts.

"Huh?"

Peter looked up with a vacant expression.

"I asked how the - (Meghan hesitated, she didn't want to say the word 'ghost') - well, how it went last night. Do you mind my asking?"

"No! No! Of course, not. No." Peter could hardly recall what the ghost crew had told him. He had to think. He felt awkward, embarrassed, as though Meghan might have overheard his thoughts. But, when he looked at her, her face was gentle and interested; he relaxed. That was all. He relaxed around her.

"Yeah, well, we have to hear the actual 'findings' from the equipment, but so far, it seems the place is teaming with spirits."

Peter took another sip of coffee, just slightly cooler now, slightly less comforting.

Meghan was silent; she stared at him.

"Oh, it's okay!" Peter assured her. "They've been here all along!"

Meghan nodded.

Emily kept eating her pancakes as though nothing was strange, studying carefully that she had enough butter and syrup with each bite.

Marblehead, 1692

Molly thought, as she admired the simple comfort of the candle flame, her mother was their Angel of Light.

Selectman Peach, against the will of his wife, and to ease his troubled soul at daily seeing the kneeling form of a plaintive mother outside his house, had a small table and two chairs, a candle and two pallets from the stables brought in to Rosie, her baby and Molly.

The candlelight cheered the women immensely; the tiny flame illuminated their tired faces with the soft light of Elizabeth's affection. The chairs brought them up off the floor. The small packages of food Elizabeth brought them, and the bundles of fresh cloths for the baby were comforts multiplied as loaves and fishes to those who had no comfort at all but the hard floor and the torment of not knowing what would become of them.

Molly cried a great deal. There was not much else to do, except to consider her new condition. Her sobs were quiet; she did not want to upset Rosie as a nursing mother, no, nor the baby Edwina either, but tears fell from her reddened eyes almost non-stop, and her cheeks were always wet. In other times, Rosie would have scolded her. But, she could not bring herself to harsh words.

"Goody Low, Rosie, I mean, do you think we are witches?" Molly asked her, one day.

Rosie snorted in derision.

"What say you? That we purposely hurt those children? Nay, child, more likely their madness comes from lack of a good hard smack on their behinds!"

"We did look through the 'scope, Rosie. And we saw him away far off in the lands of the heathen. That must be magical!"

The girl's eyes shone.

Rosie's face softened.

"Aye, tha' we did, eh, lass? An' wasn' 'e a fey young lad, my Neddie! Ye love 'im, eh? I don' blame ye. I truly do not. How could ye help but love the likes of 'im, so brave and fine a man though truly still a lad."

Rosie's own thoughts trailed off. What trials had he? What hardships did he bear? Ah, she knew that life in Marblehead had not prepared him for such situations as he found himself in now. No, nor had that same serene Marblehead life prepared her or Molly for what they were enduring.

"'Tes all madness!" Rosie thought.

Molly hung her head in shame that she had partaken of the magic 'scope, but also, she felt secretly proud that she had seen him! Yes, Rosie was right. She did love Ned. His dark eyes darkened the more with India kohl, his strange braids and scarves and the shining knife at his side, all excited her beyond belief! What had she seen? Was it real? Was it witchcraft? Did that make her a witch? She felt no different than before, except that her heart was heightened with excitement of having seen Ned through the magic 'scope and with terror at the sudden change in her circumstances. Now, she lived in the back room of Selectman Peach's house, behind his kitchen, with Rosie Low and her baby – how was that?

Marblehead, 1995

Pete and Sarah Weaver sat together at her laptop on the back porch of her house, a sprawling McMansion that had started out as an 18th Century saltbox, but had been added to bit by bit till it blocked the ocean views of the entire row of homes across the street. The back porch looked out to sea, but neither Pete nor Sarah took any notice of the perfect vista.

They were enthralled by the newness of the PowerBook with its track pad.

After they had played with all of the games that came with the machine and created a few designs in the new graphics program, Sarah asked, "Have you ever been in a chat room?"

"A what?" Pete asked before he could stop himself. Instantly, he wished he had said, "Yeah, sure." But, he really didn't have a clue what Sarah meant.

"It's really fun! All these losers - well, here - we have to go inside to my Dad's office to hook up to the modem."

He followed Sarah into the house, to her Dad's office. She continued to talk.

"I guess they all must be at work, but all they talk about is sex."

Pete froze. He suddenly felt like he was doing something stupid.

But, he didn't say that. He just leaned in for a closer look.

Sarah connected the laptop to the modem on her Dad's desk. Her dark fingers flew over the keyboard, as the internet chimed and buzzed itself on. While the screen jumped and flashed, Sarah was explaining about avatars, alt reality and how she was PinkLady online. She was wearing a pink outfit; he noticed she wore pink a lot. Pink did look nice against her deep brown skin. Sarah wore a pink headband that caught her black curls up around her face, and pink flip-flops decorated with a large pink flower between her toes.

Pete sighed and turned his attention away from Sarah's toes back to the computer screen. The chat room didn't look like much. Just lines of text that morphed as Sarah typed.

"You have to be twenty-one, but I just lie. All you need to do is type in that you were born before 1974."

Pete read some of the screen names. PartyGuy, TooHot, NiceGuy, SmartAss, LickMe, ILuvIt.

"This guy has been trying to get me to meet him."

"Who?" Pete asked. All this was way too new to him.

"He calls himself NaughtyButNice." She laughed. "What a turd!"

Pete watched as Sarah typed, "How old r u?"

"Told u, 12."

Sarah laughed again as she typed, "Whooz ur fave B Boy?"

"Watch, he doesn't know who the B Boys are!" Sarah was delighted.

They waited for an answer. It took a while.

"Not my fave." Came the reply.

Sarah cried out in delight, "Whoa! I knew it! He must be *really old!*"

Pete was loosing interest till Sarah said, "We should meet him."

"Why?"

"I wanna see what kind of a loser he is."

"Why does he want to hang out with kids?" Pete asked.

"I dunno. He's just weird."

Pete didn't think he wanted to spend his day meeting some old guy, but Sarah seemed so into the idea, he hesitated. Then, Sarah was writing, "LMIRL."

"What's that?"

Sarah never took her eyes off the screen. "Let's meet in real life."

The answer came quickly.

"GR8!"

"I'm in Lynn, City of Sin, WRU?"

"@, @3?"

"@, that's the internet café on Atlantic." Sarah explained. "It's 2:30 now. BRT she wrote. Be Right There! This guy is crazy! We can ride our bikes and be there in ten!"

"How will we know him?"

"Are you kidding? He'll be the tallest one there!"

"Oh, okay," she added. "Let's ask him to wear a red baseball cap."

Sarah typed that in, and snapped the PowerBook shut.

"Let's go!"

"What if he doesn't have a red baseball cap?" Pete asked.

"They *all* have red baseball caps!" Sarah told him.

Marblehead, 1995

Jo was in the Karmann Ghia at a stoplight just outside the office. She was getting ready to make a right turn into the driveway, when a few pedestrians started across the street.

She waited for them to pass. A couple of teenage girls in cute dresses and sandals, talking animatedly and checking their cell phones. A mom pushing a baby stroller and walking a Golden at the same time.

She looked over at Orange Dream Yogurt and thought about how the fabulous Biami had been spotted there buying frozen yogurts, and how much positive feedback she'd gotten from the sighting. She wanted to do some publicity follow-up on that. Her thoughts were already in the office as she waited patiently. She didn't notice him at first.

A man was looking into the car, she realized. He was standing in front of the car so she couldn't move and he was laughing. It was Ben Hardy.

Jo leaned on the horn. It was a comical horn she'd bought as a joke, an old a-oo-ga that she'd gotten to be funny, not mean. She hated beeping at people; she felt it was rude. Now, she regretted the silly horn. He just laughed at her more.

Jo didn't know what else to do, so she just sat there. Waiting.

Then, he did something so weird, it made Jo sick.

He came around to the driver's side and opened his mouth and licked the window that was half up. He wagged his tongue at her about an inch from her face.

Then, he simply left. He walked away.

Jo made sure the road was clear then she gunned it into the driveway, tires screaming, leaving rubber on the road.

Marblehead, 1692

Any quiet thoughts Rosie and Molly might have had, sitting now across from each other at the small table they'd been given in their captivity, were suddenly and abruptly silenced.

The door, closed for so long, now burst open and five men in black coats and two strong men from the town were suddenly in the room. The servants from the house also crowded in the doorway. Big men brought for reason of their strength alone grabbed Rosie and Molly from behind and held the women's wrists tightly. These men were one Philip Beare, a fisherman and the other, John Bennett, also a fisherman, once known as friendly neighbors to both women; now, their sullen faces were masked with resolve that was in itself a mask for payment and treachery. Oh, Rosie, thought, how angry her husband, Matty would be to know his friends had betrayed him! Chairs fell over in a sudden clatter. The baby was taken from Rosie and handed to the servant girl, Addie.

"No!" cried Rosie. "The babe will get vermin from that filthy slut!"

The men in black coats were Judge Sewall, Reverend Hathorne, Bartholomew Gedney, Selectman Peach and Reverend Parris, whose daughter, Betty and her cousin, Abigail had been attacked by Salem's witches, which included, now, Molly Treadwell.

A solemn procession strode from the dark room to an upstairs bedroom. Solemn, that is, with the exception of Rosie's struggling and hissing of profanities to the group.

"Let us go! How dare ye and where be ye takin' us now? It's not enough ye bolted us up in a root cellar, ye have to 'cort us 'round about too? Let go of me arms, y're hurtin' me!"

Molly was silent in her terror. Were they going to be hung from the bedpost right there? Some part of her enjoyed for a moment only the breath of fresh air afforded in the house from the windows that were open to the night, but these were quickly closed no sooner had she thought of it, and shutters and curtains drawn.

The door was shut behind them, closing off the crowd of servants, until only Rosie and Molly were left with the group of men.

Judge Sewall dismissed the laborers who were holding their arms.

The women stood before the officials in the master's bedroom.

"Remove your clothing!" Reverend Hathorne commanded the women.

Molly gasped. Rosie cried out that they could kill her first before she would lift a finger or remove a thread of her clothing.

A servant was called in. A female servant. Then, two female servants.

Rosie was stripped violently by the cook.

Molly was stripped by Addie Gatchell.

The servants, who had enjoyed themselves immensely, were ordered out.

Molly had never been naked before; always she had washed and bathed in her shift. The sudden shock of being naked in front of strange men made her faint dead away.

Judge Sewall caught her thin frame, frail as a bird's. He shook his head in dismay. He lifted the girl to the bed where Reverend Hathorne began an examination of her young and slender body for a third teat – they found none but her own rosy and tender nipples, just budding on the slim body. They searched the girl closely for other marks of the Devil. They lifted her legs and opened her buttocks. They opened the folds of her small vagina. They held a candle over every inch of the girl's skin.

"God will get ye, aye an' every one! Ye'll burn in 'ell an' the Devil will dance on yer bones, ye filthy beasts!"

Judge Sewall held her back, but Rosie never stopped crying out.

Rosie watched as Reverend Hathorne's chubby well-fed finger moved over the girl's skin leaving a slight trail of grease from his evening meal of roasted chicken and onions.

"Ye hogs! It's a mercy the child cannot feel what gruesome work ye're about, ye filthy, lyin' sons of whores!"

"Silence!" Judge Sewall shouted, hoping to calm the crazed woman before she attacked an official in his duty, a crime as serious as witchcraft. He grabbed a cloth on the chair that was a piece of Mrs. Peach's underclothing and bound Rosie's hands behind her back.

The judges examined Molly's limp body until they found, just under her right armpit, a mole in the shape of a crescent moon.

"Ah!" Hathorne exclaimed. "A Devil's bite! Come, let us pierce it with a needle and see if the child feels the sensation or not."

"Ah, I know wha' ye really wan', don' I! Ye want to pierce the chil' all right! Cum 'ere, I'll kill ye myself!"

A needle was handed to Reverend Hathorne, who pierced the little crescent moon's raised brown shape under Molly's arm. Molly did not flinch. The judges moaned in unison. Reverend Hathorne pierced the mole once again. Again, Molly did not move or acknowledge the pain.

"Clearly, the child has been marked by the Devil! It's a wonder ye weren't all murdered in yer beds!" Reverend Hathorne proclaimed.

"Yer all mad!" Rosie screamed. "Stark mad! The child is innocent as a newborn babe! Let 'er go! Let 'er go back to 'er mother! She's only a child! Get away from 'er body, ye lustful ol' crows!"

Rosie herself was examined standing, as she thrust the men's hands away from her with her bound hands, and they prodded and poked and opened her legs and her buttocks, lifted her arms, and peered into the hair there like monkeys looking for a tasty morsel. They bent her from the waist as she struggled and examined her anus. It was on Rosie's anus that Reverend Hathorne, the most zealous of examiners, found what he called

"Devil's tails," two small tags of new flesh that hung there as a result of Rosie's extra indulgence in ham and bacon at meals.

"She is also marked." He concluded.

Rosie farted in his serious face.

"That's fer yer evidence! A blow 'ard fer a blow 'ard!"

"A Devil's own, farting in the face of authority." Reverend Hathorne announced to his brethren who grunted in agreement.

All these findings were writ in the book of the solemn Court of Oyer and Terminer.

"Ye're all a lot of filthy whoremongers!" Rosie snarled at them as she dressed herself, and Molly, and woke the girl gently from her swoon.

***

The two women pulled their pallets even closer that night. Edwina slept in her little box as if nothing had happened. Molly wept herself to sleep, and Rosie held her like a babe whilst she felt tears fall unwillingly from her own eyes and soak her cheeks and neck.

"Now, they've found this evidence, we are doomed," She thought.

Rosie was not one to pray. She was too flippant in her nature, which was to laugh off her troubles whenever she could. She wanted to laugh. At the men, so serious in their cause, when all they wanted to do was poke and prod a naked and helpless virgin! Oh, didn't they just get erect, or maybe their old poles were too flaccid and shriveled! Ha! More tha' like, for sure! Ha! They wished they could fuck the girl! That's the whole of it, right there! And, she, herself, why she had wanted to strike them down, to kill them, one by one in that room and leave them in a bloody heap like her Neddie had done on his ship. Oh, yes, she too had seen him fight, what a buccaneer he was! She was that proud! Ah, if her Ned had been in that room, they'd never have dared to touch her or Molly! Ned would have cut their hands off, tha' he would.

Rosie's eyes closed finally, a smile lifted her mouth in slumber, as she dreamed of her dashing son.

Marblehead, 1995

Pete and Sarah were headed to Atlantic when Pete suddenly let his feet skid on the sandy ground and bring his bike to a dead stop.

Sarah stopped beside him.

"What's goin' on?"

Pete, who'd gotten caught up in Sarah's excitement, and who still wanted to impress her, had suddenly recalled the story of Polly Klaas his father had drilled into his psyche.

It was the condom they had found next to her body. That was why adults wanted to hang out with kids. Why they wanted to talk about sex when they were at work. It suddenly came clear to him.

"Look, when we see him, we need to call the cops."

Sarah just looked at him. She was breathing heavily from the ride.

"Really?"

"Yes! He's trying to kidnap kids."

"Kidnap kids? What makes you think *that?"*

"I just know, okay? And, I don't want to go on those fucking chat rooms any more. I feel like I wanna vom."

"Yeah, okay. It *was* pretty weird." Sarah agreed, though she seemed embarrassed. "Let's go get him then!"

"Okay!"

***

It was too easy, Sarah thought. The two of them waited across the street in front of Orange Dream where they had a clear view of @ with its soft blue neon sign. A tall beefy guy got out of an old green van and walked to the door of the café. He was wearing a red baseball cap.

He went in and stood at the counter. Sarah and Pete could just barely make out his head looking around the café.

"He's gonna leave if we don't go in!" Sarah exclaimed.

"No, don't go in there! I'm calling the cops right now."

"Wait, what're you gonna say? That we were in a chat room? My Dad's gonna kill me!"

"If we don't, he's gonna do this again to some other kid, maybe a little kid!"

Pete took some change out of his pocket and ran to the phone booth on the corner. He took a deep breath and dialed 911.

"911 Emergency, what's your emergency?"

Damn, it was now or never, Pete thought.

"Listen, we made a – an appointment – to see this guy online..."

"What's your name, son?"

Pete's stomach went cold.

"Peter Treadwell."

"What's the problem?"

"This guy is meeting kids. At the internet café on Atlantic right now. He's wearing a red baseball cap and he's driving a dark green van."

"Can you see the license plate?"

"Wait. Hang on."

Pete dropped the phone. He could hear the officer calling him back, but he kept walking. He crossed the street and stood behind the van. He could see the guy inside, but he wasn't looking at him. His head was down, looking at the computer screen. He was online, Pete realized.

Pete looked at the license plate and said the digits out loud. It was a trick he had taught himself to help remember stuff.

Sarah was pretty upset, he could see. She stood behind her bike, waiting.

Pete ran back to the phone and called the plate out to the officer on the phone.

"Where are you, son?"

"I'm across the street."

"Good. I need you to get somewhere safe. Go inside the yogurt store right now, okay? I have a car nearby."

"Okay."

"Wait there for the police officer. He's gonna want to talk to you."

Pete hung up the phone. Before he could say a word to Sarah, the police car whooped its siren and drove up on to the sidewalk in front of @, stopping just short of the window. Pete grabbed Sarah by the hand and pulled her into Orange Dream. Two officers ran out of the cruiser and into the internet café. In another second, NaughtyButNice was in handcuffs being led into the police car.

Pete could tell he was looking for the kid he had met online; his head darted back and forth as though scanning the street. He and Sarah hid behind a giant cone painted on the window of the yogurt store and watched.

***

Things exploded at Sarah's house. Her father took away the PowerBook and grounded her for the rest of the summer. But, Sarah had a pool and her own private beach, so she wasn't too upset. She wasn't allowed to see Pete though, no matter how much she protested that it wasn't his fault, that she had done it, and what's the big deal, they caught the guy because of her and Pete. They were heroes and they were being treated like criminals. None of her protests worked.

Peter told his son he was both proud of him and, at the same time, beyond angry. He didn't punish him. Just made him promise never to go into a chat room or do anything so stupid again. Pete said, "Don't worry, I won't." And, he meant it.

The story made the Marblehead Police Log and the Salem News. From the evidence police found in his van, NaughtyButNice, who resided in Lynn, was implicated in four kidnappings in the New England area. When Peter read that in the Salem paper, it made him sick to think of the two skinny bodies of Sarah and Pete being tossed into that van, and he said so to Pete, warning him once more.

Peter got nauseous every time he thought of it.

Except for a few lines in the Police Log, the Marblehead paper didn't print a word. It was like it had never happened in Marblehead.

Marblehead, 1995

Late one afternoon, Jo's phone rang with her ringtone, the cheerful singing and laughing of girls. She was working on some figures for Cass, so she picked it up absentmindedly.

"Simmons Hawkes. Jo Simmons speaking. How can I help you?"

Jo waited, reading the numbers.

"I'm gonna fuck your brains out." A man's voice growled.

Her heart slammed against her chest.

"Who is this?" She demanded.

The man laughed, and hung up.

Jo looked out the window terrified that she might see Hardy staring back at her. She searched the busy street with its preoccupied shoppers and orderly lines traffic for him, but she couldn't see him.

She knew he was out there.

Marblehead, 1995

Peter's heart went sick whenever he thought of how close his son and Sarah Weaver had come to tragedy. He fell almost into a state of mourning again, like he had after Beth's death. Every now and then he was shaken out of it by Emily's laughter or Meghan's face.

One summer night, when the air was sweet with cut grass and the salt snap of the sea, he and Meghan took Sarah and Emily and the dogs out for a walk after dinner. He and Meghan were together a lot with the children. Peter had gotten used to seeing her every day in his home. She had moved in a few days after the ghost hunt. Peter was really enjoying the calm she created in his life, not to mention the sheer joy of looking at her happy face and – well, Peter admitted to himself as they walked that he enjoyed seeing her red hair shine in the twilight sun and bounce on her shoulders as she walked. He admitted to himself further, that he liked to step back just a little and watch her full bottom sway. He liked the ample cleavage of her breasts whenever she leaned over to wipe the kids' mouths or – what was he saying? He shouldn't say or think such things even to himself! For God's sake, she was his nanny! He needed her!

Life had been going a lot smoother since she came. What happened to Pete and Sarah had upset him and left him with the reeling sensation that his foundation was now cracked and he wasn't sure how to fix it, or if he could fix it. Still, underneath, somehow under that split foundation, he was also impressed by how Pete had handled the whole thing. Meghan had helped him get his bearings. They were kids, she'd said, and bound to get into trouble now and then. They made some stupid decisions, but they'd redeemed themselves. She felt they'd learned their lesson. They were lucky, Peter had said. No, Meghan had told him, they were smart, and he had taught Pete well. Maybe one's foundation needed to split occasionally as it rocked with the earth. After all, Marblehead was made of granite. Though he didn't know what to make of Frank Finley's remark about granite's heartbeat, or what kind of a foundation *that* would make…

He realized suddenly, while he'd been thinking, he'd been staring at Meghan's rump swaying in front of him. Stop looking at her ass, he told himself as they walked. He should count his blessings! Meghan's ass *was* a blessing. Thank God, no one here could read his thoughts!

They turned the corner by Peach Ice Cream when Emily and Sarah both started jumping up and down, taking Peter's and Meghan's hands up and down with them in their eagerness.

"Can we get ice cream, Dad?" Sarah asked.

"Can we?" cried Emily.

"Sure!" Peter agreed and they all walked up hill, along the sidewalk of the market to the ice cream place. Peach stayed open until 11:00 p.m. to catch the crowds coming out of the movies or the restaurants, or out on walks as they were.

As they approached, Peter admired the decorations the owner, Karen Peach, Julie Low Peach's sister-in-law, had placed around the little terrace. She'd strung fairy lights over the flowerbeds and around the tables. The lights were welcoming and added a touch of – well, he had to admit – magic to the evening. Karen placed potted palm trees in summer, hung with lights, and evergreens at Christmas, also hung with lights. Once a year, about two weeks before Christmas, she invited the neighborhood kids to hang ornaments on the trees. She really was smart, Peter thought. It was a nice place to sit and relax, which is what they did.

Emily got a strawberry cone, Sarah a chocolate with chocolate chips. Meghan, a maple walnut, coffee combo, and he treated himself to something he'd never tried before, Rocky Road. It was way too sweet.

He made a face, "Should've stuck to vanilla."

Meghan laughed.

"What's so funny?"

"Sorry, your face! You look like you're eating a lemon."

"It is a lemon."

"Want to get something else?"

"Nah! I'm good."

"Wait, have some of mine."

"No, no!"

"I saw you looking at it!"

"Go ahead, Dad! Try some! Want some strawberry?" Em offered.

"No. I'll take a little spoonful of Meghan's."

Meghan filled the plastic spoon with a large sample of maple walnut and coffee.

"That's too much!" Peter protested.

Suddenly, Meghan sent the spoon and ice cream flying into his face too fast and it went all over his nose.

The kids burst out laughing. Peter wiped his nose, and blew ice cream out of his nose into a napkin which Meghan and the kids thought was hilarious.

"Oh, man!" Peter kidded Meghan. "I owe you one, big time!"

She just laughed.

"I'm glad *you're* having fun!"

They heard an angry voice approaching their table. They looked up from their laughter to see a woman, a very professional looking woman dressed in a tan suit and heels, yelling at them.

"Who the hell are you?" Peter asked, pulling the kids' chairs toward him.

"I'm the Director of Sunny Day School, Mr. Treadwell, and I'm suing this woman for slander. She's responsible for my losing the school! I've done nothing wrong and I've lost every student."

"Don't say anything." Peter advised Meghan. "We'll look into this."

Meghan wiped some ice cream spill off the table with her napkin.

"You can leave, lady. Have your lawyer call mine. Paul Weaver, he's in the book."

"You haven't heard the last from me! Steroids! Anything the students and teachers took was prescribed by a doctor!"

"Yeah, yeah, lady, go home!"

Emily started to choke on her ice cream, and then, she began to cry. Sarah dropped her cone.

Meghan jumped up and scooped Emily into her arms, and led Sarah off by the hand as the woman set off following them away from the terrace.

"Shit!" Peter exclaimed, running after his family.

He caught up with Meghan and the girls and got himself between them and this raving woman who was following them away from the ice cream parlor. He held out his hands, trying not to make any physical contact, but keep her away at the same time.

"Lady, you're way too crazy to take care of kids!"

"Crazy? Crazy? Who're you calling crazy?" She began swinging her purse, which turned out to be a large, flat, painful projectile.

Someone must have called the cops, because before Peter knew it, he heard the whoop of a siren and officers surrounded him and the woman was being pulled back from him, Meghan and his two little girls.

"She told the whole town! She ruined my school!" The woman shouted as police dragged her away.

"You guys okay, Pete?" Jimmy Martin asked him.

"Yeah, Jim, thanks."

"What the hell was that all about?"

"I really don't know, this woman came up to us at Peach's and started ranting about her school."

"Wanna press charges?"

"Oh, no, no! We're fine." He looked at Meghan, who nodded that she was fine.

The girls seemed shaken, but okay. He didn't want to go to court.

"No, we're fine." Peter reassured his friend, whom he had known all his life.

"Well, you're not the only ones here that are pissed. We got a disturbance of the peace complaint against her."

"Oh. Well, can we go home?"

"Sure, yeah. I'll be in touch, if necessary."

"Okay. You know where to find me."

He put his arm around Meghan's shoulders without thinking and pulled her to him.

"Don't worry." He told her.

"Will Missus Harper be under-arrested?" Emily asked.

"Oh, no, Em'. The police just want to ask her what's wrong." Peter comforted her.

"Mrs. Harper, huh?" Peter asked Meghan.

Meghan nodded.

"She was head of the school."

"We can talk about it later. Let's just get home."

The Atlantic, North of Rhode Island, 1692

To Ned's astonishment, there was the *Propriety* before them, as though ordered. Lowther was not in the least surprised, of course. Ned wondered if Marion had whispered into the *Propriety's* captain's ear some dream of sailing north to Salem while he slept.

The *Deliverance* overtook her just north of Newport, far off shore, miles to the east.

This time, Lowther had no patience. He did not bother with niceties, flags or planks. Lowther flew the black and bone without hesitation. He chased her down with grim intent. When the *Deliverance* was close enough, Lowther fired all fifteen guns at once at her, ten below deck and five up top and, though he was also fired upon, he accomplished his favorite trick, he rammed her broadside and she suffered a gash to her rib cage that was horrible for any sailor to see. Luckily, for them, the men of the *Deliverance* were not sailors, but thieves.

Lowther wasted no time. He beheaded Captain Vane and stuck his severed head on the man's own sword which he waved about like a trophy. When he tired of this, he had a man run the head up the flagstaff by its hair for all to see.

There were no passengers to speak of, just a young man traveling back to civilization to study at Oxford. He was thrown overboard. And a clergyman. He was stripped naked, buggered and cast into a barrel, which was then ridden and rolled all over deck amidst laughter and screams. The clergyman was then buggered again and again with a rail pin through the knothole in the barrel before clergyman and barrel were thrown overboard. Piccoli lifted the barrel himself and tossed it over to the cheers of men.

Lowther turned his attention to the cargo while all this celebration was going on. He went below with a few men to find not exactly what he had been promised: no raw gold or silver, but there were gold doubloons a plenty, one trunk of jewels, fit for a king and queen and perhaps meant for them too, lemons and limes, gunpowder and rum.

Lowther was happy. He reasoned with himself that the raw ore would have been too heavy for its value to him. He'd been debating sinking it anyways.

He took all the gold and jewels, 12 crates of lemons and limes, gunpowder and all of the rum, which were 200 barrels. He'd also found a leather bag fat with coin of the realm in the Captain's cabin.

"A fine catch!" He proclaimed.

The crew was left on board, except for three men who said they could play, that is, flute, fiddle and drum. Players were highly valued; the *Deliverance* had lost their favorite player just weeks before when the musician had gotten drunk and stumbled overboard in the night. The new musicians gladly signed Lowther's articles rather than die and joined the *Deliverance* crew.

And, in timely fashion.

Lowther ordered the *Propriety* blown up. Twenty kegs of gunpowder were left on board and the *Propriety* was lit.

The remaining crew begged for their lives. Some leapt overboard to their deaths, as they could not swim. Each man died in less than four minutes of struggling with the sea.

The *Propriety* made a lovely cloud of orange fire and rosy grey smoke reaching to the heavens and out the length of five vessels. The *Deliverance* crew cheered and danced a jig to their new music while lemons and limes also danced on the blood red waves along with arms and legs and chests of the men that bobbed up and down to song.

Lowther had his treasure. He was happy - for now.

Later, Lowther dressed himself and Ned in the King's and Queen's jewels. He balanced a jeweled crown on his head. He put pearl earrings on Ned, and long strands of rubies round his neck. Lowther draped a diamond necklace round and round his erect penis and thrust it out for Ned to suckle. Ned hated getting down on his knees before Lowther, but he knew better than to make a fuss. He did not know what position he hated most, anyways. He took Lowther into his mouth, sucking on diamonds and flesh. Lowther groaned with great enjoyment. "Ah, lad!" he cried, and patted Ned's hair till he neared his climax, when he pulled the hair tightly, holding Ned closer to him, coming far down Ned's throat, rubbing Ned's face into his rancid pubic hair. Ned swallowed and was grateful the load was already too far down his throat to taste much. Lowther groaned and stumbled on to his bed.

Ned cared not for jewels, but when Lowther was passed out with his satisfaction, he felt justified to fill his pockets with hands full of gems as money to be spent for his own deliverance; he also slipped in a string of milky pink pearls for Jordana, thinking how lovely they would look shining against her caramel skin. As for coin, he'd been collecting those for months.

Still, Ned hoped Lowther would continue north.

Marblehead, 1995

"I didn't tell you because I knew you'd be upset!" Jo explained to her husband later that evening. She also told him about the jogging encounter and the obscene phone call.

"Jeez, Jo! We have to go to the cops and get a restraining order." Bob told her.

"Ok, ok, I will."

"No, not 'I will!' Let's go now!"

The officers told Bob and Jo that they didn't have much to go on.

"Technically, Bob, he hasn't done anything illegal."

"He told her he was going to 'get her,' that 'she could run but she couldn't hide!' Are we supposed to wait until he hurts her? How close do we have to let him get? I wanna *get him* right now! Come on! You're supposed to protect us!"

"You can take it before a judge, Bob. Your lawyer can help you."

"Okay, can we at least fill out a complaint against the guy?"

"Sure, sure."

The officer filled out the paper work. Bob and Jo left the police station confused and scared.

"Jeez, I feel like I went to a locksmith for a lock and he sent me to a fuckin' bakery." Bob complained.

"I should've called Paul in the first place." Jo said. "I'll call him when we get home."

"Yeah, you're right. Maybe the complaint being on file will do us some good."

Jo didn't tell Bob how truly frightened she was starting to feel. It was odd, she kept thinking how everything around her seemed so normal: the street, the people, dogs, children, cars, most of which she recognized and saw everyday. But, she knew someone was hidden in wait amongst all that was friendly and familiar. Just like Beth. She tried not to think so fatally. She shook off her fears and leaned on Bob. He felt so solid.

"We're gonna get through this, Jo. We'll get him." He kissed her forehead.

"Okay." She needed to hear him say it.

Marblehead, 1995

About a week after the arrest at the internet café, there was a loud knock on the door at dinnertime. All the kids and Meghan looked up at him. People didn't usually come by at dinnertime, and if they came by at all, it was most often to the shop.

Peter got up from the table and answered it. It was pouring rain and he opened the door to see three men standing on his porch.

Paul Weaver stood there looking very formal, though he was uncharacteristically dressed in sports clothes, not his usual suit. He was with two other men, one a plain-clothes police officer with a badge on the pocket of his raincoat, the other a younger man dressed in a bright red beret and matching baseball jacket. The baseball jacket bore the insignia of a winged angel on the chest with the words Guardian Angels. All three men had droplets of rain on the shoulders of their coats. Peter could smell the rain on the fabric, a warning of storms at his door.

"Peter, I'd like you to meet Detective Kirkpatrick from the Boston Police Cyber Crime Division and Gabriel Thatcher of the CyberAngels. I've asked Gabriel to come up from New York, and Detective Kirkpatrick, from Boston, to speak to Pete. May we come in?"

"Come in, come in." Peter answered, somewhat overwhelmed by their presence and authority. "We're just eating dinner."

Paul took him aside in the entryway. Peter's head knocked against the framed antique head rail of his ancestor, Emilie Treadwell.

"Peter, look, sorry to interrupt your dinnertime, but we find these surprise visits to the home to be more effective than bringing kids down to the station or the court house."

"Is Pete in any more trouble?"

"No, no. We just want to make sure he gets the message about how dangerous this incident was. These gentlemen will be having dinner at *my* house later, if you know what I mean."

Peter nodded, and ushered the men into the living room. They sat down.

"Pete! Come in here please." Peter called out to his son.

Pete came in looking pretty shaken. He sat down in an armchair opposite the men on the sofa. Peter propped himself on the arm of his son's chair. Paul, from the opposite armchair, introduced the men and they shook Pete's hand and congratulated him on calling the police. They asked him a lot of questions about how he had come to be in the chat room and what he had encountered there. Pete described what he had seen, and what they had done.

"We have the url from Miss Weaver's computer, and we have already visited the site. We just wanted to hear your side of the story." Detective Kirkpatrick told him.

Pete was getting a little angry.

"You caught the guy because of us. He's a bad guy and you got him in jail. What's the problem?" He asked with an edge to his voice.

Gabriel Thatcher, who had not taken off his red beret and jacket, said. "We want to be sure you know how serious this could have been. If you had gone into the café or if he had parked in an alley, for instance, he could have tricked you into getting near the van or actually getting into the van –"

"I know not to get into a van." Pete replied, stiffly.

Peter shuddered again, envisioning his son's thin body being lifted easily and tossed into an open van.

"What were you doing online, son?"

"Something stupid I'll never do again."

Gabriel Thatcher sighed.

"I know this family has recently experienced a great tragedy. I know how you lost your mother, Pete. We want to be sure you understand how dangerous it is to meet people on the internet and –"

"My mother was killed by her friend! Her next-door neighbor! Not someone she met online!" Pete shouted.

Meghan turned her head at the sound of Pete's voice, though she still sat at the table and could see nothing. Both girls looked at her. She smiled. "It's okay." She told them.

They could hear the rain tapping on the windows then, the room was so silent.

"Okay, yup." Gabriel Thatcher was at a loss for words.

"Do you know the kind of work we do, son?"

"I dunno." He could guess from their name. "You're guardian angels. You help people?"

"Yes, we do. We search the web for sites dangerous to kids especially. Hundreds of lonely and troubled kids online in chat rooms every day get tricked into meeting predators. You're lucky to have access to a computer. But a computer can be just as dangerous as a gun if not used responsibly."

Pete nodded. He wasn't lonely or troubled. But, he understood that other kids might be looking for a friend. He supposed the investigators meant well, but he had learned his lesson. He wanted to say, "If it will get you guys out of here, I'll just sit here and nod."

The men went on lecturing for about a half hour more. Stuff about not thinking he could possibly trap more guys. That was for the police to do. Pete tuned out. He was sure their work was important, but he had no intention of wasting any more of his time in chat rooms. He knew from Justin that the ghost hunters had some pretty awesome computers and he couldn't wait to see their findings. He wanted to learn as much as he could about communicating with the spirit world, about voice patterns and thermal imaging. He knew it wasn't anywhere near as advanced as Justin's equipment, but Sarah had promised him her old PowerBook 100 with the track ball. She was using it now because her father had taken away her Blackbird. But, he was giving it back to her in the fall for school, and Sarah was going to give the 100 to Pete then. It was just the beginning.

While the men talked, Pete mused. He liked the track ball better than the track pad, even though the pad was supposed to be an upgrade. He liked to pop the track ball out of the machine and hold it in the palm of his hand. And, then pop it back in like an eyeball, a really powerful magic eyeball.

Marblehead, 1995

Later that night, Peter sat on his bed and stared at the Polaroid of Beth's spirit in his hand. He'd begun a habit of speaking to her while holding the photo. He did not speak aloud. His lips did not move. He spoke to her, telling her about the Guardian Angels and the CyberAngels, about how Pete had pretty much taken care of himself and that she would have been proud of him. He sniffed back the tears and the thinking of what might have happened and how devastated he would have been if something had –

"Daddy!" Sarah called from her bedroom. "Where are you?"

"We want a kiss good-night!" Emily shouted from the next room. He could hear the bed covers muffling her shout.

"Coming!" Peter called to them.

"I can't be afraid any more, Beth, I just can't. It's too hard." He said aloud. "I need to – trust Pete – and myself. I love you. I do, I always will. I'm so glad you came to me, I'm so very – grateful, but I need – I have to – I want -"

"Daddy!" Sarah called, impatiently.

"Okay, coming."

He kissed the photo. For some reason, he wasn't sure why, he didn't put it back on the mirror; he tucked it into his sock drawer, not on the top, but under his dress socks where it would not be disturbed.

Marblehead, 1692

It was a mercy that the two women were brought together to trial; a mercy that was in reality a simple matter of convenience of location, but for Rosie and Molly, it meant the world. Neither of them could imagine suffering this torment alone.

Rosie and Molly stood together bound hands and feet on a small cart driven by their jailers, Philip Beare and John Bennett, that rattled and bumped all the way to Salem Court House about six miles away.

Tom and Elizabeth Treadwell had traveled by foot the night before to be there when their daughter arrived.

Molly was terrified. Rosie was furious.

People followed them along the road, many of whom Rosie and Molly knew. They shouted obscenities and threw stones. They hit the women with sticks.

"Witches! Witches! Get thee back to Satan!"

"Go to hell yerselves!" Rosie cried.

Rosie shouted back at first, but she got tired of them, and crying out only made the situation worse, as fresh tormentors joined the parade at each turn in the road. As they traveled closer to Salem, the women recognized fewer and fewer of their attackers, until all were strangers to them.

Some people feigned fits; a woman fell down and vomited along the roadside. It was not clear whether she had been overcome with sickness or had driven herself into a frenzy.

Children and dogs, men on horseback, women all took part in harassing Rosie and Molly for their imagined crimes. Rosie doubted if any of them knew her. She had not recognized any one since they'd left Marblehead.

In fact, most of Marblehead was already at the Salem Court House when Rosie and Molly arrived. The baby Edwina was still at the Peach house and Rosie could not bring herself to think of her child in the arms of someone who did not truly love her.

Reverend Hathorne, Selectman Peach, Bartholomew Gedney, Judge Sewall, William Stoughton and Selectman Gale were all present, lined up in a row at a long table in front of which Rose Low and Molly Treadwell were placed. Their hands and feet remained bound.

Elizabeth nearly broke her husband's arm, she clutched it so tightly to see her daughter, Molly, standing bound and ragged. Her light blue dress, that was one of Molly and her mother's favorites because it brought out the loveliness of her blue eyes, was filthy with the wear of sleeping and living in it for weeks in that dark and dirty room meant only for crates of vegetables. Molly's usually shining hair was dull and dusty. Elizabeth shuddered, wishing she could take her child home and comfort her. It made no sense, so sense! None of it made sense! What was her dear, sweet child doing tied up and in trouble?

The judges began. Reverend Hathorne spoke.

"Goody Low, thou hast been accused, how say ye? Have ye been consorting with the Devil as yer lord and master?"

"Ye know as well as I, the Devil only consorts wi' the likes of you!" Rosie replied.

The crowd in the courtroom gasped at Rosie's answer.

"Goody Low, we caution ye to answer well and in a God-fearing manner as befits the court."

"Yer all mad! Mad as mad dogs!"

The crowd murmured and the judges seemed to agree that Rosie was the one who was mad.

"Are there any witnesses against this woman?"

"I have seen Goody Low dancing with the Devil in the woods!" Goody Pritchard stood up and declared.

"Ah, Goody Pritchard," said a neighbor, "Yer own son was seen cavorting with this she devil upon Burial Hill and rots in Ipswich as surely as we sit 'ere!"

Sick with fear, Molly realized, as through a haze of white terror, that Daniel was close by to them now. She was that sorry that she had gotten him in trouble. She wished he had not followed her that morning to Ol' Dimond's. She wondered where Ol' Dimond was now and if he could help them. It seemed impossible that anyone could help them.

Molly turned round to see her mother and father. Elizabeth's worried face broke Molly's heart, and her father's rigid jaw filled her with fear. Indeed, Molly's terrified expression drove Elizabeth mad! She made as if to rush to her, and her husband pulled her back.

Hearing her name called out, Molly turned around and faced her judges.

"Molly Treadwell, what say ye? You have been accused of cavorting with the Wizard of Burial Hill and peering through his awful 'scope. What saw ye through the 'scope, maid?"

Molly would never tell them, she decided. Oh, how she wished she had this awesome power of magic of which she was so accused!

"I saw, sir, I saw – " She hesitated. She did not want to lie: her pride and her honor bade her not to lie.

"She saw Satan! She saw his lair and his minions dancing there!" Someone shouted.

Abigail Williams was in the courtroom, and remembering how she had stolen the telescope and what she had seen in it – blood-sucking bats from another world attacking her in the night, their mouths open with snarling teeth - she grabbed hold of her belly and moaned and fell down in pain. Several of the other girls also fell down and moaned with Abigail.

The crowd roared.

Rosie realized they all wanted to see the child hang. They all envied her beauty and her fineness, which they knew they did not have and never would. They wanted to destroy it rather than see it live and prosper in another.

"Y'er all jealous of the child! Y'er all jealous of that which is better n' ye'll evva be!"

The crowd roared anew at Rosie.

"Silence!" Called Reverend Hathorne.

"I saw the ocean and the boats sailing out to sea." Molly managed to say, but no one heard her. "Only they appeared closer for the 'scope."

"Why were ye there at the wizard's house, child?"

"I went to see the morning dawn over the sea."

Now she was lying.

Rosie squirmed. She hated this!

"I have seen Molly Treadwell pinching and making Abigail Williams fall down in pain and suffering. I have seen Molly Treadwell make Abigail Williams cry out in pain!"

Who was Abigail Williams? Molly tried to recall. She knew it was significant, but, Molly was so traumatized by everything that had passed since that morning on Burial Hill, which now seemed so long ago, that she only vaguely remembered there had been hysterical girls there, crying out and somehow they had been important to her life and death, though she had never seen or heard of them before.

Then came an onslaught of accusations from the crowd.

"I have seen Goody Low talking to animals and singing in the wood!"

"I have seen Goody Low's red hair aglow in the sun with the flames of Satan's hellfire!"

"I have seen the birds fly down and speak to Goody Low on her shoulders!"

"I have see the birds fly down and fall into Goody Low's cauldron where she stirred her Devil potions!"

"I have seen Molly Treadwell up on Burial Hill where the shadows of the dead cavort, looking through the awful 'scope of the demon wizard!"

"I have seen Molly Treadwell writ in the Devil's book and she tried to get me to writ my name too!"

"Did ye writ in the Devil's book, Molly Treadwell?" Asked Judge Sewall.

"No, sir. I have not seen the Devil, nor his book."

"I have seen Molly Treadwell pinch and bite Abigail Williams!"

Again, Abigail Williams, who was Abigail Williams? Thought Molly as she reeled and fell to her knees.

The crowd gasped and proclaimed, "She must be guilty! Look she falls on her knees before the magistrates!"

"Do ye confess to the crime of witchcraft, Molly Treadwell?"

Molly was confused.

"Do ye confess?"

"Confess! Confess!" Cried the crowd.

Molly looked round to see the angry, distorted faces of her neighbors, people she had said good morrow to many times on her way to the well curb or to milk 'Cilly, the cow they had shared with the Pritchards. Now, Daniel too. She saw in her memory, his kind face smiling her way as she passed of a morning on her errands, and she had smiled back, and the sun had shone on both of them.

Molly reeled again, her body, weak from not eating and sleeping, from worry and turmoil, went limp to the floor.

Elizabeth jumped up and ran to her; Tom's hands reached to grab her back, but clutched only air.

Elizabeth picked up her child and held her close. She turned to see the crowd ablaze with fury and hate, their faces, once so kind and generous, now twisted in evil intent: they wanted her beautiful child to hang.

She looked up at Rosie, who had finally given up. Rosie's head hung down while the crowd screamed and the justices banged their gavel and also screamed for silence that did not come.

Then the austere Judges brought up the physical evidence of Molly's crescent moon mole under her armpit, which had been pierced with needles to no avail, and Rosie's Devil's tails growing from her anus.

The crowd greatly approved of this evidence; they cheered and gasped.

***

Rosie Low and Molly Treadwell were sentenced to hang by the neck until dead, and to be buried in an unmarked grave in unhallowed ground near Gallows Hill in Salem, miles from their home and hearth.

The two women were returned to Selectman Peach's root cellar to await their execution because all the jails in Salem were full to the maximum with witches.

Marblehead, 1995

"All I did was tell a friend at the coffee shop why I quit the school. Mrs. Harper actually called me at home about an hour later and screamed in my ear that her school 'wasn't fodder for coffee chit-chat' and that I had no right to talk about it."

"What did you say?" Peter asked.

He and Meghan sat down at the kitchen table to talk after the girls had gone to bed. Pete was in the living room watching television.

"I said I had every right to tell my friend why I had quit."

"You did."

"I was careful not to malign her or the school. I just told her what I told you, that it wasn't something I could support or be involved in any longer. That's all."

"Was she there at the coffee shop?"

"No. Someone must have overheard me and called her."

"Were you talking loud?"

"Of course not."

They were silent for a while. Then, Meghan asked, "What now? Do you want me to leave?"

"No!" Peter's hand shot over to Meghan's, which he held for a second to reassure her. He quickly let go.

"We need you desperately."

He was afraid to look at her. Maybe it was having had sex with Beth the other night – or the dream of it - that had sparked something, something in him that had been dormant and buried for a while, but he wanted this woman who sat beside him now. He wanted to kiss her and hold her to him and make love to her round and soft body.

Shit. The nanny. Perfect. Now, he was a cliché.

Peter took a sip of beer.

Meghan sighed.

"I'm sorry about all this fuss. I just told a friend in the coffee shop, and I called my Mom and Dad. It's not like I called all the parents or wrote to the editor of the paper. I didn't! The word just got around. I'll bet the teachers at the school talked more about it than I did."

"Yeah, and the parents decided for themselves."

"I'm pretty tired." Meghan sighed, exhausted. "Do you mind if I go to bed?"

"No, go on. I'll give Paul a call in the morning and ask his opinion. We'll go from there."

"Thank you. I can pay."

"Don't even think about it! Just put it out of your mind till we know more."

Meghan nodded. She refrained from kissing this kind man who had come to mean so much to her.

And, Peter sipped his beer, thinking how much he'd like right then and there to follow her to her bed.

Northeast of Marble Harbor, 1692

Lowther did travel north. He anchored the *Deliverance* just northeast of Marble Harbor, tucked along the seaward edge of the rocky shore. She did not come into the bay.

They were all newly wanted men by now, having taken three ships and a small snow laden with china, all of which they had thrown into the sea, before coming into New England. Lowther didn't dare Boston or Salem harbors. In fact, the *Deliverance* sailed east of them, out of sight of any bodies hanging from the outer islands - exactly where officials wanted Lowther, Ned and the crew.

Once Ned saw the familiar shape of Marblehead come into view on the horizon, his heart swelled, against his wishes, with warm recognition of home. The sharp rocks, the breaking white waves, the cold wash, even on a hot evening in July, all filled Ned with anticipation. He couldn't wait to step ashore.

That night, Ned readied himself. He had everything he needed. Jewels, knife, coin of the realm. Lowther was already gone off the ship, or so Ned thought, when he tried the door of the captain's cabin and found himself locked in. Ned's happiness was short lived. Lowther, it seemed, had other plans for him.

Ned shook the door anew, and leaned hard on the handle, nearly breaking it off. No good. The door was locked on the outside.

In a moment, he heard a crewmember go for Lowther. Then, the loathsome sound of Lowther's boots approaching.

"Ha! Ye lil' eel! Ye thought ye'd be squirmin' away from old Lowther, did ye? I decided to keep ye after all! Now, lie down and be quiet!"

Laughter from the crew.

A dilemma. Temporary, he was sure. Ned looked around for a way out. He peered out the stern windows. A crewman, Charlie Sniggs, in a lifeboat waved to him. Lowther had put him there, no doubt, to watch.

Ned went back into the cabin. He looked around him.

Good news – Lowther had left his English Doglock, a gift from the *Molly's* captain, by the bed. Ned smiled. He would certainly make good use of it. That, and a few flints and a sack or two of gunpowder he hung from his belt.

Now, he would need that boat.

To the boatman's astonishment, Ned ambled down the side of the ship as deftly as a goat down a cliff, and stood in the boat seconds later, holding a pistol to the man's head.

"Row, and quietly. I'll tell ye where." Ned commanded him.

Lowther heard the boat move and began shouting from the quarterdeck.

Ned saluted him as Lowther cursed and ranted, but could do nothing.

Ned planned to go to Burial Hill to speak to Ol' Dimond, first of all, to get the lay of the land.

"Why y'er like a private conveyance, mate! I could get used to this luxury, carriage at the door!" Ned joked.

"I've broken wi' t'articles by now, Ned." Charlie complained.

"Ah, damn the articles, man! There's more in it fer ye, if ye stick w' me." Ned confided to the man. "I need ye to take me on. Later."

As they came up to Burial Hill, Ned could see the old man in his cape silhouetted against the moonlit sky at the peak, waiting for him.

Ned turned to the boatman. "Wait 'ere fer me. I'll tell ye where t'go."

Ned climbed out of the boat, turned and showed the man an emerald.

"Fer ye, if ye follow me orders." Ned tucked the emerald securely in his pocket.

Charlie, who had been thinking of simply rowing back to the ship, or on to Lynn, widened his eyes in approval and nodded to Ned's commands. He had held naught but a lowly position on the ship and had never received more than a few kegs of rum and a few coins after booty was divided. Charlie's mind usually moved slowly, but even he began to make swift plans after seeing the emerald. He waited while Ned climbed the rocks to where Ol' Dimond stood.

From afar, he could see the old man in his cape put an arm around the younger man, enveloping him into the warm wing of fabric. He could see the two confer, and walk on, not to the house, but down the cliff side to the rocks.

Charlie waited while the old man talked to Ned. Then, Ned climbed down to where the boat swayed in the low surf.

"Go south, stay along the shore, till ye pass a long beach. Go on to the cliffs o' Lynn to the wide cove and find a place by the ancient caves. I'll meet ye there."

Charlie nodded.

"An' don't think of crossin' me, Charlie Sniggs, fer I'll think nothin' of slittin' yer throat in yer sleep, an' Lowther t'would do none the less, after he gets 'is boat back, tha' is."

"I'll think on tha' emerald, if yer don' min', Neddie. Tha'll buy me an' me common law wife a fine snug nest in Caycun!"

Ned laughed and tipped his pistol to the man.

"Ye shall 'ave it!"

Marblehead, 1995

The kids were in bed. Peter grabbed a cold beer and went to find Meghan. From the kitchen, he leaned into the dining room, not there, peeked into the living room, turned back, and saw her sitting in the dark on one of the wicker chairs on the porch.

She was looking at the sea.

Peter opened the French doors and stepped out. She turned her head.

"Hi." She said, quietly.

"Hi. Mind if I join you?"

"Of course not."

Peter sat down in the other wicker chair. He put his beer down on the matching wicker table. All Beth's decoration. Looking back at the French doors, he remarked, "You know, sometimes, I think about changing these for one of those old screen doors that make that cool sound. Do you know what I mean?"

Peter realized that was the first time since Beth's death that he had criticized any of her design decisions.

Meghan nodded, sipping a glass of wine.

"I do, though I've never had such a door. I guess I've heard the sound they make in old movies."

"Yeah, I guess, that makes me old."

Meghan smiled. "It's still nice."

Peter noticed there was something red in her drink.

"What is that?"

"It's a few raspberries. It's called an infusion now, but I've been putting fruit in my wine forever."

"An infusion." Peter repeated. "Sounds almost medical."

"It does sound medical, but it tastes great."

"Mmm, I'll stick to a good ol' beer."

"Hmm, I won't say it "

"Oh, you mean, for a good old guy?"

They laughed. Then, the view took their attention. The ripple of white moonlight over the ocean, like a path of light to the opposite shore.

"It looks like you could just walk across it, doesn't it?" Peter said.

"Yes."

"We used to try to swim across it when we were kids."

"You and Beth?"

"No, me and Bob and a few other guys."

"Sounds kind of romantic for a bunch of guys."

Peter laughed, "Yeah, we were real romantics."

"Beth dove off the roof of the fishery that used to be at the harbor." Peter shook his head. "We swam together. All of us."

"Sounds lovely. I'm not that athletic."

"You don't have to be." Peter wanted to add, "A soft body is nice too."

Instead, he continued,"Yeah, it was a good childhood. Now, kids are all helmeted, padded up, belted in, it's hard to take sometimes, but I guess, things are moving faster now, they have to be protected. Though, I'm just not sure if it works. Especially after what happened with Pete, or almost happened."

He could see Meghan was listening.

Peter sighed. He had more to say.

"Hate to bring up bad news, but we have a mediation coming up next week, Friday morning at 8 a.m."

"Mediation? You mean about the school?"

"Yeah."

Meghan took a sip of wine.

"I'm so sorry to have gotten you involved in all this."

"I'm not involved. You are. You're just borrowing my lawyer."

"Are you teasing me?"

"Yeah, I'm trying to get you to not worry."

"I'm stunned. I can't believe it's gone this far. It's like a witch hunt. I mean, all I did was tell a friend why I quit my job and suddenly, I'm being accused of doing something illegal. I would never do something illegal. Never."

Peter took a sip of beer and watched the lights of the town sparkling on the water.

"I know."

"I appreciate your lawyer helping me out. Please know that I appreciate that."

"Sure. I guess that's why I'm not worried. Paul's a good man. His family has lived here in town for over three hundred years. They came over in the slave trade, on the *Desire*, the first ship ever built in Marblehead, a slave ship. His ancestors were slaves for almost two centuries. Now, he's the best lawyer I know and a wealthy man. When we bought this house, it was actually part of a divorce, and Paul cleared everything up."

He didn't say that it had been Cassandra's house and that Beth had been the one who had questioned whether they should buy it. But, Peter had wanted the proximity to the ocean for his boat and the land to build his woodshop. Cassandra had already lost it. Someone would have bought it, why not him?

"I'm worried. When I hear you say, 'I'm not worried' I feel like I should worry for you – for myself."

Peter turned to her, "You don't have to worry. You didn't do anything wrong."

"It doesn't matter. It only matters that she said I did."

"It's a small town. Word gets around. People are bored. They love gossip. They took their kids out of that school today, so what? They'll put them in another one tomorrow."

"I know and you know, but we're going to mediation over this and they will say a lot of crap about my living with you."

"You're a live-in nanny."

Meghan looked at him.

"It doesn't matter how innocent I am. It only matters what they can say. She's gonna say I ruined her, that the witch hunt is the other way round." Meghan added, thoughtfully.

Peter sighed in agreement.

"Don't worry. It's only illegal if it's not true."

"What do you mean?"

"Libel, right? It's only libel or slander if it's a lie. Paul explained that libel is written, and since you didn't write anything about Mrs. Harper's school, you're being accused of slander. But, it's not slander if it's true. Plus, you didn't exactly put up flyers or go around ringing a bell like a town crier."

Meghan nodded.

"Don't worry."

It was then that they heard the slow rumble of a fire engine, the sound of doors opening and slamming shut, and saw tall, young firemen walking slowly and searching with the rays of their flashlights streaming before their uniformed figures. The silence and the lights, the tall, slender figures of the young men took on a beautiful and other worldly aspect for a moment; they converged upon the quiet night in a silent ceremony of communal caretakers searching for danger in the sleeping neighborhood. It was a Marblehead moment, so often falling like a gem, a mesmerizing dream, for a moment only from heaven into reality. Then, it was over.

"Did you smell a fire?" Peter asked Meghan.

"I thought it was a fireplace."

"In the summer?"

"Yeah, people do!"

Peter laughed, and suddenly a flashlight was turned on him.

"Hey, guys! I think I found the fire." One of the fireman joked.

Meghan stood up.

The fireman walked toward them.

"Don't go." Peter said to Meghan.

She lingered.

"Hey, Pete! What's goin' on?" A young, good-looking fireman asked, all the while looking at Meghan.

"I thought you guys were working." Peter said.

"Yeah, I'm working, man." Still eying Meghan. "Hey, are you single?"

"No, excuse me." Meghan left the porch.

"Looks like you struck out." Peter laughed.

"She's sweet, man. You tappin' that?"

"She's our nanny, Mike." Peter held his temper.

"Yeah, but, you know. She's a redhead, man! Those tits! She seein' anyone?"

"I really don't know." Holding his temper.

Another fireman whistled harshly from down the block.

"Yeah, I gotta go. Sorry, Pete, didn't mean anything."

"No problem."

So, she said she was not single, Peter thought.

***

The fireman, Mike called Meghan a few times after that. Peter walked into the kitchen once to hear her politely turn him down for a date.

She just kind of shrugged and smiled at him as she hung up the phone.

Peter hummed a little tune and kept walking.

Marblehead, 1692

Molly and Rosie slept the night of their trial, wrapped in each other's arms, and every night after that.

Rosie whispered to her and kissed her cheek.

"Any day or night, they will open that door and it shall be our last."

Molly had stopped crying. There were no more tears left for her. The sight of her parents in court witnessing her shame in front of the community had brought more disgrace on her than she could bear and the shock of it left her cold and silent. Her chest actually felt like ice was in it, pressing against her ribs, and lying too, in a solid, frozen block in her innards. She still did not understand what had happened nor what she had done that was so very bad. People had been going to Ol' Dimond for as long as she could remember, and now, she was being hung for it.

She had stopped looking for an answer. The question just remained there, like a lump in her throat that would soon choke her to death.

Rosie, for her part, busied herself with looking after the baby and Molly. She had faced death before with each new pregnancy. She had faced the possible death of her dear husband, Matty, with each new voyage to the Grand Banks in Newfoundland, with each storm and every time he or the children left her field of vision. Now, she faced death again. She was solemn, but she was ready. It mattered not to her that her death was needless or foolish, no, she was used to people being mad, used to it. Yes, used to it.

Rosie sighed, and pulled Molly's sleeping form closer to her. Ah, unbidden by her, tears filled her eyes (so, she was *not* used to it!) and slipped down her cheeks that she was not to see her other children again, no, nor her dear friend Elizabeth, who had cried so much in the courtroom, she was that sorry to have seen her suffer so, and her son, Ned now so long at sea, oh, what she would give to spy him once more through that fateful glass!

Just as she formed that thought in her mind, and near drifted off to blessed sleep, a sound, a scraping sound and a door opened, not the door to the room, but another door, in the far corner, behind some empty baskets waiting for the harvest and a few old and broken tools, a door creaked open and there stood he – oh, her tired eyes must deceive her and she must be dreaming!

A tall wiry figure, lean and taut, dressed oddly in leather and linen, with weaponry upon his belt, and dark eyes, blackened with India kohl and long black curls to frame his chiseled jaw. Though only eleven years, how dark and wild he did appear!

"Ned!" Rosie sat up, and Molly did too.

Then Rosie stood and ran to her son who embraced her, but all the while, looking with his dark eyes, over his mother's shoulder, into the deep blue of Molly's. Molly was sure she was dreaming.

"Ned! Y'ev cum fer us!"

"Aye!" He turned his face then to kiss his mother's cheek. "But, we 'ave business first. Where be the master of this house?"

Rosie looked frightened. "Why, he be upstairs in his bed. Why d'ye ask, Ned?"

"We 'ave business w'im. Be he not a magistrate, a selec'man?"

"Aye, but he be our jailer and not a man I want to bother tonight. Can't we just slip away now the way ye cum?" Rosie tried to peer over Ned's shoulder to see where he'd come from. "Be there a door?"

He had closed the hidden door behind him.

"Aye, aye, in time. Now, I want my revenge, and other business too. Come, both o'ye, gather what things ye have, including my l'il sis, an' we must knock on 'is chamber door this night!

Cum wi' me!"

This last he directed at Molly. He took in her light, and she had a second only to be riveted by his dark beauty.

She did not understand how he had come there or where they were going now, but she was too stunned to do anything but obey Ned's strong command.

The trio, with Edwina fast asleep in Rosie's arms, got ready.

"Now, turn round and stand back, as far as ye can to the wall! And be ready to go quickly!" Ned told them.

The women did as he said, and to their horror heard a gunshot like thunder explode the wooden door that had kept them prisoners all these weeks.

Ned reloaded.

Marblehead, 1995

Jo Simmons had just gotten off the phone with her husband, Bob. He called from the coffee shop where he was getting an end of day pick me up. They'd had one of their "silly" conversations, as she liked to call them, conversations full of silly inside jokes about their lives. Cass was showing a house. It was a Friday after five: and for a few moments, there were no visitors or clients, no passers-by waving hello, and she was glad no one had been in the office to hear her gibberish about "hunky bunky dunky," it would have been a major embarrassment if anyone had overheard her love talk about Bob dunking his donut in his coffee. Nothing had happened for a while, and she and Bob were starting to relax and get back to their happy lives.

Jo was smiling to herself when the office door swung open violently and the gentle chimes she and Cass had hung to welcome customers smashed to the floor.

She looked up to see that guy, Ben Hardy; it'd been weeks and sometimes, for a moment, like now, she actually had forgotten about him! He looked so like Girelli that she froze in shock. Jo was always in such control that she just couldn't believe it was happening. She sat rigid in her chair as the man strode quickly toward her.

"You! You can't be here! Get out!" Jo managed to scream.

He kept walking.

Jo screamed again, "I have a restraining order from a judge! Get out!"

"This is a public office. I can come in. I want to buy a house." Hardy said, laughing at her distress.

Jo's hand fumbled its way over to her desk drawer where she had placed the little pearl-handled Chanel gun that was half a joke, but now seemed her only recourse.

She pulled out the pistol and pointed it, her hand shaking, at the man who now stood over her.

"You won't shoot me!" He taunted. "You want it! You want it!"

Jo shot the gun, but the safety was on.

"Ugh!" She had to take her eyes off him to fumble with the safety, and he tore the gun from her hands. He smacked her hard on the head with the gun and she fell to the floor behind her desk.

Ben Hardy stood over Jo's unconscious body and laughed. He took the time to walk back to lock the door. He noticed all the people walking by on their errands. Hilarious, he thought; he liked having them so close, it turned him on.

Marblehead, 1692

Quickly, the three ran up the stairs to the master's bedroom, another door that Ned kicked in this time.

He ran to the man who sat up in the bed and placed the pistol to his skull. Mrs. Peach squealed like a pig and made to get out of bed and run. Ned quickly drew his knife and sliced her upraised hand which bled perfectly, as far as Ned was concerned, in a spring of blood that made his point exactly, brought the servants running and caused all to take heed of him as the one in charge.

"Now, git back into yer warm cozy bed, ye great sow in a lace bonnet." Ned motioned to the servants. "Come in, come in, join us."

Addie, the cook, a maid and footman, all in their nightdresses came into the room, fascinated by the sight of this young boy with a gun to the head of their master.

Ned seemed to lift Selectman Peach from bed with his pistol, while motioning to the servants to get on the bed.

"There now! Aren't we cozy! Ye never thought all o'yer lowly slaves would be cuddlin' up to ye in yer fine coverlet, now, did ye mum?"

How funny they did look to Rosie, all in their nightclothes, and all, unwelcome on the bed of their masters. She could not suppress a joyous giggle.

Molly reeled again at the chaos around her, but she stiffened her resolve not to faint. She breathed deeply and stayed as brave as she could.

"Now, come Selc'man, we're to 'ave a ceremony."

Ned guided Selectman Peach with his gun over to the small writing desk in the room.

"Wha' a fine piece of furniture tha' is!" Ned exclaimed. "And does it hold a piece of paper or two?"

Selectman Peach, who had been silent till now spoke up. 'Yes, it is made for writing."

"Made fer writing! How fine is tha'? A table fer just one purpose.

We're going to write on it tonight. Take tha' quill – now, write as I say –

This is to certify that Edward Low and Molly Treadwell, both of Marblehead, are married on this the 28th day of July, 1692. Write it! And we shall 'ave a wedding!"

Ned turned to the people huddled together on the bed, all of whom, Mrs. Peach was trying not to touch, except the cook, who was wrapping her bleeding hand in a piece of sheet she had torn for the purpose. Addie actually looked interested and smiled a bit.

"We're goin' to 'ave lots of witnesses, now, aren' we, Selec'man?"

Selectman Peach took a piece of fresh paper out of the desk, and it made a sound that Molly had never heard, sharp and clean, the luxurious snap of quality paper. All the paper she had known was soft as cloth with damp or crumbly as the pages of a Bible. The Selectman wrote on the paper then and all were silent as the quill scratched. He handed the paper to Ned who could not read.

"Well, now, I've never 'ad time to develop the skill." Ned said, looking around the room, thinking if he could hold a gun to Mrs. Peach's head, if she would read it correctly or not, when Molly spoke.

"I can read." She said.

Ned looked at her. Peach for a moment thought of trying to grab the pistol, still cold against his skull, while Ned was looking away, but he hesitated too long.

Molly walked over to the desk and took the paper from Ned's hand.

She read it and handed it back.

"It says what you told him to write."

Their eyes locked for a moment only.

Then Ned stood beside Molly and faced the official, holding the gun directly on the man's gut.

"Now say the words and sign it and seal it official-like."

Selectman Peach then married Ned Low and Molly Treadwell officially and with a legal document.

"Now, take another piece of paper and pardon my mother and Molly Treadwell."

"I have no authority to do so!" Peach protested.

Ned shot the pistol over their heads. Screams and squeals ensued from the bed.

"Ye do now!"

Quickly, Selectman Peach wrote the words as best he could to pardon Rosie and Molly. While he did so, Ned gave Rosie his knife to hold to the man's neck while he reloaded the pistol. Again, Peach shuddered under the touch of cold steel.

Ned handed the newly writ page to Molly and she nodded.

"Sign it! Seal it!"

Peach did so, turning his personal seal into the scarlet wax.

Ned took both papers and tucked them safely into his vest.

"Now, I'm sorry, but we must go!"

Ned, Rosie, the baby and Molly went out the door, which Ned then covered with a large cupboard in the hall.

"Don't think of followin' us, ye fools!" He called back. "Ye wouldn't like where we are goin'!"

"Back to the root cellar!" Ned whispered.

"Back?" Rosie argued.

"Aye! Cum wi' me!"

Marblehead to Boston, 1995

On the drive in to the mediation, neither of them spoke much. Peter didn't like leaving the country life of Marblehead for the city life of Boston. He couldn't go barefoot or wear sandals to a mediation. Meghan was quiet with her own terror that what could go wrong probably would go wrong. She didn't trust people meddling in her life, especially people of the professional, authoritative kind. Suits.

"Suits." Meghan repeated aloud.

"Beg pardon?" Peter looked up from his own thoughts.

"Suits," Meghan repeated again. "They tell you what to do."

"Yeah, but we've got one on our side too."

They parked in the garage, which Peter also hated, and found the Government Center building easily enough. Peter had the information written down on a post-it-note in his chicken scratch. He squinted at it now.

They stood in front of the list of offices like two country bumpkins; he, in his wrinkled tan linen jacket and blue tie that Beth had bought him at L.L. Bean for "formal occasions" and Meghan in her blue flowered dress and sandals. They matched, Peter thought, miserably. He had shaved for the occasion. He couldn't wait to get home.

The elevator opened and they stepped in. Gratefully, they were alone.

"What time do we have to pick up Emily from your mom's?" Peter asked. He couldn't wait to get home, he thought again, sulkily.

"Whenever. She can eat dinner there, if necessary. Pete's gone to the beach and he'll just get something at home."

"And Sarah?"

"Sarah's at Jane Pritchard's. She's sleeping over tonight."

Peter groaned.

"I hate sleepovers. I like her to be home."

"I know."

"Polly Klaas was taken at a sleepover in her own house." Peter said. Ah, he knew he was being stupid. He hated being in this place, but this lawsuit had to be taken care of.

"I know." Meghan turned her serene face to him. "You can't be with her every second."

Peter grunted.

"Yeah, that would suck – for her."

Meghan laughed. She touched his arm, for just a second, stroking him re-assuredly.

Their eyes met. A softness seemed to travel between them.

The elevator doors opened.

Marblehead, 1692

Ned plucked two cloaks from pegs in the entryway and tossed them over the shoulders of the women.

"You'll need these. We've a way to go."

Rosie was completely confused as they re-entered the dark, root cellar. Ned took them to the far corner where Rosie saw a small wooden door open, soil fell from the façade of this door, and a faint light glowed from behind.

Edward Dimond stepped forward with a lamp, illuminating himself suddenly in chiaroscuro as a welcome angel.

"Cum, then." Dimond instructed.

"Where?" Cried Rosie as she peered into the darkness beyond the door.

"Into the snakes." Dimond replied.

The party stepped out of the dark room, whose dangers were known, into darkness whose dangers were unknown.

"Snakes?" Rosie repeated, questioning.

"Aye," Dimond told them. "The ol' snakes be the smugglers' tunnels and the hide-aways of pirates. This house has a tunnel that do lead out or in."

Ned shut the door behind them, and they really were out of captivity.

Rosie and Molly stepped tentatively forward to where they could not see the ground and, at first, their feet hovered timidly trying each step, but soon, they were hurrying along the damp and slippery tunnels, following Ol' Dimond and Ned through twists and turns. The old man led the way with the lantern, then Rosie clutching the baby tightly, then Molly and lastly, Ned holding up a candle he'd taken from the room. Creatures of the dark and damp places scurried over Molly's shoes, and she could hear Rosie curse now and then, and she knew she too had been touched by rats or snakes or spiders or God knows what. But, they did not have time to shudder, only to keep on.

Sometimes, they came to deep water, and the group had to wade. Sometimes, they only splashed through puddles. Sometimes, they climbed. Sometimes, they slid downward. The tunnels echoed with dripping water. The close air was musky with brine. Droplets of water settled on their clothing and glowed in the candlelight, and to Ned's eyes from behind, the party bore halos of light surrounding their forms. Molly's hand thrust out to regain her balance slid on wet slime. The women were afraid that at any moment, the sea herself would fill the tunnel, rush toward them, and they would see their last.

Rosie cried out, "Will the sea overtake us?"

To which Ol' Dimond calmly answered, "We are far above the tide."

They kept on. Always, they smelled the sea. Somehow, the faith the women had in the two men who led them (Yes, men, though Ned be only eleven years, his mother relished the idea!) kept them moving forward, as well as the terror they had left behind, now falling from their backs, more and more, making them feel lighter and lighter even as they grew wearier and wearier.

***

Indeed, they traveled for nearly eight miles, resting now and then at the turns.

Molly was thirsty, but she said nothing. Rosie, too, but she did not speak of it. The baby needed to be nursed and would wake soon. They had been walking for hours.

Suddenly, they all heard a loud crack of thunder. Ned felt a whoosh of air over his face. Ol' Dimond's back went stiff, for he had heard that very sound once before in his life. He knew something awful had occurred. Dimond turned to see Rosie's astonished face, and clear through the line to Ned's blanched cheeks.

"Where is she?" Ned cried out. "Where is Molly?"

"What was that we 'eard, Ol' Dimond? What's 'appened to the child? Where'd she go?"

Dimond said the worse thing he could.

"I dunno."

Boston, 1995

They were at the right place, as several people, including their own lawyer and Mrs. Harper stood in the hallway.

Peter and Meghan stepped out of the elevator.

"Well, looks like we're all here." Paul Weaver said. "Shall we?"

He motioned them all into a bland conference room with a fake veneer table that Peter instantly didn't want to touch, matching chairs with leatherette seats and a neutral grey carpet. Peter couldn't believe people would choose to spend their days in such an artificial environment of plastics and fake wood. He decided not to think about it and took a seat next to Meghan and Paul, facing the mediator, a small, neat woman in a crisp navy blue suit, and the opposing group, also wearing stiff dark suits in which they seemed perfectly comfortable and ready to do battle.

Meghan and Peter exchanged a glance.

"Suits." Peter remarked under his breath.

"Suits of armor." Meghan agreed.

The mediator began after everyone settled into their seats.

"We are here to try to come to an agreement in the lawsuit of Mrs. Doris Harper vs. Ms. Meghan Merritt, a matter of malicious slander and loss of the business, The Sunny Day School of Marblehead, Massachusetts. We'll hear from each side, whereupon I will ask questions if need be and as a judge of the court I will decide if there is a case for slander and if the parties should continue to litigation or try to settle their differences here or in further mediation."

Peter listened carefully as the different points were made. Meghan had said the children and staff were taking steroids. Steroids were prescribed. Meghan had said the children were sobbing all day. They were children. Children cried. So far, Peter didn't see where the slander came in.

"So far, facts have been stated and confirmed. We've seen evidence of several prescriptions and statements from physicians. My client was simply stating what you have proven with your evidence. I see no case for slander at all." Paul Weaver, a tall, elegant man, who also sat tall in his seat, seemed to echo his thoughts.

"Ms. Merritt implied the use of steroids was rampant and illegal, causing parents to pull their children from the school." Replied Harper's lawyer, a large man with bulbous lips and a huge stomach upon which the bulbous lips seemed to rest.

Paul Weaver went on. "Implication derived at by the parents was not slander from my client. I have here a sworn statement, signed and notarized, of the friend my client was speaking to at the time of the alleged slander. This friend is ready to appear, if need be. She is away on business at this time, but can appear if summoned. However, you'll find that the statement is complete: my client simply told her close friend why she had left her job. No malicious statement was made toward the school or the teachers. My client merely stated that she felt uncomfortable there and needed to make a change."

A paper was passed to the mediator.

She looked it over silently.

"May I also submit several other sworn statements from the teachers and parents saying that their steroids were prescribed?" Said the lawyer for Mrs. Harper as he also passed papers to the mediator.

"It's imperative to note that my client made no other attempts to speak about the school after telling a close friend and her parents why she left her position at the school. She made no slanderous remarks in public or to the media about the Sunny Day School."

Peter knew this statement from his lawyer wasn't exactly true, as Meghan had told him why she was leaving at the ice cream parlor and she had been visibly upset and had cried and anyone could have overheard her, but, of course, he wasn't about to blurt that out. Again, nothing Meghan had told him that day was untrue. He had been grateful to her then and he was damn sure grateful now, he thought.

At that moment, about an hour into the mediation, the door opened and Meghan was amazed to see several of the teachers from the Sunny Day School entering the room.

Each held a paper in her hand.

Marblehead, 1692

"We must find her!" Ned insisted. He grabbed his knife tightly at his belt.

"Your weapons won't help you, lad."

"What's 'appened?" Ned looked around him frantically, only to see rock everywhere. "Molly! Molly!" Panic engulfed him, as never before, not even in battle had he experienced such terror. His face went cold. His heart slammed against his breast.

Faintly, he heard her sweet voice answer him, "Ned? Ned! Where are you?"

He screamed and his lungs tore out of him. "Molly!"

To hear her voice so far from him was excruciating.

"Ned! Ned! It's so dark here! Where are you?"

Rosie understood nothing. She clutched the baby to her.

Ned took hold of Dimond's shirt as though to choke him.

"Find her!"

"I canna, lad."

"Where is she? What can we do?" He screamed, searching the cave walls. He banged on the wet rock as though it would open.

"You canna fight it. The snakes took her."

Ned went silent.

"I've seen it once before in my life. A loud crack and then, a man who was once beside you is gone."

"This is not a man! This is my wife, sir!"

"Ned, we must go on. We are too low to linger."

The idea that the tide would take Molly, alone, without him to help her was too much.

"We need to look for her." He demanded, pointing his pistol at the old man.

Marblehead, 1995

The doorknob rattled.

"Jo?" A male voice.

Rattle, rattle.

"Jo? It's your horny, happy hubby!"

"Jo!"

"Jo! Come on, what's going on?"

Bob Simmons thought his wife had been so cute on the phone that he couldn't resist driving by to give her a surprise kiss. It had been ten minutes since they'd spoken, and – he peered into the office – her desk was empty.

Then, he saw what looked like a hand, a hand with big rings and bracelets – it was Jo – on the floor behind her desk – and Bob could see another figure, a man also sprawled on the floor, but across the room. His back was jammed against the wall and his pants were down around his ankles.

Marblehead, 1692

Dimond was undaunted by Ned's gun.

"Very well. We'll look for her. Call her again."

"Molly! Molly! Call out that we may find ye!"

"Ned!"

Was her voice louder?

"Molly!"

"Ned? It's so dark."

"Can ye still smell the sea, Moll'?"

"Ned! Ned!"

Fainter again, fading.

Water poured in suddenly and swirled around their feet.

"We need to move, lad."

Dimond began to walk forward. Rosie followed like an obedient child.

"Molly! Molly!" cried Ned.

No answer.

He had the urge to shoot his pistol at the walls, but he knew it would do no good, and possibly kill one of them. He began to sob in frustration. Tears slid down his cheeks. The water at his feet pushed against his legs, higher now.

He banged his fists against the stone.

"Oh, God!" He sobbed, helpless. "Where is she?"

"Ned!" Her voice was a whisper in his ear.

He opened his eyes to see her beside him.

She held her hand out to him. He reached for her and took her in his arms.

"Moll', are ye really here?"

"Yes, Ned. I think so."

The others came rushing back. Rosie kissed Molly, it seemed a hundred times.

Ned wiped the tears from his cheeks, his hands trembling.

"What happened to me? It seemed I was here but you were not." Molly cried, her tears and Ned's on her frightened face.

Dimond's old face was inscrutable.

"Let's from here." Dimond said.

"Aye!" Ned answered. "Quickly!"

He held Molly close to him and walked with his arm around her. Dimond knew that would not be enough, if the snakes were to take her again.

Marblehead, 1995

He wasted no time smashing the glass panel above the doorknob and breaking open the door. He ran into the room and saw that the man, though half-naked, seemed to be out cold. He hurried to pick up Jo.

"Jo, honey! Jo!" Bob picked up her limp body and hugged her to him. He saw that Jo was fully dressed, her white slacks clean and belted.

Jo moaned and started to come to, shaking her head; she threw her arms around Bob.

"What the hell happened?"

"I, I don't know, he burst in, he locked the door, my gun didn't work…"

"Gun? What gun?"

"I have a gun. It's a Chanel."

Jo sat up, weakly; she put her hand to her head. Bob was already smacking numbers on the office phone to call 911. The police station was a block away; hardly a second went by before they heard sirens.

The man began to stir and Bob went over to him, checking over his shoulder to see if the cops had come. They were just pulling up, so Bob took the opportunity to kick the guy's head back into the wall.

Uniformed cops poured into the room to find Bob holding Jo on the floor and an unconscious man, with his pants down and genitals exposed, crumpled against the wall.

On the road to Boston, King's Beach, Lynn, 1692

They emerged from the tunnels at dead low tide. For a while, they walked a long beach, and saw an old man and woman clamming. The two old people looked up from their task, startled, afraid they might see officials, for clamming was illegal along that beach. Their two old hearts were startled anew when they saw the peculiar party hurrying along – an old man in a hooded cloak, a dark young man strangely dressed in India scarves and leather breeches (dressed like a buccaneer!), a fair young maid, and a red-haired woman carrying a babe, who looked askance lest she be looked at. Indeed, both aged folk dropped their heads back to their task. They knew the weird group would never speak of them, being none too legal themselves, though they would soon speak at tavern to what they had seen! To be sure! Their old eyes glistened at the idea of having a new morsel to share over a pint.

Bad luck, thought Ned, though unavoidable. They would be seen where they were going, but go they must!

Once, the group heard, or thought they heard, screams coming from the open ocean – a woman crying out, so like the woman on the beach that fateful night in Marblehead, two years ago, that they stopped a moment and listened.

Had they heard something? They listened, but there was nothing but the surf. The group went on. Rosie and Molly were shaken; Ned frowned, he was sure he'd heard it. Edward Dimond, looking as wise as ever, solemnly continued the journey.

After the beach, they entered another tunnel through a cave and, then, up. The group climbed for several minutes, and just as dawn broke, entered a small shelter made of stone. An ancient shelter, Molly and Rosie could see, with stones stacked neatly and tightly as the finest seam.

The sun broke through a small opening in the back of the cave, which faced the sea, filling the stone enclosure with a warm, orange glow. The party gasped in unison, Ned included, they could not help it, for the very stones did seem to vibrate with fire, they looked at each other in surprise and great awe of it.

"Where are we?" Molly asked. Her ears seemed to ring with a high-pitched bell that faded after a few moments to a noise like a buzzing bee, then, nothing.

"'Tis a sacred place for the ancient people's worship of the sun." Ed Dimond told them. "'Tis where they came to pray and worship their pagan gods on the first spring and winter morns to give tribute to the life-giving sun. At holy moments, this sun t'would be naught but a spear of light marked 'pon the stone."

"We are in Nahanten, where two islands meet." Ned answered Molly. "And, we will leave 'ere very soon fer Boston."

"I will leave you now." Ol' Dimond said.

Rosie was surprised; she'd been thinking he was getting out too.

"Where will ye go, Ol' Dimond?" Rosie asked.

"Back to my home."

"Won't they catch ye?"

Dimond chuckled. "They canna, Rosie dear. Nevva ye mind, fer they canna."

"I will see Ol' Dimon' back to the beach." Ned told them. "Don't move from 'ere and when I return, we will go on."

The women nodded, still somewhat amazed by all that had transpired.

Ned and Ol' Dimond walked back, into the tunnel. Ol' Dimond turned to Ned.

"Ye don't have to cum back w' me. I know the way, remember, I'm the one who brought you." He laughed.

"Aye, ye did. But, I have questions fer ye. Do ye mind answerin'?"

"Aye. If I can."

Ned looked back. He could still see the orange glow in the cave; he walked on a bit more till he could no longer see the light.

In the darkness, Ned whispered to Dimond.

"How long before they can return to Marblehead?"

Dimond sighed deeply.

"The frenzy will go on for some time. It has not reached its peak. In September, Giles Corey of Ipswich way will be crushed to death for refusing to dignify the court by testifying. In September too, old Willmott Redd will be hung fer her pond and acreage. John Proctor, too. After that, despair will overwhelm the judges and remorse will take over where fear once reigned."

"Can they return then, in the winter?"

"Better in spring, like 'Sephone 'erself."

Ned nodded.

"Can ye tell me, wha 'appened in the tunnels?"

Dimond looked at the young man.

"'Tis a mystery to me as well. I've only seen it once before. I can tell you only that the snakes returned her to you. Ye were lucky, lad."

Ned was shaken, but convinced. He was only too glad to be out of the tunnels, where he hoped he would never have to go again.

He thanked the old man and turned to leave. Then, he bethought himself.

"Will ye tell me, Ol' Dimon' – how do I end?"

Ol' Dimond told him.

"Ye swing."

Ned smiled.

"And Lowther? How will he?"

"He cuts 'is own throat rather than be taken."

Ned grinned widely.

"Ah! An' I thought I would 'ave to do it fer 'im! Cheers, Ol' Dimon'!"

"Good luck." The old man said quietly, as the young one left him alone in the snakes.

Boston, 1995

Paul Weaver stood and welcomed the new witnesses to the mediation, all young women in their mid 20s and 30s wearing summer dresses of various colors, looking like a bouquet of flowers. A very powerful bouquet of flowers, as each held a statement collaborating what Meghan had said about the crying children.

"Please take a seat." The mediator gestured to the women. A small commotion followed as they sat down and faced the group.

The mediator asked each woman what she had witnessed.

"The children are very young. They don't understand that they will be picked up in a few hours. The concept is too sophisticated for their young minds; they panic and sob, and press their bodies against the gate we keep at the door to keep them safe."

"It's very hard to bear, for everyone. The other children get frightened and confused, thinking there's something wrong, that they should be crying too."

"Even if you're not in the classroom, your own classroom is disrupted."

"It takes more than one teacher to take care of the toddlers."

"I couldn't take hearing it all day myself. I quit after two weeks. They cried so much; I got sick from their mucus getting all over me. I had the flu for a month. I decided not to go back.

I think that's why the teachers are on steroids. You need an edge to stay well in that environment."

"I couldn't take it. In my opinion, most children need to be cared for in a home environment, by their mothers or by a family member or a familiar caretaker. The school environment is just too impersonal and too long a duration for many children. The children I saw at Sunny Day School seemed too traumatized to be away from their home environment all day."

"Is that your personal opinion?" Mrs. Harper's lawyer asked.

"Yes, but I am professionally qualified to make such an assessment. Since leaving Sunny Day four years ago, I furthered my education and am now a practicing child psychologist."

"Harvard." Was her answer to the lawyer's next question.

"Crying is natural in a day care situation." Mrs. Harper's lawyer defended. "Most children cry at some point."

Paul Weaver summed it up. "I believe the teachers are agreeing with my client and their written statements show that the crying was excessive enough to disrupt other classrooms, and to upset the other children."

The mediator nodded. She collected all the papers in her hands. She stacked them neatly and put them to the side.

"We should break for lunch. But, I can tell you now I see no real case here for slander or for malicious intent or loss of business. Mrs. Harper, you're lucky this lawsuit wasn't against you and your school."

After a tedious and stressful lunch, which Peter and Meghan spent trying to get waited on at a sidewalk café, and wound up getting sandwiches – hot dog for him, tuna fish for her - at a food truck outside the court building at Government Center, the mediator heard briefly from each lawyer and sent them all home without a case.

Mrs. Harper spat her words out as they were exiting the ugly room that Peter and Meghan were thrilled to be leaving.

"This isn't over! You're a slut and a bitch!"

The mediator overheard this and said, "Be careful, Mrs. Harper or you'll find yourself back here again, only the shoe will be on the other foot."

Mrs. Harper nearly spat again, "She's living with this man! She cost me my school!"

It seemed for a few awkward minutes that no one was going to get out of the room without a fist fight breaking out between Doris Harper and the harassed mediator, but Paul pushed through the bodies collecting at the doorway, taking Meghan by the arm, and Peter.

They could hear voices behind them and security being called.

Paul ushered them into the elevator. As the elevator doors closed, he asked, "How about a drink?"

Nahanten, 1692

When Ned returned to the ancient cave, he found Rosie and Molly asleep in each other's arms, and the babe too, also asleep. Molly, snuggled inside the spiral of Rosie's body, dreamed she heard an ancient heart beating like a soft drum from deep within the rocks. The three were curled in among each other like small animals in a nest. Golden light poured into the small cave through the opening aligned with the sun.

Ned nudged them awake. There was much to do and they had to take the chance of moving during the daylight hours.

Just as they reached for their bundles, the trio heard voices and footsteps above their heads. Ned put his finger to his lips, and took them backwards into the dark tunnel.

The voice of John Bennett spoke. "Ah, P'il'ip, I dunno if I care to catch 'em er not. After all, we wuz paid, wuzn't we? I dunna like trappin' the wife of a fellow fisherman all tha' fer a selec'man. 'Twas one thing when she was already caught, now tes 'nuther."

"Aye, yer right, let's say the trail went nor', then, an' go havva pint down by the wharf at home."

Ned's hand rested on his knife, and his hard eyes seemed to listen as the fishermen spoke. Molly and Rosie hardly dared breathe.

Then, suddenly, hearing the fishermen talking, the baby Lena let out an exclamation, "Dah!" From inside the tunnel, her sweet baby voice echoed and boomed, "Dah! Dah! Dah!"

"Wha' be tha'?" Beare asked, turning his head from side to side.

"I heard not'in."

"No, it soun'd li'a l'l babe. An' didn' they havva babe wi' them?"

"Aye."

Ned gripped his knife tightly,

"I don' 'ear not'in now, P'il'lip, an' lis'n'n do make me awful thirsty."

"Aye, then, I'm just go'in ta peer down this rock a ways."

Beare's face appeared at the mouth of the cave, upside down from above. The cave was dim now, as the sun had moved on. Still, Beare could discern lumps of clothing, and a bag.

Beare considered for a moment the turmoil and the pain he would receive at the hand of Ned Low should he raise an alarm. He had heard from Addie Gatchell what Ned Low had done the night before in the Selectman's own bedroom. This pain he compared with the joy and ease of settling himself down with a pint by the fire in the tavern. He chose the pint.

Beare stood up, brushed himself off and said. "'Twas nuthin but a rock cave, John. Let's to home, then."

Ned peered out of the opening in the rocks to see the backs of the Bennett and Beare stumble exhaustedly along the path away from the cave and then clamber awkwardly down to the beach. He watched till the two men passed the clamming pair to be sure they did not speak, or surely the two old people would share their adventure of seeing such a strange ensemble traveling along the beach.

Ned waited as the bent forms and walking forms met - and the men passed. They did not speak to each other.

"Time to go!" Ned informed the women. To himself, he recalled Marion's warning, "Hide her in the sacred temples…along the path of the snakes."

Back in the cave, they bundled together what little they had, cloaks and child and made their way out of the ancient shelter and down the rocks to where the boat and Sniggs were tucked away in a cove.

The women got into the boat, and Ned took a minute to wash the kohl off his eyes in the surf, and remove the India scarves and jewels around his neck. He hoped he looked more normal. Molly and Rosie were amazed to see him look more like the Ned they had known.

They set off, rowing as far out as they dared so as to appear small and faint. When they came to the port of Boston, they were all exhausted and in need of a night's sleep.

Ned paid Sniggs with the emerald he promised. The man seemed surprised to see it gleaming in his hand.

"I never dared believe it." Sniggs said.

He thanked Ned and ran off as fast as he could, lest his good fortune be jinxed.

Ned left the boat tucked under an old pier. He took the oars and hid them behind some rocks. He did not take the time to do more, as he might not need the boat.

He took his mother and his wife then to an inn he knew that was avoided by pirates because of its official appearance and avoided by officials because of its known respectability, The Rose & Crown, a place none would expect a pirate.

Ned thought of handing the innkeeper a gem, but changed his mind. He wished he had known how to write before this venture. He'd have forged a letter of credit. Ah, he'd save it for another time. Instead, Ned paid for two rooms, one for Rosie, one for him and his wife with gold coin of the realm, which he had been pilfering from Lowther for months.

The innkeeper looked impressed and gave Ned his best rooms, thinking he must be an eccentric young lord, traveling in the colonies with his mother and young bride. The man's imagination filled in all the blanks very nicely for Ned, who was beginning to learn that, the slightest lie - or gold and no explanation - was the best because most people provided the details on their own.

Rosie was that grateful to have a soft, warm, dry bed to fall on, and this she did without though of food or drink. The baby slept soundly by her side, being the only one of the two fed that night.

Boston, 1692

Ned closed the door behind himself and his bride. Molly, who had entered the room, hardly believing she was there, turned to him as the door closed behind them.

"You'll want a bath and dinner." Ned said, looking into her soft blue eyes with his own black gaze.

Molly felt weak again, her knees buckled slightly and she caught herself.

She could only nod. The idea that Ned was now her husband was one she repeated to herself as Ned left the room to give instructions to the maid.

Molly looked around her to see a fire burning warmly in the hearth. Two stuffed chairs faced the fireplace with a shining table next to each, as though to place a cup on. The luxury of this made her smile a bit, as she recalled the little writing desk, the table just for writing in Selectman Peach's bedroom that Ned had remarked upon, it seemed, so long ago – imagine such a thing as a table only to write letters and another only for a cup!

She turned again to see a clean, soft bed, so stuffed with soft covers it rose high off the floor. Rich curtains hung over the windows, making the room private and cozy. Deep carpets softened the floor beneath her tired feet.

Ned returned then and Molly faced him in anticipation. She who had grown up in nature knew what to expect, but she did not know what *her* experience would be like. She especially did not know what Ned would be like.

The maid entered with two men carrying a tub. They dropped the tub in front of the fire. It resonated slightly like a bell dropped on tiles. The servants then proceeded to carry in pails of steaming water and splash them into the tub.

Ned and Molly smiled secretly at each other.

Towels were brought and hung over the stuffed chairs to warm. A cold dinner of bread and chicken, apples and butter twinkled in china dishes.

Then, the servants left. The maid curtsied, and closed the door quietly.

The two faced each other in the candlelight.

Ned regarded her. Her delicate beauty struck him anew; her fineness, that he would dare to touch her.

Molly still could not believe any of this: not her marriage, nor her escape. What had happened to her in the tunnels, she did not know, and did not think on except as a dark cloud of danger as any other, circling.

Ned approached her. Her heart pounded.

Slowly, he began to unlace her bodice. The filthy dress, now caked with mud and sand, old vomit and weeks of wear, fell away from Molly's slight form, and to the floor. He sat Molly down on the bed, and removed her mud-soaked shoes, one, then the other. At his touch, so rare and new, her skin shivered with excitement. He removed her stockings, slowly sliding his hand up her leg then pulling the stockings, one, then the other, down. Her whole body began to pound with her desire. She felt a new sensation between her legs, as she came alive there, pulsating.

He took both her hands in his and lifted her to stand. He knelt and lifted the hem of her shift from her ankles, up over her head.

She stood before him naked, slender and fragile.

He picked her up then, and carried her to the tub, where he washed her. He drew water over her golden hair and washed it till it shone, like he remembered it. He wanted the Molly he recalled, all light and rosy of flesh.

She was new to him. He touched her all over and he thought of her fineness, how now, at last, she was his. He began with her hands, holding each up to the firelight to see the glowing red light around her fingers and palms. He lifted her arms, also thusly, and saw them glisten with water droplets and fire. He stopped now and then to look into her blue eyes and her sweet face, almost to reassure himself she was really there.

Molly was breathless at his hands stroking her and his dark eyes gazing into hers. She saw the blood of other men under his fingernails lingering there from the fighting and the soil also there from the journey. These never left his hands, and she knew he was different than she was, and would always be.

She let him wash her; she watched every move he made. He then stood before her; he pulled off his shirt, boots and breeches. She saw his penis erect, the first she had ever seen.

She stood in the bath, and he covered her with a towel. She stepped out and into his arms. She felt him against her. Ned kissed her mouth, the little red bow he had longed to kiss, for the first time; he kissed her again, opening her lips for his tongue.

"Give me your tongue." He told her, and she did.

Molly and he felt the same excitement rush over their bodies and flood their minds till thought was near impossible.

He stopped himself from taking her then. Instead, he carried her to the bed where he touched her again with awe and she pulsated inside with each touch as though Ned's fingers caressed her inner most place. He touched her, his own hands trembling, from her fine hands, wrists, elbows, inside of her elbows, stopping to kiss her soft skin every now and then, at the warm well of her throat, the bud of her breasts newly formed where he lingered, slightly rounded tummy, delicate knee, behind the knee, and her slender feet. He opened her legs, there he kissed her, finding her already wet for him; he thrust his tongue into her, so that she arched her back and exclaimed. She ached for him, hardly knowing what it was she desired. He opened the folds of what seemed to him a pale red rose moist with dew, and stroked her lovingly with his tongue until she squirmed and groaned on the bed. He then met her and pushed inside her; she closed about him tightly and he seemed to swell the more, he kissed her open mouth as he took her virginity but not her innocence, for that had been lost the moment she had looked through the telescope and had seen him in the Jamaicas, hundreds of miles away.

**

In her bed on Isla Hispaniola, Jordana felt every loving caress on her own skin, on hands, wrists, elbows, breasts, tummy, knees, even the soles of her feet, and knew immediately from whence this adoring touch had come and what it meant. He had never touched her, Jordana, with trembling awe. No, he had not.

Marblehead, 1995

"Oh! He hit me." Jo said, holding her forehead. It was then that Bob noticed Jo had a large welt on the side of her head.

"Jeez! What did he hit you with?"

"My gun." Jo answered. She felt nauseous. She fell forward and vomited.

Bob caught her in his arms. He called to one of the EMTs who were putting the man on to a gurney.

"Hey, fella! My wife is injured."

"Oh, no, I'm fine. I just want to go ho –" Jo vomited again.

"That's a nasty bump." The EMT told her. "We'll send another bus."

"I can take her in." Bob said.

A police officer approached Jo. "Mrs. Simmons, we have a few questions."

Jo vomited more, all over the cop's shoes.

"It can wait! I'm taking her to the hospital now!"

Bob pushed past the cop, who wasn't someone he recognized, hoping that he wasn't assaulting an officer, but he had to get Jo out of there.

He and Jo got into the Karmann Ghia and sped off to Salem Hospital.

Boston, 1692

As soon as Rosie woke, she began to chatter and did not stop. When she saw that she had servants, she ordered everything she could think of – a bath, breakfast, towels, more towels, fresh diapers for the baby. She chattered non-stop.

Ned was glad to hear her nonsense, until breakfast when she began to go on about the trial, being locked up and the examination. Until she came to the examination, Ned and Molly exchanged smiles as they ate hot sweetbreads and drank tea from china cups.

With her mouth over-full of bread and ham, she prattled. "Oh, tha' foul magistrate put 'is greasy fingers all ovva the two o' us! My how he relished the fair chil'!"

Molly and Ned stopped eating.

Rosie did not notice.

"Aye, tha' man wen' ovva every inch o' her skin lookin' fer a mark of the Devil and 'course he found wha' he was lookin' fer, right under her luvly armpi –"

She stopped.

Molly had burst into tears; she ran from the room into the one she shared with Ned.

They heard the door slam shut.

Ned glared at Rosie. His black stare made Rosie's stomach turn over with all that she had eaten lying like lead.

Ned calmly got up from the table and went to the door. He could hear Molly's sobs from the next room.

A maid walking by turned her head towards the sounds of crying.

Ned smiled at her. The maid smiled back. He closed the door quietly and turned to his mother.

Rosie chewed the food that was left in her mouth slowly as she watched her son walk back to the table. He stood over her.

He leaned down and put his hands on the table.

Rosie looked at his hands. She didn't dare look into those eyes.

"Madam!" He said firmly.

He had never called her that before.

Rosie swallowed and the food did not seem to go down. She looked at her son.

"I'm going to ask ye what ye were jabberin' about tha' has upset my wife so –"

Rosie began to speak again, but Ned's hand went up to stop her. She shut her mouth abruptly.

"Ye will tell me quietly. Then, ye will keep quiet until we leave this inn, do ye hear? No more fussin' about wi' orderin' the servants, d'ye hear?"

"Aye." Rosie nudged a morsel of ham out of her tooth.

"Now, wha' the blazes 'appened? Are ye tellin' me there was some sort of physical z'amination of my wife and mother by the justices?"

"Aye."

"An' who 'xactly touched Molly?"

"Reverend Hathorne did."

"Where?" Ned snarled.

Rosie did not know how to answer. She hesitated.

"Where?" Ned said, more dangerously than before.

"D'ye mean-?"

"Where?" Ned whispered.

"All ovva, and, and - at - at S'lec'man Peach's bedroom!"

"Why didn' she tell me?" Ned said almost to himself.

"Tha chil' didn' know, Ned! Soon as she was n'k'd, she fainted dead away! She nevva woke tha whole time!"

That was why she ran out, Ned realized. She also was hearing it for the first time.

They were silent for a full two minutes while Ned thought and Rosie wondered if she could resume eating.

Just as she was about to pick up a nice juicy slice of ham, Ned turned round and she put her hand down.

Ned sighed.

"Finish yer breakfast, Mother, but remember wha' I said. Lie quiet unless ye wan' to be returned to jail."

"But, I thought we was pardoned, Ned."

Ned shook his head. "Mother, dunna be so simple. Tha's just for lay folk to see, it dunna hold no weight wi' the justices and magistrates of Salem or Boston. We got to lay *low*." He emphasized low, hoping she would understand, but she nodded like a five year old and kept eating. He'd have to explain it to Molly too so that she could keep watch over his childish mother.

"Now, stay in the room, Mother, an' be quiet. I have to go out."

"Aye, Neddie!" Rosie replied with a mouthful, as she gulped more tea.

He kissed her head.

"An' cover yer hair wi' a bonnet."

She nodded again, like a little child.

***

Ned opened the door to his room to find Molly sobbing face down on the bed.

He closed the door behind him and locked it. He lay down beside her and pulled her to him.

He kissed her wet eyes, and cheeks and lips.

Molly wanted to say she was sorry, but she didn't dare. She didn't dare say anything that would make him feel as she did, that it was her fault.

Instead, she looked up at him with her blue eyes.

"Y'er mine, dear one, d'ye hear?" Ned said quietly.

He kissed her wet lips again with joy of her.

"No one can take ye from me now. Not justice or magistrate or reverend, no, nor snakes neither, nay they canna."

Molly sobbed anew in his arms, deeply abandoning herself to him.

Marblehead, 1995

Cassandra was showing the basement of a charming two-bedroom cottage overlooking the harbor when she stopped in mid-sentence.

"It's a partially finished basement, but I think you'll see, it has a lot of potential. There's room here for – *A pink mist entered her vision, disappeared and re-appeared, a pink flash of light, another flash, broken chimes, the office and Jo pointing a small gun straight at Cass, she wanted to laugh, but it wasn't her own laugh, someone else's, that guy, that Ben Hardy, the look-alike, he laughed, he grabbed the gun, hit Jo, and he was standing over her, opening his zipper, when Beth's anger, in a sudden wind, picked him up like a rag doll and sent him careening, she spun him, smashed him on the ceiling, he cried and cried, she smashed him against the wall and ceiling once, twice more, and finally, threw him against the opposite wall where he slid down and stopped, legs askew, pants down around his ankles, three ribs broken and one leg bent weirdly forwards at the knee..."*

Cassandra took a deep breath; and used what she'd learned speaking to outsiders, as she now called them. "Lots of room to create a laundry area or even a play room or a family entertainment center. Let's check out the half bath that's down here."

Boston and Salem, 1692

Ned had to buy a horse. The boat would not be fast enough. Using English coin, he bought a strong young mare with black hide and mane.

Ned rode hard, though he did not have the skill of horsemanship, and nearly fell from the saddle a few times. He hung on by pressing his knees against the animal's ribs, hugging her neck with his arms if he had to, pulling the reins tightly and, reassuring her with his voice.

He rode to Salem, directly to the docks, where he knew a man who could tell him what he needed to know. It was not long before Ned Low rode past Reverend Hathorne's fine mansion.

He rode to a small, neat common across the street from the Reverend's house, where a handful of cows grazed. There, he let his horse graze and drink from the trough. He then walked her to a copse of maple trees where he waited for nightfall.

Ned watched the house. He watched as servants lit the chandelier in the dining room. He watched as servants lay dinner before the Reverend and his wife and three children. He watched as the family adjourned to the parlor, where lighted candles awaited them. Ned moved closer to the house. He saw the Reverend reading aloud from the Bible whilst his children and wife knelt. He watched as the nurse took the children up to bed. He watched the upstairs window suddenly glow with candlelight. The children's room. He watched as the wife sighed and told her husband she was going up to bed. He watched as the Reverend nodded and kissed her forehead goodnight. Ned watched as another room upstairs became lighted. He wondered if the Reverend and his wife slept in the same bed. He waited. He watched as the Reverend grew tired, looked at his pocket watch and also sighed and got up and went out of the room.

Ned watched as another room became lighted. The Reverend slept alone. Ned waited until the Reverend was sound asleep.

Salem, 1995

"Mr. Simmons!"

The cops were in the waiting room at the hospital, but Bob pushed past them again to get Jo admitted.

"I'm not goin' anywhere, guys! I have to get my wife admitted, okay?"

The nurse put a cold pack on Jo's head and got her prepped for the emergency room doctor.

Bob sat by Jo's side on the emergency room bed. Behind a flimsy blue curtain, a woman in another bed sobbed about being in pain. Bob heard a nurse tell her they would be able to give her something for the pain after a doctor had examined her, but the woman wouldn't be comforted. She cried louder.

Bob tried to be cheerful. "You look cute in that gown." He whispered in his wife's ear, kissing her cheek.

Jo smiled.

"I might vom again."

"I'm not sure that's a good sign for a head injury."

"Head injury? This bump?"

"Yeah, it's pretty bad."

Jo sighed, and lay down on the bed.

"I'm so tired suddenly."

The doctor came in, moving very quickly through the curtain.

"I'm Dr. Hennessey. Heard we have a head injury here?" He spoke rapidly.

"Yes, right here."

"Hmm. Okay, let's get you to the MRI right away. It's kind of close to the temple."

"She's been vomiting, doctor."

"Hmm, okay. Well, we need to check you out for fracture or bleeding."

"Okay."

The doctor examined Jo's eyes.

"Your eyes seem good. Good sign."

The nurse came in and asked a few questions about their primary care doctor and insurance. Bob could see that Dr. Hennessey was observing how Jo answered the questions. She did well, as far as Bob could tell, lucid and prompt.

"We have a little cocktail for you, Jo." Dr. Hennessey told her. "And the nurse will bring you a paper to sign."

The nurse got the injection of contrast dye ready.

"In a few minutes we can get an image that will tell us a lot more."

"Wait!" Jo realized the dye might be dangerous. "I might be pregnant!"

"Pregnant?" Bob repeated in shock.

"Yes." Jo looked at him, fondly. "I was going to buy one of those home pregnancy tests."

"Pregnant." Bob repeated to himself. He grabbed Jo and kissed her.

"Well, we can skip the dye then. Let's just get an image. I want to check for bleeding before I send you home." The doctor pressed his fingers around Jo's abdomen. "Hmm, a few weeks? And, you're forty-eight?"

Jo nodded.

"Don't worry about the fetus. An MRI so early on is fine."

They wheeled Jo off to radiation while Bob hustled alongside the gurney, clutching Jo's thin hand in a kind of stupor of absolute rapture mingled with terror.

Salem, 1692

All seemed peaceful to Ned, but he could not know the torment Reverend Hathorne endured at the will of Bridget Bishop. Slowly, as the Reverend tried to rest from his daily mission of looking for the Devil, and the Devil's own, slowly, the odor of rotting apples would fill the room - the parlor, his parlor, where he prayed with his wife and children! Slowly, the sweat beaded up and fell from his brow as he prayed. Why did not the Lord intervene on his behalf? Why was he tortured as the damned in hell? Why was not Bridget Bishop in hell? Why was she still there, in Salem?

"Apples!" He heard her whisper in his ear.

Oh, yes, he had taken her lovely apple orchard as his own. Why not? Who else would take on the acreage and the responsibility of the farm? Who else had the resources?

"Apples! Apples! Apples!" In that sweet voice he had once loved to hear calling his name. He could still feel her warm, naked body under his.

He could hardly stand to pray. His voice wavered so. Finally, his wife went to bed. How he feared she would hear one night! He had requested his own bedroom because of that voice! He'd told his wife he was restless and did not want to wake her.

"John!" Bishop's wanton voice teased.

He got up to go to bed.

God only knows what she had waiting for him up there! Her voice flew round the room all night and her shadow with it.

Salem, 1995

Cassandra drove straight to Salem Hospital after her showing. She'd gotten a good strong offer on the cottage. She knew that would please Jo, whom she also knew would survive and be well. Her spray-painted orange VW bug darted along the road with a loud grunt and scrape at every bump and turn. She had the sunroof open. The searing city sun roasted the top of her skull, and there was no relief of Marblehead breezes in stifling Salem traffic. *Cassandra sighed and imagined the VW bug lifting up and continuing on its way like a very large lady bug flying over the endless line of cars and trucks and buses and motorcycles that coughed and choked into the summer day.*

When she finally reached the hospital, Cassandra hastily pulled into the lot and dashed into the building in time to see cops and lots of other folks from Marblehead whom she knew by sight: friends, realtors and park workers, all come to show their concern and support. Peter Treadwell was also there, wincing over a cup of bad coffee.

The technician had forced Bob out of the MRI room, so he waited in the hall with his friends. When he saw Cass, he called out to her.

"Cass! Jo is —"

"I know!" Cass replied, hurrying down the hall toward him. "She's gonna be okay."

"She is?" Bob queried, unsure of what they were talking about. "You mean her head?"

"Yes, and the baby."

"Jeez, you knew?"

There was nothing simpler, really, than noticing a woman was pregnant, Cassandra thought. She didn't say so; she was learning when to be silent as well as how to speak.

Anyway, she wouldn't have gotten a word in as the crowd in the hallway burst into laughter and congratulations, patting Bob on the back, and making comments like "You dog! You old dog!" and "Break out the champagne!" "Woo!" and "A dad? At your age?"

Bob blushed a shocking pink and stammered something about a hot wife.

He sat down to catch his breath.

Cassandra sat next to him.

Bob began to shake, and before he knew it, sob. He covered his face with his hands and shook with sobs.

Everyone was silent, mumbling a little, and turning away to give him privacy.

Cassandra took Bob's hand, and waited till he recovered himself.

When he stopped crying and wiped his face with his bare hands, she whispered.

"It's a boy."

Bob looked into her face, threw his arms around her and hung on to this mad, sweet woman for dear life.

Salem, 1692

Ned tucked his horse just under the garden wall, which he climbed. From there he climbed to a wide limbed oak tree, where he faced the Reverend's bedroom window.

He faced the window for but a second. A sneer lifted his top lip.

Then, he held on to a tree limb and swung his long legs and burst through the glass window and fell into the Reverend's bedroom. He ran to the bed, slit the man's throat before he could scream and climbing on to the bed, stood over the justice, and said in a whisper, "Tha' from Ned Low fer touchin' me wife an' me mother, Rosie Low, wi' yer greasy, foul paws!"

The Reverend gurgled and gurgled, his eyes wide in the terror of death.

"Wait fer me in hell!" Ned whispered harshly.

Ned leaped from the bed as the household came running, jumped out the window to the tree, scrambled down the tree and over the wall, on to his horse and rode off.

The night meant nothing to him. Darkness was nothing. He had learned to see in it. Ah, he thought as he rode his black mare, the training of getting away from Lowther had done him some good.

Marblehead, 1692

He had another errand before he could return to the inn. The truth was, he did not like to leave his bride for very long. Saying farewell to Molly, even for a day was hard. He had never been one to linger a bed, but he found himself doing so now. He loved to touch her. Her skin, her sweet face, her hair, which defied softness, it was so very fine!

She was teaching him to read and write. In the firelight or the sunlight, in bed or at table, he spent more time watching her delicate hands and her pretty lips than the words on the page. But, he would get it right soon enough. Reading and writing would be valuable skills, this he knew.

He was getting better at riding, he thought, as he rode up to Elizabeth Treadwell's cottage, a place he had last seen the morning of that fateful night Lowther had kidnapped him on the beach.

Ned jumped from the horse, tied her to a tree, and gently soothed her by patting her nose. She snorted in approval and began grazing on grass.

He strode into the cottage and there she was, his mother-in-law.

Marblehead, 1995

The police still wanted to talk to Bob. They told him he needed to get down to the police station immediately to make a statement or they would have to arrest him. They knew that Jo was not strong enough to have caused Ben Hardy's injuries. Apparently, Hardy's statement had included being "grabbed by some guy and thrown around the room till he passed out." Bob asked Peter to go with him, and his lawyer, Paul Weaver, and his buddy, Wainwright Parker, or Wain as he was called, who'd been with him in the truck, and Cass, who offered to come.

Jo was still in the hospital for observation, though the MRI had revealed no internal bleeding at that time.

Bob didn't want to leave Jo. He had no choice. Cassandra assured him Jo would be fine, and that, she, Cassandra, would be needed at the station.

"I saw what happened." Cass told him.

Shit, thought Peter, here we go!

Marblehead, 1692

He stood before her and reminded her so much of the pirate who had once stood in that very spot and demanded she hide him when she was a young, married girl that Elizabeth truly started with fear. Was she reliving that moment?

"Who are you?" She began to say, then realized who stood before her.

"Ned." Elizabeth said.

"Aye!"

He was taller than she remembered, and in full pirate regalia. His eyes were darkened with kohl. She saw the India scarves, leather vest, golden and jeweled chains, diamond earring; she saw his belt, and the knife, pistol and gunpowder that hung from it. Something else had changed. Elizabeth did not know exactly what, except that he was manlier, and more frightening.

"Why are you here?" Elizabeth asked him, warily. For Rosie and Molly, she knew were missing from the dark room where they had been awaiting execution. She had heard tales of what had occurred, but she honestly had not known what to believe.

"I am here, Madam to give you this for safe-keeping."

Ned took the papers out of his vest and handed Elizabeth two rolls. These she slowly unwrapped. She noticed the Selectman's seal on the pardon.

She nearly cried out in happiness and relief, but held back as something told her all was not right.

She opened the next roll and read carefully. She fell slightly, grasping hold of the table. The same table where Molly had served and eaten all her meals, where Rosie and Elizabeth had kneaded bread, where the children now ate, and…

"How is this possible?" Elizabeth managed to whisper.

Ned was silent.

"Molly is ten years old."

No word from Ned, who simply regarded her in his victory.

"She agreed to this marriage?"

"Aye!"

"She, she hardly can know what is best for her! She is shocked by these events, she is –"

"It may not be best for her, Madam, but it is done!"

Elizabeth grappled with this new idea.

"Have you –"

"Aye!"

"She was supposed to marry Daniel Pritchard." Elizabeth said, as though recalling a dream.

Ned laughed.

"Wasn't he arrested with her?"

"Yes. He is in Ipswich."

"Has he been to trial?"

"Not yet."

"Tell him to confess, then. Tha' is me best advice. They will release him if he confesses. After all, he was on the Hill tha' day."

Elizabeth could not believe his coldness, even towards a rival.

Ned took out of his pocket three large rubies, four emeralds and a black pearl. These he dropped on to the old wooden table.

"I am entrustin' you, Madam with these jewels as insurance of the future of me young bride and 'er family. I am also entrustin' you with these papers, as the most honest and capable woman I know."

Elizabeth nodded.

"Where is she?"

"I intended to tell you. We be at The Rose & Crown for the time being, in Boston. It's a respectable inn. Molly and me mother're there, also the infant. They're more than comfortable."

"May I see her?"

"Of course! Come visit us! Soon we shall take a small house in the city where ye may also come, but be careful to give another account of where y're goin'. Be also careful, I don't need to tell ye, not to tell anyone where we are. We cannot fool everyone with this pardon, ye might know."

"Can she ever come home?"

"Ol' Dimond says it will all be over by Spring. She and my mother may return then."

"Spring."

"Aye."

"Then, you will leave her for the open sea."

"Yes, mum. But, I also will return to her. Believe me or nay, she is my dear heart."

"I believe you, Ned, for she is mine also."

Marblehead, 1995

"Now, let's go over it again, Ms. Hawkes." The police detective began. "Where were you when you witnessed the alleged rape attempt?"

They were all sitting in the clean and spacious brand new police station that glittered with glass and blonde wood. Their chairs were Scandinavian and the table they rested their hands on was blonde wood and shining chrome. Peter had to remind himself that he was in a police station and that the conversation was not as harmless and pretty as the furniture and building belied.

"I was showing a cottage on Nanepashemet Street." Cassandra answered.

"So, now, let's be clear. You were no where near the real estate office on Atlantic Ave. when you saw what happened?"

"Bill," Peter began to say.

"Detective Murphy."

Peter almost laughed. His old friend was being so serious; it was almost comical.

"Bill, this isn't an episode of Law & Order."

Bill Murphy shot Peter a nasty look. 'I don't go down to your wood shop and tell you how to saw a log."

"Yeah, that would mean I was asleep."

Bill ignored him.

Paul Weaver advised the men to be quiet and just listen.

Peter scratched his head. He felt a kid in school.

"Why don't we just ask Ms. Hawkes what she saw?" Weaver suggested. "Then, we can see if it fits the evidence."

Detective Murphy sighed.

"Okay, let's hear it."

"I was showing a house, when I saw Beth." Cassandra told them.

"You *saw* her?"

"Yes."

"All the way from Nanepashemet?"

"When I say that I saw Beth, I don't mean that I saw her physically."

Detective Murphy just looked at Cassandra, without speaking.

Then he said, "Go on."

"She was furious. She told me -"

"Wait! She *told* you?"

"Yes. I got the message. She didn't have to speak."

"Speak?"

"Yes, the dead speak without words."

"Go on." Murphy sighed. He didn't even want to ask how they accomplished *that*.

"She was angry because Jo had tried to save her. Jo had seen her getting on the boat and she had run to her house and told Peter to go after her."

Detective Murphy was silent. Thought abandoned them, all of them, except thoughts of Beth and her terrible murder. Out of respect for Beth Treadwell, Detective Murphy listened to Cassandra as she went on with her story.

"Beth showed me what was happening. He was standing over Jo; he unzipped his pants…

Bob stiffened in his chair; Peter put his arm around his friend.

…He leaned down to move Jo, when suddenly Beth took him. She lifted him from behind and tossed him about the room."

"Just how did she do that, Ms. Hawkes? Even if Beth Treadwell were alive and physically present, she would not have been strong enough to lift the man in question."

"She's strong enough now."

"How so? How did Beth lift this man, if she did?"

"With her rage." Cassandra told him as though she were telling him it was four o'clock in the afternoon.

"Okay, look," this time Detective Murphy scratched his head. "Did you *see* Beth?"

"Yes."

"All the way from Nanepashemet?"

Bob was just a bit peeved by all this "see her" talk.

"She's dead, Bill." He wanted to say, but he didn't. He could see that Peter was getting uncomfortable too. "Move it along, Bill." Bob thought.

"I saw the man fly around the room and I saw Beth." Cassandra told the officer.

Everyone looked at Cassandra. Some, like Peter and Bob, silently agreed with a nod. Wain frowned. Paul Weaver waited patiently. Detective Murphy scowled. Peter, and especially, Bob were so relieved about Jo and so happy that the perpetrator had gotten what he deserved, they were almost giddy.

"Look, Bill," Wain offered, leaning forward, "Bob was in the truck with me. He went in, and not two minutes later, you guys showed up. How the hell could he have had time to beat this guy up? Besides, what the hell are we talking about anyway? This guy isn't dead, right?"

"No, Wain, he's not dead. He's in traction."

Bob couldn't help it; he burst out laughing. Peter too.

Wain added. 'I can testify I saw Bob the whole time and he never touched the guy."

Bob made a sound something like a suppressed giggle.

"Did you touch him, Bob? Can you honestly tell me you didn't pick this guy up and slam him against the wall a few times for trying to rape your wife?"

Bob went dead serious. He almost stood up and hit the detective. In a second, Peter's hand was on his shoulder.

"Bob." Weaver spoke, his voice a steady warning.

"I wish I did, but I didn't. And, yeah, I can tell you I never touched the asshole."

"We found gravel in his mouth, Bob. The same gravel that's on your boot right now."

Bob shrugged.

"Maybe he ate the floor."

More general laughter ensued from the friends. Even Cassandra couldn't help smiling, though she kept quiet.

"Look, Detective, you've got a convicted sex offender with his pants down and an unconscious pregnant woman. I think this situation describes itself." Weaver told him.

"Get the hell outta here, all of ye'!" Detective Murphy hollered. "You're all nuts!"

"I'm goin' back to the hospital, if you need me." Bob told him.

"Nah!" The Detective repeated. "I got a convicted sex offender with his pants down. I'm goin' with that."

Peter, Bob and Wain left the police station giggling like three kids dismissed from the principal's office. Weaver told them they had nothing to worry about.

***

Cassandra went back to the office to write up the buyer's offer, as best she could, without Jo's help.

She pushed past the police caution tape and sat down at her desk.

"Thank you, Beth. Thank you." Cass whispered.

She went to work.

Marblehead, 1692

Just as he took his leave of his new mother-in-law, Ned passed Tom Treadwell outside. Tom seemed paler and weaker than ever. He was stopped, looking at the strange horse.

"Hey, Tom, ye ol' fool! How be ye?"

Tom said nothing; he looked surprised to see Ned.

Ned mounted the horse, and just before he rode off, he called to Tom.

"Y'er lucky, Tom, y'er me brother now! Lucky as all the day!"

Marblehead, 1995

Three weeks after the ghost hunt, Justin, Frank, the crew, Pete, Peter, Meghan, and Cassandra sat down in Peter's kitchen to discuss Justin's findings. Peter had long since gotten over the fact that Justin was fifteen years old. He was rapt with attention to hear what this young person had to say.

"We took a lot of Polaroids." Justin began. He spread the photos out on the old wooden table and Peter was amazed at what he saw. "You can see there is a lot of activity right here in the kitchen." Justin explained.

The whole kitchen, which was dark when the photo was taken, was alight with globes of light that seemed to float.

"You can see, where we've done a few close ups of these photos on the computer, that these globes are not just empty light. You can see the activity within each of them. We think these are real orbs, or spirits."

Peter looked at the enlargements and saw what seemed to be small worlds glowing, globes of the earth with sparkling oceans and landmasses of light mapped out.

"Of course, it is impossible to tell whom each of these orbs represent. But, judging from the activity we experienced in one night and the fact that you and your children have experienced very little in the house up to now, we think these are actually visitors."

"Visitors?" Peter asked.

"Yes, we think these spirits, whom we have photos of in various other areas of the house that night, we think they came to visit because – Justin sighed as though expecting to be laughed at – they heard about our being here to listen. It's happened a few times before, but I have to say, it's pretty rare because it does require some really strong spirits who are not attached to a particular place but can travel."

Justin breathed out, waiting to be rebuked.

Silence.

Then, Peter asked, "Well? Who were they?"

Justin smiled, and nodded, "Okay, okay! To determine that, we'll have to go on to the tapes."

The crew, whom Peter had not noticed till now, a pale, thin young man with bad skin, short blonde hair and hands that worked very sure and fast to set up the recording devices for listening. He pressed ON and stepped back.

All Peter could hear was static. Then, louder static and a moan and a high-pitched whistle and another moan. It was unnerving and incomprehensible.

"Okay, I didn't get anything." Peter admitted.

Justin brought out his small laptop computer.

"Oh! That's one of those laptops I saw advertised on TV!" Peter exclaimed, thinking he was being supportive.

Justin smiled to himself, "You haven't seen this one on TV."

Frank added, "We've got some special stuff here, Peter. Still in the experimental stage otherwise."

"How so?" Peter inquired innocently.

"Can't say. Or, we'd have to kill you." Frank told him.

Peter felt he wasn't kidding about the equipment.

"Well, I'm glad you're on my side, then."

Justin opened the laptop, which Peter saw had a U.S. Army insignia stamped on it in gold; he pressed a few keys and what Peter knew as voice identification bars came up on the screen.

"Let's listen again." Justin said, pressing a key.

More static, then a voice. Static. Voice. A female?

"That's Bridget Bishop." Cassandra offered.

"Yes, listen again."

Justin played the voice again and this time, Peter heard a faint, breathy whisper, "Apples!" in a female voice.

His skin crawled with goose bumps. The voice seemed very alive, distinctive, deep and lusty.

Justin said, "There's more, if you're up for it."

"Yeah!" Peter exclaimed.

Justin moved down the line to the next voice. Again, Peter just heard static. Then, suddenly, a voice, clear for a split second only - "Killed - static - in my bed - static - by- static - "

"Whoa! Who was *that*?" It was obviously a male. An older male, Peter thought.

"Well, we can't be sure, but if you listen again here, he says who murdered him."

A hell of a lot of static, Peter thought, then the same male voice cried out, "Ned Low! Pirate!" as though he expected all who heard to get him justice.

"Wait, Ned Low, the pirate, didn't Beth tell me he was related to her best friend Julie Low Peach?"

Peter realized with a shock that that was the second time he had mentioned Beth comfortably and with an interest in something else since she had died. The first had been thinking of changing the French door to a screen door.

Everyone looked at him, then, Cassandra broke the silence.

"Yes, Julie Low Peach is his descendant."

Peter asked her, "Did he kill this guy?"

"Historically, we have no way of knowing." Justin told him. "However, we do know that Reverend Hathorne was murdered in his bed, his throat slit, by an intruder in 1692 just after he sent several so-called witches to their deaths. He had plenty of people who wanted him dead, and many who could have had the opportunity of breaking into his bedroom smashing the glass of a closed window. We know that's how it happened through legal documents, diaries and letters. However, we have no proof it was Ned Low."

"Besides, he would have been eleven at the time." Justin added.

"Eleven?" Peter repeated incredulously. Again, he had to give it up on the whole thing of kids not being capable of this or that.

"Eleven." Justin also repeated, as though he also couldn't believe it.

But, Cassandra believed it. She could see and hear the whole thing. She decided, if there was ever a time to speak, this was it.

"It was him and yes, he was eleven."

Everyone turned to her. She began her story.

"On a hot night in July, 1692 Ned Low waited outside the Reverend's house; he watched while the family ate dinner, then knelt in prayer, then went to bed, one by one, the Reverend's children and nurse, then the wife, then the Reverend himself. Ned observed which window lighted when the Reverend went to bed. He climbed a tree and waited till the man was asleep, then he sprang, like a cat, swinging on a branch and thrusting his booted feet into the closed window. He jumped on to the bed, startling the man. He cried out, 'This from Ned Low!' and slit the man's throat from ear to ear before leaping back out the window and down the tree. He had a horse waiting."

"Are you *serious*?" Peter asked, without thinking of being polite.

"Yes." Cassandra replied, quietly.

"Why did he kill him?"

"The Reverend had touched his wife."

"Wait, what? He was eleven!" Peter couldn't believe this! All this was so new – first, he had come to believe there were spirits in his house, but *this*?

"It was a different time. Marriage was an economic necessity. Children were married as infants, or as young as two or three. By comparison, Ned and his wife were almost middle aged. They were married right after he rescued her from internment as a witch."

"She was how old?" Peter asked.

"She was ten."

"Wow!" Pete and several of the others cried out at once.

"Who was she?" Frank asked.

"She was Molly Treadwell, one of Peter's ancestors."

"Molly." Peter spoke her name.

"The little cap on the wall belonged to her sister, Emilie." Cassandra told them.

They all looked at the little white cap with the small brown stain on it that Beth had framed.

"What – what had the old man done to her?"

"He had examined her as a witch. In other words, he had touched every inch of her nude and virginal body looking for a third nipple, a Devil's mark or a crescent scar."

"Did he find one?" Peter asked foolishly and everyone laughed nervously.

"Yes, as a matter-of-fact, he found a crescent moon birth mark under her arm."

"So, that meant she was guilty?"

"Yes, that confirmed it, but she had been caught up on Burial Hill looking through Ed Dimond's telescope. It was considered a magic telescope, which it was. He used it to watch for ships in trouble on the high seas."

Peter just shook his head in amazement.

"This man is in my house?"

"Ed Dimond is, but not the Reverend Hathorne. Not usually, just the other night. He wanted to be heard." Cassandra assured him. "I think that's why Bridget came too, because she knew he was here."

"And, what about Ned Low?"

"Do you mean, is he here?"

"We don't think so." Justin replied.

Cassandra spoke up. "He is much too powerful a spirit to need any reassurance or justice from anyone. He is content where he is, in the afterlife with his bride."

"What happened to him?

"He was hanged for acts of piracy when he was thirty-five."

"Any regrets?"

Cassandra smiled knowingly.

"Absolutely none."

"He was a pirate at eleven?" Pete asked. "Not a cabin boy?"

Cassandra thought it was not appropriate for her to speak the truth about that to Pete.

"He was not a cabin boy." She explained. "He was too good a fighter and was promoted almost immediately."

"Wow!" Pete was impressed.

"Who the hell else was here that night?" Peter asked, causing them all to laugh.

"Well," Justin said, "let's see."

They went over more voices, but nothing clear enough to understand. Only Cassandra said she heard something. She said two men, John Bennett and Philip Beare, who were arrested for drunkenness in July 1692, said they saw witches in a cave, but did not report it to the authorities, instead went to get a drink. None of the team could make out any more words from the recordings, only static, though voice spikes were definitely visible on the computer screen.

Justin also showed them Polaroids with weird writing on them. The photos looked like someone had come along and written on them with a white finger paint trail. One photo of the living room French doors had the word, "Happy" scrawled across it in very bad handwriting. Another, taken in front of the bookcase read, "Go fish."

Peter was also shown a film taken in Emily's bedroom in which a teddy bear was petted – Peter could actually see the fur flatten and pop up as an invisible hand passed over it - and then, the little stuffed bear fell over. Thermal imaging showed a distinct temperature difference between the bear and the space beside it, which was twenty degrees cooler. Peter was fascinated to think that the liquid blue shape morphing and floating on the computer screen might be Beth. His son, Pete was spellbound. Other cameras had been set up in the other bedrooms, but the only other activity had been the French doors in the master that had popped open, seemingly, by themselves. The white curtain lifted in the breeze and Peter couldn't help thinking of Beth standing there, naked.

"Has that ever happened before?" Justin asked.

"Never!" Peter exclaimed, like a kid caught thinking about something forbidden.

Epilogue, 1692

Before he could return to the *Deliverance*, Ned had one more errand. He could not go back to Lowther empty-handed, not if he wanted any trace of freedom to remain in his new life. He wanted to stay a fighter on the ship; he did not want to be stuck trying to make his way in a city. Land was naught but friendless violence, ever-present hunger, threatening harm and endless jeopardy. Nothing was worse than life on land at the mercy of the moneyed and ruthless. The only thing he was fit for was murder. Even at his age or because of it, he could be hired to kill, but how long before he was found out and swung, as Ol' Dimond had predicted? Someone would gladly turn him in for a reward. He had no loyal compatriots on land. At sea, he was protected. If he remained careful and clever, he could be reasonably free.

It was not hard to find a hungry little boy. The dark streets of Boston were full of starving children. He saw several huddled together under a stairwell, waiting for an opportunity to run out and steal a wallet or a watch. He saw their eyes glowing white like the eyes of rats in the darkness.

He wanted a small boy. He did not desire a struggle, and most of all Ned wanted a boy who would last Lowther a long while. He needed one of no more than six years in order to ensure some years to come. And, he needed an innocent. Ned did not want Lowther to complain of a face worn with sores or the pain and wisdom of experience.

It was not a happy night. Unlike the wild streets of Isabella, there was no music or shouting, no jugglers or dancers, no cockfight or monkey on a leash. The street was dimly lit with a few lackluster vendors' fires and tavern lights. The weather was a soft drizzle that had just finished and left a dirty mist that blurred what light there was.

Ned strolled until he saw just the sort of boy he sought, there, in the company of several other street boys outside a near empty tavern; their faces were lighted by the flames of a street cart where a man was turning a pig on a spit. The greasy aroma of roasted pork filled the corner. The man, who called his product's virtues out into the street, held a fork with slices of meat dangling and dripping.

"Swee' pork, sir! Swee' pork to wet yer lips wi'! Swee' pork, sir! Just a tease 'afore dinner!"

The boy nearly ate the slice of meat with his eyes. Round and blue, they were indeed hungry eyes under a canopy of dark blonde curls glistening with light and the oil of many unwashed nights; eyes that gleamed the brighter for the dark circles that surrounded them and the blackened skin of a face that had rested its soft cheek on the filthy ground for a pillow.

Ned approached the child who took no notice until Ned blocked his view of the dangling, juicy meat.

"Are ye thinkin' o makin' off wi' tha pork then, me lad?" Ned taunted the boy.

"Ge' o' the way, 'less yer thinkin' o buyin'." One of the older boys chided.

"My pleasure, sir!"

Ned turned to the vendor then and gave the man enough for the whole side of pig, enough to feed all the boys present, eight in all. The boys shouted with greed and joy; they reached to grab handfuls of meat that dripped juices through their clenched fingers. The vendor could not cut fast enough. The boys mobbed the cart. Soon, the hunk of meat was on the ground and boys bodies grappled for it so violently, Ned had to step back.

He took the youngest boy by the collar then and lifted him out of the fray. The boy kicked and complained that he hadn't gotten any food. Ned placed him down, still holding him. He paid the vendor another coin and stuffed a pig's foot into the small boy's mouth. This he took eagerly, making moaning sounds and slurping till Ned could not help but wonder if he would continue to make such pleasurable groans when eating Lowther's pork sword.

"Where 're ye frum, then, lad?"

The boy looked up, incredulous.

"Wha? Frum?"

Ah, better than he dared hope. The boy was dumb as he would be dumb.

"What's yer name?" Ned tried.

"Ned." He replied with his mouth full.

Unacceptable.

"I'll call ye Lil' Tom."

The child shrugged.

Perfect.

Ned chatted a while, telling the child of his glamorous life at sea, telling of riches and foodstuffs to make your eyes pop and your mouth die of pleasure. The boy's eyes grew wider and wider. Ned told of mermaids with breasts like apples, long flowing hair but no legs, just the tail of a fish. He spoke of treasure, gold and jewels, fine clothes to dress himself, and a sword - ah, yes, he should have a sword with a jewel-encrusted handle, bearing his initials. Would he like that? Lil' Tom nodded, and nodded again, enthusiastically, when Ned asked if he wanted to join him in the carefree life of a sailor with the sea salt spray and the free wind on his face.

The boy drifted off to sleep while listening to Ned spin his tale.

Ned let him sleep for nearly half an hour before he thrust his knife into the vendor's fire and walked off with the boy in his arms. The vendor hardly blinked. Ned took him to a dark and quiet corner in a graveyard behind a church, just steps from a busy tavern quarreling with activity, where he held the boy's tongue with one hand and sliced it out of his mouth with the other.

A caller strolled by, a little old woman in black rags, calling out the deaths. She carried a torch that illuminated her pox-scarred face; she sang of death. She looked directly at Ned and called out in her craggy voice, "A small boy! A small boy! An unknown boy!"

But, she was wrong, Ned thought, the boy was not to die.

The child came to, rolled his eyes and passed out just as Ned cauterized the wound.

The thought occurred to him as he carried the little boy, that one day, with Molly, a child like this could be his own, that he might farm and fish in the free air and open sea with Molly by his side. But the idea was fleeting as breath itself, for he knew, the world would not allow it. If he stopped for a day, they would find him and hang him.

He kept on.

Epilogue, 1995

From the crest of the hill at Crocker Park, Cassandra could see the whole harbor. She loved to look out to the open sea, over the tops of the sails, over the many nesting boats, small and large, fishing and sailing, white and green and blue against the sea. The day was overcast and muggy, turning the harbor to a grey wash. The sun, in pale yellow streaks, kept trying to break through. Two young women stood on paddleboards that were paint strokes of bright orange and turquoise smoothly guiding their way out of the crowded moorings. Cassandra saw a strong, young Naumkeag standing, gracefully paddling his canoe alongside the two women. A man and his dog puttered by in a motorboat. An older couple sailed out in a small white yacht. A constant sight in town, Bobby, a man who'd had cancer for years, his long grey beard covering his thin chest, easily rowed a red kayak toward the open sea. Bobby biked or walked or kayaked every day, all day, not wanting to miss a minute of sun or rain, fresh air or life. Every minute, he grinned with enthusiasm.

Clearly, Cassandra could see two swimming figures beneath the kayak: a young girl and a young boy, both of them naked. The two figures swam like little frogs, like happy fish around and around the kayak. Bobby paddled with his ever-present smile. He looked ecstatically out to sea.

Cassandra loved this kind of vision. The two figures were Bobby and his girl friend, Deidre, when they were teenaged lovers, healthy and strong. Deidre had died before Bobby, in her fifties, from a heart condition. Bobby was in remission; he never stopped moving.

***

Peter told himself he shouldn't have been worried; it happened more easily than he had thought. They'd lived together now with the children for several months. School had started and evenings were slammed full of meetings to attend, homework to help with, and quick dinners to finish in time for other, more pressing, school events.

Once, while clearing the table, Meghan had let her hand slide over his shoulder almost as though she were saying, "Come with me." He'd turned his head to see her busy at the dishwasher, surrounded by two little girls jabbering together, competing for her attention.

He wanted her. Since the night her hand had trailed over the cloth of his T-shirt, he'd felt her warm touch on his skin; over and over, her hand trailed in his memory, building his passion till he could hardly stand it.

He was in his shop when he saw her drive up after dropping Emily, who was now in kindergarten, and Sarah off at school. His son Pete rode his bike on his own. Peter followed her movements as she unloaded the car of groceries and carried the bags into the house.

He followed her into the house, walking along the covered path parallel to her movements.

He found her in the kitchen, unloading the groceries. Her red hair stuck to the side of her face a bit from sweat, as the day was warm for September. She smiled at him, but continued working, distracted.

"Thirsty?" She said, talking into the bags. "I made some cold lemonade with organic lemons this morning. It's in the fridge."

She stopped unpacking the groceries then, and took a long sip from her own glass of lemonade, tinkling with frosty ice.

He went to her, and touched her shoulder as she had touched him, lightly, lovingly. He took the glass from her hand and took his own long sip from it. He put the glass down. Then he leaned to kiss her.

"Oh!" She turned as he took her into his arms, holding her as closely as he could, kissing her mouth, not too hard in his enthusiasm, gently, he told himself, gently.

She loved to hear his breathing; his breath so close to her own excited her, she could hear his passion as his breath came hard and quick. She could taste the cold lemonade in his mouth and her own.

Meghan's blouse, a flowery frothy sort of thing, had shifted exposing her neck; there he buried his head, kissing her throat.

"Come with me." He whispered, hoarsely.

He took her hand and led her to his bedroom.

They kissed and he began to undress her, the frothy thing fell from her shoulders; it wasn't a blouse, but a summer dress that fell to the floor and she stood before him in blue lace underwear that stunned him.

"My God!"

He wasn't usually affected by clothes, or underclothes, or was he? He couldn't remember. Her skin glowed with its healthy tan through the blue lace, her breasts filled the bra and spilled over the top in a way that excited him beyond words.

He touched her breasts, letting his fingers travel over her cleavage. He cupped her breasts in his hands and pushed her down on the bed.

She was thrilled by this sudden roughness and she held her arms open for him.

He leaned over her, kissing her mouth and neck, her ears, where he lingered, putting his tongue inside her ears; she could hear his tongue licking her, caressing her, it felt wonderful, wonderful, as the liquid from his lips seemed to fill her and open her, she ached, she could no longer think, her thoughts became aching.

"I have to see you!" He gasped.

She sat up and reaching behind, unclasped her bra. Her beautiful breasts spilled out and he reached out for them, sighing as his hands felt how heavy yet how very, very soft they were. He stopped only to grab and pull her panties down. He already had seen her dark red pubic hair through the blue lace, but when he saw her, so full and dark, the sight of her nearly drove him mad.

"I've waited long enough." Peter said, quickly pulling off T-shirt, jeans and underwear, lowering his body to hers.

"*We've* waited long enough." She said, softly.

"You're so wet!" He cried as he entered her and she enveloped him.

He reveled in the strength of her thighs around him, pulling him closer to her, deeper inside her, he tasted like mint sometimes, sometimes his flesh smelled of sawdust, her mouth tasted like apples, as though he had interrupted her eating the crisp, white flesh, her belly, her breasts, soft roses, *why had he waited so long*, at last she was in his arms.

About the Author

Patricia Goodwin grew up in an Italian-American neighborhood outside of Boston. "A Child's Christmas in Revere," a chapter from her novel, *Holy Days* was published in the anthology, *Under Her Skin: How Girls Experience Race in America* (Seal Press, 2004). Her poetry has been published in *Marblehead Magazine*, *IndeArts*, *Runes*, *nthposition.com*, *Pemmican Press, Radius: Poetry from the Center to the Edge* and *The Potomac*, among others. Her poetry books include: *Marblehead Moon* (Plum Press, 1993), *Java Love* (Plum Press, 1997) and *Atlantis* (Plum Press, 2006). *Dreamwater* is the sequel to her novella, *When Two Women Die* (Plum Press, 2012). Patricia lives with her husband and daughter in a historic seacoast town in Massachusetts.

For more information about the author, including new work, events, and videos, please visit patriciagoodwin.com.

Also by Patricia Goodwin

When Two Women Die

Atlantis

Java Love

Marblehead Moon

Under Her Skin: How Girls Experience Race in America
(anthology)

Far: Ahead Of Its Time
(blog)

Available at patriciagoodwin.com